GUARDIANS
OF THE
THRONES

BOOK 1 OF CLANS OF DRAGONS

KASSY R KNEPP

Trigger Warnings

This story contains content that might be troublesome for some readers, including:
-Explicit Language
-Detail sex scenes
-Childbirth Death
-Domestic violence
-Body dismemberment
-Child death
-Blood/Gore detailed scenes
-Choking
-Biting
-Murder
-Suicide
-Burning alive
-Forced oral
-Parent death
-Possession
-Torture
- Decapitation
-Spitting
-Self harm
-Stabbing
-Eating bodies
-Bone breaking
-Hair pulling

Kassy R Knepp

Dedications

To my grandpa (Pappa)
Grandpa: You better do something with this book before I pass.
7/21/1940-10/04/2017
-Cecil

I am Sorry it took me so long, Pappa, but I finally did it; I even changed the
name of the main character after you.
I am missing you, always.
-Your Galoot Kassy.-

To my husband: Thank you for the support in keeping me going in writing
my book, and for buying me the laptop so I could write it, and for the
support in pursuing my childhood dream to become an author.
I love you, and I will always find you.
-Your Wife.-

To my Mom: Thank you for your support and believing in me, when a lot of
people thought it was just a silly childhood dream that wouldn't be reality. I
know it took a long time, but I did it, and there will be more to come in the
future.
-Your daughter.-

And lastly, to my readers: I hope you like my book and, you are able to
escape reality for a bit.

Chapter One

Every night when she awoke, she could smell that sweet scent over the sea coming from the different islands. The smell would get stronger for her as the days went on. Her sense of smell differed from the others. Stronger, more powerful. It made her wonder, why me?

She couldn't understand why the world had gotten this way. She hated what she was. A killer, a soulless non-living parasite, a creature with no soul not connected to earth, but there was a lot more to her than she knew.

She didn't have a choice. When she was born into this life, into this family, it was already chosen for her. Now she just needed to find the right way, the way to fix things, to bring peace to all the lands.

Whichever path she chose, hopefully it was the right one to save them. She hated her parents for bringing her into this world while this war was going on. She didn't ask for it and didn't want it. She never met them until she was older, or so she thought. She was raised by vampires and had to figure out the truth on her own.

....

"What do you want for this creature, life or death?" asked the deep voice in the shadows.

Like they really had an option, it's a trick question really; either way, it is death.

"Life," Cecilia replied. As they ripped me out of her warm arms, my father, Marcus, was filled with anger and lost total control of his emotions.

"No, you shall not have our baby! Give her back!" Marcus yelled as he grabbed me and tried to yank me out of the man's arms.

"Do you dare question and rebel against me, you fool? It would only take a second for you to become a cold, lifeless, stiff corpse. The only reason you creatures live as long as you do is because we let you. You're lucky everyone in this room is not dead from the blood dripping on the floor from the birth of your creature," said Efron.

My father glanced at the scissors that had been used to cut my umbilical cord; he grabbed them as quickly as he could and stabbed Efron in the chest.

He took a step back. The scissors were sticking out of Efron's neck. Efron started laughing hysterically. Then Efron yanked the scissors out of his neck and tossed them to the floor.

"Stupid human creature, you can't kill me. Do you think we would have put silver in those scissors? You could have lived another day, but now you will meet your termination," he said cockily, at the top of his lungs. He couldn't understand why a useless creature thought it could kill him.

"She will rebel against you and take back what is ours, freeing the humans. She will be nothing like you, and she will kill you and your kind!"Those were Marcus's last words. He now had a look of fear in his eyes, knowing it was his last moment on earth.

Efron walked toward Marcus, who stood frozen, shivering in sheer panic. He then threw him against the wall, covering my father's mouth, so that his screams could not be heard. Efron exposed his fangs and bit into my father's neck. He yanked a chunk of my father's throat out and spat it out with the flick of his tongue, and it hit the floor. There was blood gushing from the wound. He then continued with my father's demise.

My mother watched on in disgust, almost vomiting as Efron made a meal of my father. He seemed to enjoy it, and my mother could feel his energy growing as he drank my father's blood. She lay there on the bed knowing what was going to happen next. Her mate had been killed, so now she had no one to breed with, so she too must die. She was not scared, more relieved if anything. She would be free and no longer a prisoner that must do what she was told by a race with no soul. She had despised the vampires for taking away her life. And for changing the one she loved into a vicious bloodsucker. She couldn't believe that was him standing in front of her.

"Do you have a name you would like to give this child?" Efron asked, Cecilia couldn't focus from seeing Marcus's blood dripping off Efron's mouth and chin. Efron then wiped his mouth on the sleeve of his shirt. His shirt was black, so the blood just faded into it like it was never there.

"Tell me now if you have one. Or we'll give her whatever name we see fit." He demanded.

"Luna," she said. "Please let her keep this blanket I have made her and my journal so she can know of her real parents."My mother pleaded. Luna was a familiar name he once knew. Efron said nothing, staring Cecilia in the eyes with a warming gaze. He nodded, taking the blanket and wrapping Luna in it.

"What happened to you, Efron? This is not you," she said, with tears in her eyes.

"You don't know who I am anymore. The thirst takes over; it's like nothing you have ever felt, the power. It's unimaginable, like a high you don't want to come off of. You knew it was going to come to this. What did you expect when you made the choice you did? You chose to be a breeder. Did you think I wanted to do this?" he said in a husky voice and then huffed and scowled at her.

"I didn't want to become what you are, to never love, have children, or have a connection with a human," she replied.

"I am not as bad as you think. I am sorry it has come to this, but I have no choice to do what must be done; they are the rules. I have to do this; you don't know the cost otherwise."He whispered.

"I know they are, but I also know it is the demon in you that is going to take my life, so I forgive you.""But there is something I must tell you before you do it." She pleaded with him.

"No, we have talked too much; it will make it harder. I will always remember our time we had together forever. You will always have my heart's love and last beat," said Efron.

Then, as fast as a bullet, he put his mouth to her neck and killed her without another word from either of them. A tear ran down his face as he never thought he would be the one to kill her. To take her heartbeat away, he had never forgotten her from their childhood.

He stood there looking at her lifeless body and wanted to die. Maybe I should have told her I was still in love with her, he thought. But he wanted to show no emotion; so he said nothing.

She was still as beautiful as she had been back then. She had long golden hair; it was almost white when it hit the sun a certain way. She had sparkling bluish/green eyes. Her skin was warm and had a glow to it from the blood running through her veins.

He didn't suck her dry, for he thought she deserved a better way to the end of her life than as one of his entrées. Efron stood there for a few minutes gazing at her to collect himself. He didn't want anyone to know he had ever been in love with a heart beater. If they knew, his road to becoming an enforcer would be ruined. He wished he could take back the choice he made and be with her, but it was way too late. He was an immortal now.

Efron carried Luna, put the journal in his coat that Cecilia gave him; he grabbed a picture of Cecilia and put it in the same pocket as the journal. He exited the house with Luna. The operations boss was outside waiting. Efron had the creature in his arms and gave her to Vilhauer, the second hand man of the Vampire Society.

"What took so long, Efron?" Vilhauer demanded

"There was a problem with the man creature, so I had to take him out, and per the rules, her as well." replied Efron.

"What was the problem?"

"Nothing too big — he just had an opinion and stabbed me with the scissors. He thought he could kill me," Efron said with a smirk on his face and chuckled a bit. Although, you could see the pain in his eyes that he was trying to hide it. He was hurting deep inside from having had to kill Cecilia.

"Seems like it was a big problem to me," replied Vilhauer.

Vilhauer walked into the house and into the birthing room. Efron followed him and looked as if he was going to have a breakdown, but he stayed strong and hid his emotions. Vilhauer saw Marcus on the floor, lifeless, and Cecilia on the bed. She was not pale, still glowing from the blood running through her veins. He could still hear her heartbeat as well.

"What is this? If you kill someone, you are supposed to suck them dry, so it is an easier clean up and they are not as heavy to carry." Vilhauer demanded.

"I didn't know that," said Efron.

"Yes, you did. It says in the rules, and I know you read them and studied them to no end, or I wouldn't have brought you here, so do it now!" he demanded!

"I won't do it. I can't. Not to her. She deserves better," he said, being argumentative.

"There is a reason we gave you this house. We all knew about your love affair and sleeping together before you were transformed. This is your punishment for breaking the rules. Finish, her, off!" He demanded.

"We knew you would lose it and kill the heart beater she was breeding with because of your jealousy. You need to be like us, and once you drain her, you will lose all hope and that love feeling you have will disappear, which will make you a better enforcer and a better vampire," explained Vilhauer

"I hate you all, I will never forgive you. You gave me this house as a punishment? What kind of punishment is killing someone you love?"

Being away from her for nine months was punishment enough. If anything, the transformation made the feelings stronger. He had so much hatred in his body he shook. The blood that he had drunk, rose to the top of his cold skin, and he almost looked like he was a human for a minute. He was boiling with despise.

"It was not my idea; The Society thought it would be a good idea. Right now, you have no choice. You must do it, or you will be terminated. That will be your consequence. And I will kill this creature so you will have nothing left of her. You will learn to live with this. We all do things we don't like at first, and then we learn to love them in our own sick little way," said Vilhauer.

Efron walked over to her and gazed at her as if she were sleeping. He remembered when he used to watch her sleep in the orphanage, and his favorite memory was the first time he kissed her when they watched the sunset. He put her hair behind her ear and then put his mouth next to her ear. He whispered ever so sweetly in her ear.

"I have always loved you, and I am sorry for not choosing us." Then he bit her neck and sucked as hard as he could, with tears running down his face. He looked like he was in pain while he drained her.

Right in that moment, when there were no more drops of blood to take, he released venom out of his fangs and spit it into her. He instantly felt a bond deeper than the love he had felt for her. He didn't know if it could change her, because he had never changed anyone before. He could only hope that he had done it right, and that he would see her open her eyes, and that she would be alright.

"You are sucking to long, she is drained," said Vilhauer, Efron pulled off of her neck with a smile on his face, blood dripping from his mouth and took a step back. She looked pale now, and all the life had been drained out of her.

"Why, yes, she is," he replied. With a smirk on his face.

"Oh, you didn't." Vilhauer had a look of disbelief on his face. "No one is supposed to change creatures except, The Society," said Vilhauer.

"You're right; I did do my reading of the rules. Once a vampire has been created, they cannot be killed by anyone but The Society, or both vampires shall be terminated. Only The Society makes the choice of what will happen given the facts of the situation." Efron defined.

"You misunderstood the rules. It says nothing about just any vampire creating vampires. There is a reason everyone has the same vampire genetics. We are all the same family. We all have the same Creator. You are now a Creator, and they don't want other creators. One is all that is needed. If there is more than one, there will be too many of us and things will get out of control." Vilhauer had a look of fright on his face about the unknown. Thoughts were going wild in his head.

"Well, things will soon change around here." Efron said with confidence.

"So you think. You didn't think your plan through correctly, she is going to hate you now," said Vilhauer.

"I don't care. At least she will be alive, and I don't have to live with her death," said Efron. He looked relieved.

"That's what you think, Efron. You have made a grave mistake. You have to live with her human death." Vilhauer sighed. "You didn't read the rules correctly. Or you misunderstood them. The very first decision is made from what your parents would like for you to be. The second one is if you chose to override your parent's choice and you chose to go the opposite way of what they wanted for you. You chose to become one of us. And the final choice is The Society's decision on all the facts and what would be the best fit for us and for you.

It is The Society's choice of who is born into our world, or who is a breeder, or who becomes a course meal. For you to take that action without consulting them could mean the final termination. But no one has ever done it before, so no one knows what will happen. I can't believe I vouched for you to be one of us. You have made me look incompetent." Vilhauer said assertively.

Vilhauer had a look of shame on his face. If he didn't get the final termination from killing Efron, he would kill him. Vilhauer thought maybe they would terminate them both because he was in charge of Efron; being his adviser. He cared for Efron like a son; he had raised him as his own, taught him the vampire ways in nine months. Efron had never disappointed Vilhauer before, so he was still surprised and in shock for what he had done.

"I should have just let you become a breeder like your parents wanted you to be in the first place. He scolded him, you need to clean up this mess, and fill out the proper paperwork and get this house ready for the next breeders. The Society will deal with you tomorrow night. I don't have the time to deal with this now," said Vilhauer angrily.

"I will have it done before the sun comes up," said Efron

"Good, that's what I like to hear. You would have been a great enforcer. But now, who knows what will happen," said Vilhauer. "What do you mean would have? No choice has been made yet." Efron looked confused, as if Vilhauer was keeping something from him.

"If I have anything to do with it, you won't. Look at your fall through. You now have a weakness; you're so naïve," said Vilhauer.

Vilhauer exited the room with Luna in his arms and headed outside to wait for news from the other enforcers about their rounds of deliveries. Efron followed protocol and had the house cleaned up and all their belongings and the male mate burned in the fireplace. He put some of Cecilia's belongings in his bag to take with him, so she could have them later. He even had time to clean Cecilia up and still had four hours until sunrise. He looked at her and realized she was transforming. She was already beginning to heal but had not awakened yet. Her pregnant belly receding back into place; the stretch marks she had accumulated while pregnant disappearing. She looked the same as she had nine months ago, when he had last seen her. Wow, it worked, he thought. He kissed her on the forehead and said, "You're going to be alright. We can be together forever now." But he wondered what lay ahead for them, if anything at all. One thing was certain; his future was going to change.

He walked outside to accompany Vilhauer. "Cecilia is healing."

"Well, you get to carry her back then. I don't want to hear any complaining from you, and I hope the best for you, because I care about you, but I am not sure what is going to happen. I have never seen anyone go against the choices of The Society."

"Thank you, Vilhauer."

Efron gave Vilhauer a hug a she apologized for his sudden action and for getting him into any kind of trouble.

"When will she awaken?"Asked Efron, he had a look of excitement on his face, but he was worried as well.

"Twenty-four hours is the normal time, but you drained her dry, and they normally leave half the blood in the body, so it's an easier transition. So it probably will be in twelve or so hours. Currently, the venom has no blood to go through, so it goes straight to the organs and will be quicker and more painful. You better be ready when she wakes because she will be hungry for blood no matter who it is. And nothing will stop her. And since you are her creator, you must watch over her and teach her our ways.

"Usually, The Society will appoint someone to her, but we are not on Vampire Island, so it is your job to watch her until we get to the island."

"Vilhauer!" yelled a voice of desperation.

"There is no way the woman creature that I am assigned to is going to deliver before the sun comes up," said Cronus.

"Well, what are your options?" Demanded Vilhauer. Cronus was in a panic.

"I am not sure. I think the baby creature is stuck," he said.

"Did you do your research before we came into town?"

"Yes, some of it I did, but not everything. I believe it is her last time to deliver a baby creature," said Cronus.

"So what is the problem then?" Vilhauer looked agitated and rolled his eyes.

"I don't know. I am not sure what to do. Nothing is coming out of the hole."

"Do I have to do everything myself?" said Vilhauer.

"No. Let me take care of this, Vilhauer. It's the least I can do after everything," said Efron.

"I guess so; I might as well use you while I still have you here. Make yourself useful," said Vilhauer, as he rolled his eyes, thinking about what else Efron could mess up tonight.

"I will show you how it's done, Cronus; this is why you vouched for me, Vilhauer."

Cronus took Efron to the woman creature and her mate. There was blood everywhere all over the room. Efron could tell it was amateur work.

"Well, I can see why she can't deliver on time. You killed her mate, and fed on her until she was unconscious," said Efron, shaking his head in disbelief.

"Well, I couldn't control myself. I was so hungry, and her mate was not enough for me."

"You are supposed to wait until after she delivers; to kill them both. Do you have any idea what could happen to you if anyone finds out about this? There are protocols in place for a reason." said Efron.

"Well, I was just so turned on with her in pain I just went wild, maybe this is not the right job for me." said Cronus with a smirk on his face.

Efron walked over to the pregnant women and put his hands on her abdomen, he tore her stomach open. She let out a scream and started to seizure. Cronus ran over to her to feed more, and Efron punched him straight in the face and through him against the wall.

"Wait until I get the creature out, you idiot," he demanded.

This woman was bigger than most of the others. He was having a difficult time pulling the creature out, so he had to snap the woman in half. You could hear the cracking of the bones, one at a time. It sounded like a gun popping. Pop! Pop! Pop! Blood gushed everywhere. Efron was getting a little hungry but was able to hold himself together because he knew what it meant to get the creature out.

"I am in heaven. Or really hell." said Cronus. He was laughing uncontrollably, as he dove on the floor almost tripping himself and started to lick up the blood off the floor.

Efron reached in her mangled body and pulled out the creature. He was staring at the dead women's stomach, because it was odd her abdomen was still moving. Well what was left of it anyways? He reached in again and felt around, he felt something that felt like a little head, and he pulled out another creature. There were two creatures, matches as they called them, one boy and one girl.

"Did you happen to ask the mother what she wanted to call them Cronus?"

"No I didn't get to that part; I had already lost control and killed them"

"I will pick the names then "Phoebe and Orion." Efron said.

"What should we do now Efron?"

"Me? I am not doing anything; I am taking these matches to Vilhauer. He will be pleased there were two creatures instead of one. You will clean this mess up before we have to head back to the boat." said Efron.

"So what am I to do with all their stuff?"

"Burn it in the fire place and get the house ready for the next ones, and fill out the proper paper work. Did you even read the control book?"

"No," Cronus said, with a look shame on his face.

Efron shook his head, grabbed the matches and headed outside to the dirt street where Vilhauer was waiting by the small carriage carts to take the creatures back to the boat. Vilhauer looked confused, but excited at the same time.

"Matches?" he said.

"Yes, apparently Cronus didn't do all his research before coming into town. The woman breeder was quite a bit larger than the others. It was also her last time mating, and the birth was a big mess. He lost control and let his hunger guide him."

"Well The Society will be happy there was another, but I don't think they will go in your favor because of it. You have done me a favor by stepping in with Cronus, but that doesn't get you off the hook for you going against protocol and breaking the rules." said Vilhauer angrily. "It is time to meet at the gate, gather the others and grab Cecilia.

Efron nodded his head and ran around the colony and made the signal that it was time to meet at the gate and go. He went back to the house that had Cecilia in it. He gave her a kiss on the lips and then picked her up and placed her over his shoulder.

She was a lot heavier now since he had changed her. He thought it would be effortless carrying her, but he was wrong. He left the lights on and the door unlocked so it would be more welcoming for the next breeders. He shuffled down to the gate. Almost tripping over his own two feet a few times.

There was about an hour to go before the sun came up. All three enforcers and their assistant's gather by the gate that surrounded the city. There were six assistants including Efron. Three women and three men. Each enforcer was in charge of two assistants, but it was becoming an ordeal, and the enforcers couldn't keep up with supervising their assistants and doing their responsibilities in time before they had to leave.

This was all their first time out. So it was more difficult than if they had already been trained and knowledgeable about what to do. It made Vilhauer nervous, for if they messed up he would take the raft for it because he was the Head Enforcer.

There had been six deliveries, but seven creatures. They were not expecting seven, so they had to make do. No one knew what Efron had done, but they all had an idea because he had Cecilia over his shoulder.

"Protocols," piped Cronus as he looked at Efron.

"This is different, mind your own business. You're lucky I helped you out."

"Efron, what are you doing? Are you mad?" asked Siren.

"This doesn't concern you Siren."

"Oh, it sure the hell it does, when I am your mate. Who is that woman?"She shrieked.

"Quite everyone or you will become ashes where you stand! We have less than an hour to get out of here. It is time to collect all the creatures and head back to our community. If you want to stay and argue then you will die when the sun rises." shouted Vilhauer.

"Yes sir", they all said.

Everyone was accounted for, so the gates to the colony were closed and locked by the human keepers that watched The Island for us. The only reason they agreed to do this is that their families would be left alone and safe from the soulless ones. They allowed us to keep this island and the colony to breed the humans because if they didn't, the world they knew would be no more, and we would control the humans that got to be free. If there were to be a disturbance in the balance, the Soulless ones would take over all the islands, and no one would be safe anywhere from them.

No one really knows about the Soulless Ones in the free land. The humans in the cities there don't know what we are capable of; they just know that we come in the night and collect some of the older children. If they don't give the children away willingly, the whole family would be slaughtered and eaten.

They have grown accustomed to giving away their children and have never tried to rebel and take us head-on. At least they haven't since I was a boy. But that was also the first time they came, and no one had known what they were dealing with.

There is only that but one story of us invading, and no one remembers anymore. At least that's what the stories are, but who really knows if they are true.

The mortal children were then taken to our Vampire Island for which they have no choice and be raised to the age of maturity. After they become of age, they are bred like animals so we can eat to stay alive.

If the humans really wanted to leave the island they probably could, but they would need a boat. Although The Free Land is way too far away for them to travel by small boat, the only boats allowed by our Colony are The Society boats. If any other boat is out at sea by either of our two islands, they always disappear and no one knows where to.

Even if the humans made it off the Colony Island, they could only go as far as our island. Anywhere else, we would be able to smell them before they were out of our reach. And if anyone ever got to our land, on arriving, they would be killed as soon as they stepped foot on the land. But I don't think anyone wants to leave anyway, what they have is the only life they know.

I glanced back at the gate one more time before arriving at the docks. It's hard to believe those old gates could keep the humans in. Humans, I haven't thought of the creatures as that until I saw Cecilia again. It's like she is bringing my soul back to me. As soon as I stepped onto our boat, I heard someone shout.

"Wow, you idiot, Efron!" I thought to myself. So what, I love her. No one could ever understand the love I have for her. I changed my choice. I was in love with her our entire childhood. Even after I had been transformed, my love for her never changed; it may have even grown.

Baby Luna should have been ours together. That should have been our house; I should have protected her. Being a human, I wouldn't have been able to protect her or any baby we had from someone like me. But I made a mistake because I was too afraid to die. What if I have doomed us both now?

"Efron, you comfy carrying your bride?" said Adonis. The entire crew burst out laughing. Except one, and that was Siren.

She had no clue who this woman was, although she knew one thing, that she hated her. She knew that if Efron broke such rules he must love her, but how can he love with no soul? She thought.

I must get to the bottom of this, and get rid of her; no one is going to steal my life mate, not even her. I am supposed to connect with him, and share eternity with him. I already gave myself to him; it's too late now, he can't turn away. If I can't have him, no one will.

"Efron, it's down to the cages for you and your bride," said Vilhauer.

"But why would we need too? I thought we were okay for now?"

"No, you still broke the rules. Now, you will be put in a cell next to Cecilia."

"Come on, Efron, let's go," said Adonis

"Fine, at least have a meal ready for when Cecilia wakes," he huffed.

"You. Get one out of the closet for her; make sure it's that chunky one that won't stop babbling. He is driving me crazy with his wailing. It will be a delightful treat for her."

"Ha-ha," said Vilhauer. "Everyone! Down under deck; the sun is about to rise. Creatures, do your jobs; remember, your families' lives are at stake if you don't."

All the soulless ones walked to the stairs to go underneath the deck, as human slaves locked the doors behind them. Adonis walked Efron down to the cells and then placed Cecilia on a concrete bed. It had a blanket and pillow he used to cover her up and walked out of the cell.

Adonis then escorted him to the food closet, where the meals were kept. You could hear the chunky one down the hallway saying, "Please don't eat me." Efron opened the door and stood in front of the humans. He let his fangs pop out, and his eyes were black as night with black veins on the sides of his eyes popping out.

"Back up now, or I will kill you all," he said.

He grabbed the chunky one in the corner that was crouched down on the floor.

"One more sound and you will be my dessert." The chunky one nodded his head and shut his mouth. His eyes were swollen from crying all night.

They headed back to the cells, and he put the chunky one in with Cecilia. "Sit here and be quiet until she wakes. You will be eaten. There is no reason to cry about it. You can't change it. You are going to die. Just be glad it will be finally over!" Efron walked over to his cell and sat on his bed and stared at Cecilia. Adonis locked Cecilia's cell, then locked Efron's cell. Seconds later, Siren appeared.

"Not now, Siren, he can't have visitors," said Adonis

"Just a few minutes. You can even stay if you want."She smiled; he knew what she was signaling.

"What do you want, Siren?" Efron said with a sigh.

"Do you love this woman? I mean, you broke the rules for her. How stupid are you? You want to be terminated? You are supposed to be my life mate."You could see the anger on her face.

"Yes, I love her. I always have. I am sorry we can be no more. Just because The Society said for us to spend eternity together doesn't mean I will or that I have to."

"That's not how it works; we will fight to the death for you. I laid with you first, so you are mine." Siren grabbed the key to his cell. Adonis tried to pry it out of her hand, but Adonis was human, so really it wouldn't matter what he tried to do.

"Relax Adonis; I am not letting him out. I am going in." Siren got in Efron's face and said, "What's the matter did the stupid creature get to you?" She bit him on the neck and grabbed him close to her, and put his hands on her butt. They were both hot and still turned on from the killings.

"You know what the blood does; it's the only way to get rid of this heat I feel in you. It's too warm and will make us sick if we don't release this tension. You need to lie with me right now, right here!"

"No, I can't, I am going to wait for her to wake." Siren kissed him one last time; it felt like her tongue was going to come out of his neck.

He pushed her off. She could see that something wanted her, and it was in his pants. She took a step back and ripped off her dress.

"It's hot in here, don't you think?"Her body was perfect, and the belly ring made her even more desirable, and her supple nipples were pointing out as always, he thought.

"Get out, Siren. I don't want you anymore. Why don't you fuck Adonis or something? I am not for you anymore. I have made my choice. You are no longer mine. The bond isn't with you anymore."

"We will see about that, prude." Siren walked out of his cell and didn't take her dress. She was about to walk passed Adonis, but he grabbed her, pushed her against the wall with his body and kissed her and yanked some of her hair out.

"Well, you know how to turn a girl on. Enjoy Efron; you are going to wish this was you, you little pervert." She had excitement in her eyes, as they turned black as night.

"You're damn right I do, now bend over my desk and take it, you whore." Adonis slammed her down on his desk; his papers went flying everywhere. He broke his belt on his pants because he was so excited. It had been over a year since he had had intercourse. For such a big guy, he had a small one, she thought.

He stuck it in her and slammed her head down on the table repeatedly as he was thrusting in and out of her. Wow, she does feel like a virgin; he thought. She was tighter than he could ever get his hand to go. He was moaning like some old cat that was dying on a hairball. Without realizing it, he started to twitch and orgasmed in less than a minute. Efron was in his cell watching and started laughing hysterically.

"That's some good sex to watch. I am totally jealous. I have had more fun masturbating then watching you two go at it." he chuckled.

"Sorry it's been a while."

"Yeah, I guess. Get off me, Minuteman. You have a small penis too; no wonder no one wants you." Siren was so embarrassed her cheeks were still red. Efron threw her dress at her. She put it on and ran out the door. She had nothing else to say, she just wanted the humiliation to be over.

"Well, I got mine sweet cheeks, with my little penis," yelled Adonis.

Adonis picked his paper work up off the ground and sat down in his chair. He had a smile on his face now that he didn't have before. "I should just stick to what I do best," he thought. Who needs women, I got my lefty. He kissed his hand and said, "You will never insult me will you."

"Wow, you got issues Adonis." Adonis ignored Efron and went back to his paper work. About a minute later Adonis went to his lair to rest.

Efron lay there wondering when Cecilia was going to open her eyes. The chunky one just sat on the ground next to the concrete bed looking at the wall. Efron had forgotten he had been there because he was so quite.

Efron sat there trying to not laugh at what he just saw. But he couldn't help it for every time he thought about it he wanted to laugh. It was little things like that, which made his life worth living.

He glanced over at Cecilia and noticed she moved her arm off her side. Is this it he thought, it must be time. He could feel her energy, her every emotion, he could feel that she was hungry as well. He didn't know being a creator could make you feel these things, he could feel the bond, he wondered if it was normal.

She lifted her arm, moving her hair out of her eyes with her hand. She opened her eyes, stared, and saw what she feared most.

Chapter Two

He could feel every ounce of anger she had in her body. He had never felt that from her before, or anyone. He could also feel all the sadness in her body and the pain in her heart even though it was not beating anymore.

He felt mortified about what he had done to her. Really, he was selfish for turning her; she didn't want it, but yet he didn't care. He wondered whether she would hate him now. He was afraid to talk because he didn't know what she might say, and he didn't want to hear the words I hate you come out of her mouth.

Her hair was still blonde and as bright as the sun. Her eyes were black, but every blink, her eyes would turn red and then back to black. She had red veins on the sides of her eyes; he had never seen it like that before. She looked dead and pasty white, like she was about to pass out.

He got up off the concrete bed in his cell and walked toward her. She scooted away from him. You could tell it in her eyes that she was afraid of him, and didn't have remorse for him.

"You must eat," he said in a timid voice. "You will feel sicker if you don't; I promise you will feel better." She rolled her eyes at him.

"Eat what? A human?" The look of fear was on her face. She didn't want to, but she thought he smelled sweet. The chunky one was shivering in the corner; you could see the sweat dripping off his forehead.

"I will make it easier for you, I will kill him first for you, so you don't have too."

"Wow, thanks," she said sarcastically. She was just a human only hours ago. She couldn't imagine killing a human, let alone eating one. She started to feel nauseated, so she leaned over off the concrete bed and puked all over the floor. Her puke was steaming, it was venom.

"I am just trying to help you out." He explained.

"Help me out? You should have left me dead and did what you were supposed to do. Now, I am… I am this." Her eyes got watery and tears starting rolling down her face, but it wasn't water it was venom and it burned. She wiped them away with her shirt and grabbed her eyes in pain.

"Yes, you are a Vampire. I couldn't live with the guilt of killing you." His eyes were moist, as if about to cry. "I still love you. I never stopped loving you, and I have loved you as long as I can remember."

"You love me? Ha! Shut up! You turned me into a Vampire, a disgusting Vampire. A slaughterer, a heartless bloodsucker!" She was so livid you could see the veins popping out of her neck. She then stood up off the bed and walked toward him, but her legs gave out, and she tumbled to the floor, falling right in her puke. You could hear her knees crack and pop as she hit the ground.

"I think I just broke my knees," she said with a groan of pain.

"I'm sorry," he said. His cheeks turned blushes of red, you could tell he was embarrassed by the look he had on his face. The chunky one got up slowly knowing they were not paying any attention to him. He walked toward her. Lifting his leg up, he smashed her with his foot with all the strength he had to the side of her body. You could hear another crack from her bones as soon as his foot hit her hip bone. She screamed with pain. She was dead and broken; the pain was more excruciating than anything she had ever felt before. She could see her hip bone sticking out of her body. But she had no blood oozing from her wounds, because she had no blood in her body, for he had drained her completely when he transformed her.

"You're not going to eat me, you infection of death," he yelled. He was standing over her, thinking he had won and that she was going to die. She didn't have enough strength to get up and do anything. He was standing just close enough to the bars of the cage for Efron to reach out and grab him. The chunky one had a look of terror on his face. In the blink of an eye, Efron reached over and put his hands around the man's throat and snapped his neck. It was a loud pop, like someone had fired a gun. His body went limp and fell to the floor. Cecilia was whining in pain. She knew what she had to do, but she didn't want to. At least she didn't have to kill him, she thought.

"Now eat him, or the pain will stay and get worse."

She put her arms down on the concrete floor, which felt warm to her. She remembered how concrete floors used to feel somewhat colder to her, but her body temperature had changed to ice cold. Even Efron could feel she was a slight bit colder than any other vampire he had been close to. He thought once she gets a drink, she should warm up a bit.

Cecilia started scooting her broken body toward the lifeless body on the floor. The closest thing to her was his stomach; she didn't feel like moving closer to his neck, which was the ideal place to eat from.

She noticed that the closer she got to the warm body, the better he smelled, and the more desirable he got. She felt a rage come over her she had never felt before. She felt hungry, angry, and powerful. She pulled up his shirt, and his tummy jiggled a bit. She couldn't help laughing.

She looked at Efron one last time before taking a bite and sank her teeth in like she wanted his approval or something. He gave her a nod, and he sat back down on his bed and watched her devour the chunky one. The blood tasted just like it smelled, sweet. It was like taking a drug for the first time; it got better with every swallow. She could feel her hip bone sliding back into place, and her knees healing from the inside out. She felt like she could take on an Army of Dragons and kill them all. Efron also noticed she wasn't as pale anymore. Her skin was filling out, and her body curved out more like an hourglass figure. She was stunning, the most beautiful woman he had ever seen, he thought. She stopped sucking for a minute, licked her lips and looked at him.

"Did you say something?"

"No," he said. He had a look of confusion on his face. Then he thought for a second. No one had said anything. Adonis had been passed out sleeping, and there was no one else in the room but them.

"You should hurry and suck him dry before he goes bad," he said with a grin on his face. She turned her head back down, and her eyes were as red as the flames of hell. He knew she was feeling better and had been healed. But it wasn't normal for her eyes to be red. He thought she might need more but figured the chunky man would be enough for now.

She lifted her head, looking up at him again. "No, I don't. I am fine," she said irritably.

"No, you don't what?" he said with confusion again on his face.

"You said I might need more, and I said, no, I don't."

"I didn't say anything. I was thinking it." Wow! The legends are true, he thought.

"What legends?"

He was in total disbelief. There's no way they would kill her now if that's what they chose to do. She is too valuable. What will they do with her now? His mind just went wild thinking about the many different things The Society would do with her.

"What do you mean? Who, what, when, give me some answers," she demanded.

"There is an old spoken story that goes way back, before we were born, of a Dark Guardian who could read minds and had unspeakable power. No one could control him. He controlled others, he controlled our world and he could walk in the day light. Legend says the second the Dark Guardian is terminated another one is created in that same second, and they would receive his powers. You have one of those powers. I have heard of other powers as well, but it doesn't seem like you have any of them."

"Well, if that's true, then why didn't I hear the fat one thinking about killing me? Or hear your thoughts before hand when I first woke?"

"Maybe because you hadn't tasted blood yet; I don't know all the answers. It has been told how he wrote all the protocols and all the rules. He is supposed to be the one in charge of The Society. But if you have his powers now, I'm not sure he is even alive anymore." Efron was in shock; how come out of all creatures that were changed she got it? She has no idea how powerful she is; she could change everything.

"You must say nothing about this to anyone. You must wait until the time is right. They have to find out The Dark Guardian has been terminated first."

"I don't want this power; I don't want to be a Vampire! Don't think for a second I'm not mad at you anymore. I am still furious!" she said. All he could think about was how sexy she looked when she was mad, and how he was turned on by her and just wanted to take her right there.

"Stop thinking about me; I can still hear you!" she sighed. "You are never getting a piece of this again."

"Be quiet and keep this to yourself. We will also see about that," he smiled. Looking into her eyes, which were back to normal after her fangs protruded, she still had red veins around her eyes. He could tell she still had feelings for him; the sparkle in her eyes gave it away when she glanced at him.

"There might be more powers to come later when you are stronger. They build as you grow. I am not exactly sure. Only The Society knows all the details of The Dark Guardian."

"Oh great, more things I don't want."

Cecilia looked around. She could smell something sweet. The red in her eyes returned; they looked like fire. She was still hungry. She could hear a heartbeat and got excited. She didn't want to get excited; she was ashamed of it. But there was something else in her body taking over. A predator's sense. She swallowed and could feel a burn in her throat.

The door to Adonis's lair opened, and he stepped out, walking over to the cage where Cecilia was. She was gorgeous, he thought. He had never seen a Vampire like her. Stunning, thin, perfect breasts, hourglass figure, and plump buttocks. He was picturing her naked and smiled as he licked his chapped lips and grabbed at his groin.

"Yuck," she said with disgust on her face. She wanted to eat him even more, knowing what he was thinking about her.

"Control yourself, Cecilia." Efron was nervous she would spill the news that she could hear Adonis' thoughts.

"What's all this commotion out here? I was trying to sleep. I see your bride has awakened."

"Bride?" She looked even more enraged than she already was, her face getting even redder.

"It's nothing, just a dumb joke. Everyone on the crew thought it was funny to call you my bride."He gave Adonis a dirty look.

"Mind your own business, Adonis. Go back to bed. No one has anything to say to you. You're just a vampire slave. You're lucky we don't kill you."

"Well, by the way it looks, kid; you will be gone before me. Who's the one in the cage here?" Efron sat in silence and gave him a look that could kill. Adonis was glad Efron was behind bars, or he would have been attacked. Maybe not killed but enough to make him not open his mouth again and talk such nonsense. Adonis walked back into his lair.

"Keep it down out there!" he yelled, then shut the door and went back to bed.

"Oh, well, they're dumb. What can you expect from a bunch of dead people? They just wished I was their bride; they are so jealous. So, are we just going to stay in these cages forever? Or what?" She looked around and thought, how revolting this cage was.

There was a dead body on the floor that was taking up most of the walkway in her cell; she couldn't even go to the bathroom if she had to. Plus, he was starting to stink because he was decomposing from the inside out.

The fact that she had fallen into her own vomit didn't make it any better. There were no showers in here, so she had to live with the repulsive smell on her clothes. With so much going through her mind, she couldn't really focus. She was still trying to accept that she was now a Vampire. On top of all that, she could hear others' thoughts.

She didn't know what powers would come next, or if she would be able to spot them, and control them before someone knew she had them. She was still trying to figure it all out. What will she become, but with Efron not knowing much, she didn't really get any answers.

"No, we won't stay in these cages for long, but you should get some rest. You will have a long night ahead of you. We have to face The Society, and they are not going to be happy with me." Efron sighed. You could tell he had anxiety and was apprehensive about the whole situation. But he acted as if he had no issues in the world. He was a strapping infant, not even a year old yet. He had spiky black hair and brown eyes. He dressed well for a young Vampire. He's got that can-do attitude and will do as he pleases, but he still has some humanity left in him and has a weakness when it comes to his love for Cecilia.

"Rest, rest? You are joking, right? How am I supposed to relax with all that has happened tonight? Speaking of things that has happened tonight where is my baby? Can I see her; will I ever see her again? I know that if I wasn't transformed I wouldn't be able to see her and I would carry on. But now I am a Vampire, it will be different, right?"

"Whoa with all the questions, one at a time, please. I can't really answer all of that right now. The Society will make the choice of what will be done, and you will know from there. I am sorry I don't have any answers for you."

"It's fine for now, I guess. I just want out of this cage." The smell was making her lightheaded and dizzy. But she still had a hint of the sweet human smell. She sat down on the bed and stared at the wall. She could feel a burning sensation on her arm; she immediately jumped up and said, "What the heck was that? It felt good." She looked at her arm and saw a line of green-looking scales that had appeared on her arm where the sun had touched her. It healed immediately.

"There is a small crack in the wall. The sun was coming through, so you have to be careful. The sun will burn you and make you explode into ash, so stay away from it."

"Thanks. I should have known that. It's just hard to think with everything going on." She grabbed the pillow and moved the blanket so she would have some support under her on the concrete bed. She sat back down on the bed and shook her head. I will never see the sun again, or the bright blue sky with the clouds, she thought.

Efron took off his shirt and handed it to her. "Here you can wear this so you can take off that biohazard shirt." She smiled and giggled a little. She glanced at him for a minute; it was like his six-pack on his abs had enhanced since he had been transformed. He looked better than he did when he was human. She never really stopped to look and notice because she was so mad at him. She wanted to stay mad at him; she didn't want her feelings to resurface. She looked away real fast before he caught her looking.

"Thank you," she replied. She took off her shirt and noticed she had a bra on. She couldn't remember putting one on before giving birth to Luna. She took it off, for it didn't matter she was wearing it; she was busting out the sides of it.

"Well, my breasts got bigger." It was like she wanted a compliment, or something, but her back was to Efron, so he couldn't see, and he wasn't trying to look either. Efron sat there in silence. He didn't want to upset her or make her anymore annoyed than he already had. But he remembered she could hear his thoughts, so she knew he was thinking of her breasts. She put his shirt on. She took a big sniff when she put the shirt on. It smelled like him, which made her feel safe. She lay back down on the bed, although this time she lay on the opposite side of the bed, away from the sunbeam. She started to cry quietly. Efron was lying down on the concrete bed in his cell. He put his arm through the bars and around her side the best he could and held her. She wasn't mad that his arm was there; she wanted to be held. It made her feel safe, and she hadn't felt that since he last held her nine months ago. Efron thought, "If only I could make her understand why I couldn't kill her, maybe she wouldn't hate me so much."

"I don't hate you. I'm just extremely mad and upset at you."

"Well, that's a relief."

"Just be quite please. I just need quiet. It makes me feel like everything is okay."Soon she was able to doze off for a little while.

She had a dream where she was sitting in a dark room with no windows. There was a table and a few chairs, with a pitcher of blood on the table with two cups. There was a man across the table in black clothing; he was wearing a trench coat and a black mask so you couldn't see his face. He lifted the mask to the tip of his nose so he could take a drink of the warm blood. She asked herself, "Is this real?"She patted herself on the cheek.

"The destiny is yours now. Choose what you want to do with it, but choose right, or all will come crumbling down around you. You can have anything you want and make them do as you please. You are in control."

"Who are you?"

"Someone you are not ready to accept yet, but you have been chosen. Time will change you, and you will learn who you are." The man disappeared, and the room changed to outside, where she was standing in the middle of an open field. She looked up into the sky; the moon was full. As she was looking up, she saw something flying in the sky. It was big and yellow. She felt a connection to it. Then it disappeared into the darkness over the hill. She could feel the breeze from the wind, and she felt free. This is so strange; it feels so real. The man reappeared again.

"How did I get here? How did you get here?"

"You can go where I have been. I can only tell you certain things. The rest you have to learn on your own."

"How do I get out?"

"Think in your mind where you want to go. Make it happen. You have to really want it."

She thought about lying in bed. She was now staring at a wall. Turning around, she was now standing in a corner, in a room that looked so familiar to her. She looked at the bed and saw a child in it. It was her before the Vampires came and took her to the orphanage. How is this possible? She heard her name being called from the other room.

"Cecilia!"

She knew that voice well; it was her mother's. She had somehow jumped back into her past. "Had the Dark Guardian been here before?" She thought. She saw the door handle moving, and the door opening. "What if she sees me?"

She again imagined lying next to Efron in the cage. She could feel breathing on the back of her neck. She opened her eyes and was back in the cage. She moved Efron's arm off her and sat up.

"Did you get some rest?" he asked.

"I guess, if you could call it that. I had a dream. I thought we didn't sleep."

"We don't."

"Well, I did. I saw a man, dressed all in black, and said I was not ready to accept what is. I also jumped into my past."She looked frightened.

"What does this mean?"

"I don't know. I can't answer that for you. Maybe it was the Dark Guardian? But it seems like you are getting more powers."

"I don't know who it was. He wouldn't tell me. He said I wasn't ready."

"Well, try not to worry about it; if you are the new Dark Guardian, you shouldn't be afraid of anything."

They could feel the boat shift, and a loud bell went off. They had finally arrived in the blood lands, where the Vampires lived. Adonis opened his door and walked over to his desk and grabbed the keys to their cages. He unlocked Efron's first and then left the room for a moment. Coming back in, he placed the keys on the desk, and grabbed the paperwork off his desk.

"You two need to wait for Vilhauer to come in here and get you." Then he headed out of the holding space.

Efron walked over to the desk and picked up the keys and unlocked Cecilia's cage and picked up the chunky one and put him in the brick fireplace, where he would burn.

Cecilia just sat on the concrete bed, looking amazed that Efron had no emotion on his face while he put that man in the fire to burn. Efron then grabbed the mop and bucket by the sink and filled it with soapy water. He went back into Cecilia's cage and began mopping up the puke. He didn't ask Cecilia to help because she had been through enough last night.

Just then, Vilhauer walked through the door.

"Thank you for cleaning up Efron; you didn't have to," said Vilhauer.

"I know. I wanted to help," said Efron.

"Well, it's time to go. Please follow me, and don't make any problems along the way, or I will handcuff you. So that means while we all walk together, you need to keep control of yourself, Cecilia."

"Where are we going?" asked Cecilia.

"I have to take you guys to the holding cages in The Society house until they are ready to see you and choose what is going to happen."

"Oh."

"No more questions or talking, just come with me."

Vilhauer walked out of the room, Efron and Cecilia just followed him silently.

They made their way down a dark hallway and stopped at a door with a padlock. All the other Enforcers were there along with a few human slaves, who were carrying the babies. Cecilia could smell the blood, and Efron grabbed her and held her close. Cecilia saw that one of the slaves was holding Luna. Cecilia felt angry; she wanted to take her baby and run. She loved her baby.

Vilhauer walked to a door on the side of the boat and knocked on it three times. Then there was a return knock of three as well. That was the signal that they were in the right place, and it was safe to open the door and disembark from the ship.

Adonis stepped in front of everyone and took his keys out of his pockct and unlocked the padlock. He then opened the door to double-check that it was safe. As soon as he did, he stepped aside and let Vilhauer and all the other vampires walk ahead of him. He pinched Siren's butt as she passed by him. She smacked his hand and hissed at him.

All the Vampires turned left when they came into the underground tunnel. There was a side door that took them into the underground buildings. Vilhauer, Efron, and Cecilia, along with the human slaves that had the creatures, kept walking down the underground tunnel. Only important vampires, human slaves, and The Society could use the underground tunnels.

They stopped by another door with the word orphanage on it. The human slaves took the seven creatures and walked through the door, closing it behind them. Cecilia hadn't seen that door since she had left to become a breeder. She remembered saying goodbye to Efron on the very steps of the door. It was like yesterday. Suddenly, her feelings came rushing back to her. It hit her like a brick wall. She felt it. The bond was there. She looked at Efron and smiled. Now the only ones left walking in the tunnel were Vilhauer, Efron, and Cecilia. They stopped in front of another door that was guarded by two men dressed in black.

"I have to put these two in a holding cage," said Vilhauer.

"The boss is not going to like this," one man said, as the other one rolled his eyes. The men moved out of the way and opened the door for them.

They walked up two flights of stairs. They again knocked on another door that was closed. A woman in a black dress opened it. They walked in and closed the door behind them. Cecilia couldn't believe her eyes.

The house was huge; it was like the fairy tales she used to read about. The house was spotless; the curtains were draped on the floor. There was a crystal chandelier hanging in the living room. She was confused as to why it was dark outside even though it was daytime. They walked to another door, but this time Vilhauer just opened it.

"It is the holding cell. It hasn't been used in ten years, so it was turned into a guest room, but it still locks from the outside. So don't try any funny business. You wouldn't get far if you did anyway," said Vilhauer.

"Wow! This is some kind of holding cell," said Cecilia.

"Stay in here until The Society is ready to see you. It could be a few days. I will come by to drop meals off every five hours or so. But you really need to be resting."

Vilhauer closed the door, but he didn't lock it, which meant he still trusted Efron. Cecilia looked around the room. She noticed there was a wardrobe closet and opened it up. She looked through the clothes and found a green dress she wanted to try on. She grabbed the dress and walked behind the dressing wall. She threw Efron's shirt at him. She put the dress on and walked out from behind the wall. She then walked over to the mirror. She thought she looked stunning in the dress. Efron thought so too.

"Thank you."She said with a smile. Cecilia then walked over and sat on the bed. It was huge, probably king size, she would imagine. She had never seen one this big before. She didn't understand why there was a bed in the house, because vampires didn't sleep. Efron walked over and sat on the bed.

"So why was it still dark outside? I thought it was daytime."

"There are domes over the Island that block out the sun. They only rise during the day. It's so we can walk around and not have to worry about being turned to ash."

"Oh, that makes sense, I guess. I hate this waiting game. Why don't you put your shirt back on? I gave it back to you."

"I am kind of warm right now. After killing and eating, we get aroused, and our body temperature is warmer than it is supposed to be."

"So what are you trying to say then, Efron?"

"There is only one way to turn the heat down, and that's to have sex."

"Wow, really that's a cheesy line if I ever heard one. Why am I not hot then?"

"You should be. Maybe it's because you didn't kill, you just drank." Efron grabbed Cecilia's hand and realized it was cold to the touch. He then put her hand on his chest so she could feel how warm he was. Her face blushed a little bit. She pulled her hand away and turned around.

"I know what you're trying to do, and it's not going to happen. If you're so warm, go take care of yourself."

"It doesn't work like that. All vampires have a life mate. The Society chooses who men mate with, and the woman has to do what they say. If we want to have sex, you do it. If we want to give you to someone else, you do it. Do you want to be with someone way worse than me?"

"I am not falling for any of these lies."

"No, it's true. Why would I lie to you? I am trying to help you and make you educated about how we live. If you don't mate with me, some other vampire will force it on you, and you won't have a choice."

She sat there for a minute in disbelief; she couldn't believe this was happening to her. She wanted to smack Efron across the face, but she didn't. She lay next to him on the bed and rested her head on his chest. She could feel the heat coming from his body. She was debating what she should do.

"You won't force me to do it, will you? I am just not ready right now. What if we just pretend that we did?"

"No, I won't force you, but we can't pretend. We can tell if there has been a connection between two vampires. Also, what do you mean you're not ready? We have slept together before?"

"Well, that's great to know. Also, that was nine months ago. Things have changed."

She still had something she wanted to tell him, but she was too angry with him. She didn't want to tell him, she didn't know if she ever would. She didn't think he would care, only for the fact that he had no soul.

"Give me a little while," Cecilia said. "We will be in this room for a few days."

"Fine, if that's what you want to do. I respect you and will wait."

While they were lying there, they heard a loud noise coming from the hallway, like someone was throwing stuff against the wall. The door to the room swung open. It was Siren. She was enraged, and her eyes were black as night. Cecilia sat up and looked frightened.

"What's this, Efron? You're supposed to be in holding. What kind of holding is this? The guys at the tavern told me about this woman, and where she is from, and about your affair."

"I let you go Siren. You are no longer mine. You don't need to worry about what I do anymore. I no longer want or need you."

Siren was getting even more panic-stricken with every word coming out of Efron's mouth. Cecilia looked horrified.

"I am sorry; I had no idea about you." Cecilia said apologetically.

"Who do you think you are? You just waltz into our lives and steal my mate. I'm going to terminate you right here, you whore."

Siren came at Cecilia. She didn't know what to do. She didn't know how to fight with her new body. She put her arms up and pushed her hands outwards and imagined Siren stopping in her tracks.

All of a sudden, Siren stopped in her tracks and everything near her was hurled against the wall. It was unbelievable, like something that could only happen in a dream. Siren's jaw dropped, and her eyes became normal again. Siren was suddenly lifted into the air, and then shoved up against the wall. The harder Cecilia pushed her hands and thought about it the more pressure was put on Siren. Siren looked like she was going to be flattened. Cecilia started shaking and screamed, her eyes turning red, glowing with rage.

Chapter Three

Efron could feel the anger coursing through Cecilia's body. To be honest, Efron hadn't been that scared in a long time. He had never seen anything like it. There was no questioning it now; she was The Dark Guardian.

Siren looked like she was going to pop like a balloon. Efron wasn't sure what to do. So he thought if he stepped in front of Cecilia's force it would push him and she would stop.

He stepped in front of her, and nothing happened. The screams of Cecilia's voice started to make his body go numb. All the mirrors and the windows in the room were cracking and breaking.

She was powerful. He walked over to her and yelled as loud as he could.

"Cecilia! Stop this now! You don't want to kill her! Please stop!" Cecilia put her hands down, and everything fell to the ground except Siren. She was partially embedded in the wall, blood dripping from her mouth. Cecilia was still thinking about squishing her, like a bug.

"Cecilia, The Society is already mad at me, and I am not sure what they will do. If you kill her, they will kill you. They are the only ones allowed to choose who lives and who dies," exclaimed Efron.

Finally, Cecilia thought about Luna. She started releasing the pressure. She watched as Siren fell to the floor. She still had some humanity left in her. Cecilia just sat on the bed and started to weep. Tears rolled down her face, but they weren't just any tears. They were red and filled with blood, and it frightened her.

"I don't want this," she said.

"Oh great! She's the new Dark Guardian? What did you guys do?"

Siren had the look of disbelief on her face. Efron jumped off the bed, grabbing Siren by her neck before she could even react to him coming at her. Siren's eyes looked like they were going to pop out of her head.

"Shut up Siren! You have no idea what you are talking about, and keep this between us. If you don't, I will terminate you permanently."

"Fine." Siren grabbed her throat and rubbed it from the pain. "This isn't over. Your new mate is crazy, and you can have her. Besides, I don't want to be terminated for killing that thing, whoever she is."

"Shut up. If anything, you're the whore. You took my leftovers. I had him first. So technically he was never yours to begin with." Cecilia screamed at her.

"I am out of here. This isn't over, freak. I will get you when you least expect it. Then what will you do?"Siren scowled at her.

"If I were you, I would just leave me alone. The way things look now, it won't be me that gets terminated permanently. For the record, next time, I won't stop." Cecilia smirked.

Siren glared at her and then stormed out of the room. Her gut hurt because she was scared, but she wouldn't let them know. All she could think about was how Efron had betrayed her for that woman. She hated her and wanted her terminated.

Cecilia was no longer scared of Siren or of anything for that matter. She felt as if she could take on the world.

Efron went and locked the door behind Siren. He then went and sat on the bed next to Cecilia. He was still in disbelief. He was somewhat shaken. The heat from his body had left. He picked his shirt up off the bed and put it back on. He lay back down.

"Are you scared of me now?" she asked.

"No, I'm just kind of in shock. I have never seen anything like that before."

"Well, I didn't know I could do that, but I tell you, it felt amazing and powerful. I could feel her energy disappearing as if I were taking it. I am somewhat scared, because I don't know what I am truly capable of."

"Well, don't lose who you are. Remember, you don't like killing people. You are sweet and kind."

"I don't know who or what I am anymore. How can you say that is who I am?"

"Because I know you, and that's why I fell in love with you in the first place."

Efron slid closer to her, leaning over and kissed her. She didn't pull away. She decided to let him have her. To mate with her, to be one with her. It was better him, than anyone else she didn't know.

Once their spirits connected, they would never be separated again. His spirit had already been with her. That's why he was never able to fully move on. He loved her and would die for her. After everything she had just been through, she just wanted to be close to someone. She had all these emotions going through her at once. She felt like she wanted to cry.

She missed her baby. She didn't want this life. It didn't help that she had a secret she had written down in her journal that no one knew but her. She thought it would be best to keep it to herself for now, because with all these new powers, she didn't know if it was best to say anything. It could complicate things more than they already were.

"Are you sure you want this now, Cecilia?"

"Yes."

"It is better to do it after a feeding when the heat is going through our bodies. There will be more of a connection."

"I thought you already were feeling the heat?"

"It went away."

"You talk about this connection, but what you don't realize is, it was already there. You can feel my feelings, and my love, so what is stopping you?"

"Nothing, I guess. It's just different now. And how did you know I can feel it? When we do it, you are going to feel different and do things, things you normally wouldn't do as a human."

"Because I can hear your thoughts and feel them too. Well, I'm okay with that."

"Well, alright then."

Efron began kissing Cecilia again, and after what felt like a moment, there was a knock on the door. Five hours had gone by, and they hadn't even realized it. Efron got up and unlocked the door. Opening the door, he found Vilhauer on the other side.

He had brought two meals; both were really old and wanted to die. They normally don't take people who want to sacrifice themselves, but there was an exception with these two. They couldn't get around much anymore and asked to go together.

Vilhauer handed them over to Efron and left without a word spoken between the two of them. Efron shut the door and locked it again, in case Siren came back. But really it didn't matter if the door was locked, because she could burst through it.

He sat the old folks down on the bed, before he could even ask Cecilia if she was hungry, she was latched onto the man's neck. He could feel her energy growing and excitement at this point, she seemed not to care anymore; that humans were just food to her.

Efron grabbed the old woman, brushing her hair out of the way of her neck. He could see her veins, which he liked. Neither of the old creatures was afraid. He noticed Cecilia looked like she was enjoying herself. She started making little noises as she ate.

Efron bit into the old woman and she tighten up her muscles, which made eating more difficult. But he managed to hook onto a good vein.

Cecilia felt powerful being able to kill people. She didn't think she would be able to do it. Maybe it was because of the situation and how the woman just wanted to die, but it wasn't right, she thought. Although, she loved the taste of blood, and couldn't help herself. She wanted more.

She sat up after finishing and could smell something sweet coming from the door. She was at the door in a second. Before Efron could say stop, she had busted through the door. Whatever it was smelled like cotton candy. She was down the hall in a flash and stopped in front of a door. Efron was after her, but not fast enough. There was a lady sitting at a desk by the entrance to the room.

"Can I help you, miss?"The lady looked a bit nervous; she knew that look.

Cecilia said nothing. She looked at her like prey. All she could think about was her sweet smell and how good she would taste. She never smelled one as delicious as her. She started creeping toward her, and her pupils got big with excitement. The lady had a look of fright on her face. She knew she was going to die.

Efron ran after Cecilia and reached out to grab her, but Cecilia pushed her hand back, and he went flying against the wall. He wasn't strong enough to stop her; nothing could.

She latched onto the lady's neck and sucked the life out of her. Cecilia dropped her to the floor like she was nothing after she was done feeding on her. Blood was dripping from her chin. She had a satisfied look on her face.

"What have you done? You can't just eat whomever you want. She worked for us, and you're supposed to leave the human servants alone," said Efron, in an angry voice.

"Well, what do you expect from a new vampire? I can't control myself yet."

"Your right. Why would Vilhauer put us so close to humans knowing you can't be controlled?"This makes no sense.

"Maybe he is testing us?"

"I don't know. Leave her and touch nothing."

They were back in their room in seconds. Unfortunately, the door was now busted. They sat on the bed and looked at each other.

"Are you done yet, Efron?" said Cecilia. She had finished and was waiting for him to be done eating as well. She had a heat rush over her body she had never felt before. It was uncomfortable, she thought. He pulled away, blood dripping down his face. Before he could wipe it off, Cecilia was licking it.

"It gets better with every taste she said. I thought we could go days without eating?"

"Well, you're newly transformed, so you need to eat more often for the first week or you will be uncontrollable."

"Oh. Well, I can feel the heat now. It's a burning, throbbing sensation."

"That would be it," he said, with a smile on his face. "I thought you said you didn't want to kill? You had no problem pouncing on this old man as soon as he sat down."

"I can't help it; the smell is so magnificent. It's what I am now. I'm a killer. The only way to survive is to eat."

"Well, just don't lose who you are, Cecilia."

"I won't; don't worry about me. I can take care of myself."

She grabbed him by the arm and threw him onto the bed. She ripped his shirt off. It had been too long since they had been together. It felt kind of awkward at first, but she wanted him more than anything right now, so she wouldn't stop now.

He looked like he was a little frightened but intrigued. She unzipped his pants and threw them across the room. She ripped his boxers off and sat on him. She didn't take her clothes off because she was uncomfortable.

Efron pulled her breasts out of the top of the dress she was wearing and started rubbing her nipples. It felt like she was dreaming, their bodies becoming one. She hadn't felt this kind of connection since the last time they had intercourse nine months ago. She felt safe once again. She loved Efron more than anything — well, almost anything — except the taste of blood. Her eyes went red, and she started shaking and moaning.

Efron thought she had found her release, but she was still riding him, so he was just lying there enjoying himself. He had never seen someone's eyes go red like that. So, he was confused. All these things happening to Cecilia were new to him. He wasn't sure what to do or what she was capable of, or what she was becoming. He didn't think she would hurt him, but it seemed like she was having an out-of-body experience.

She grabbed his hand, bit it, and then started sucking his blood. It seemed to make her more excited. The biting didn't hurt Efron; it was a turn-on for him as well.

Efron never let Siren bite him because he didn't want her to be one with him because he didn't love her. But Efron was already one with Cecilia; she could feel how he felt and hear his thoughts, so he had nothing to lose. He felt human again.

Cecilia was getting out of control. Suddenly, her fingernails extended into claws as she dug them into Efron's chest and scratched him all the way down to his abdomen. Her eyes were glowing like the sun's fire.

Cecilia was standing in the middle of the field again. This time, the sky was a reddish-yellow color. She felt the presence of another person. Turning around, she saw the man in the dark robe again.

"Have you figured it out, yet?" he said.

"Figured what, out? Who are you?" she replied.

"You need to take everyone in a new direction; the future is yours to control," he retorted.

"I'm no one. Honestly, I'm actually dead. So how am I supposed to know what to do?"

"It will come to you. I know what you must do, but I will not give you the answer you seek. You are new and young, but you possess all the power you need to accomplish anything in the world. You must learn to control yourself before you can control others. I know who you are and what you are capable of. You must figure it out on your own." He was gone when she blinked her eyes.

"Wait, will I see you again? How will I find you?"

She looked up at the sky on the windy, starry night. She saw flames of a fire coming over the hill, but it wasn't on the ground; it was shooting up in the air. She felt drawn to the fire and needed to see where it was coming from, but she was afraid, for light and fire could terminate her. She began imagining herself in the holding cell with Efron.

When she came to, his stomach was cut open, and he was unconscious. His blood wasn't red; it was black as the night's sky with no stars. She jumped off him and panicked. He was healing as soon as she took her claws out of him.

Wait, claws, she thought. Vampires don't have claws. Her claws retracted back into regular fingernails. He came to.

"That was the best sex I have ever had," he said.

"Excuse me?" Cecilia said. She had a look of horror on her face.

"I told you; things would happen that you're not used to. The woman vampire has total control. I didn't expect to go unconscious, but the pain was so excruciating, and so very enjoyable. Depending on how strong the bond is, a woman vampire could completely kill her mate."

"What? So why would you want to have sex then?" she looked shaken.

"Because the heat from killing someone and drinking blood can make us explode."

"I don't want to kill you during sex or anytime."She said frantically.

"You just have to stop. You can stop, can't you?"He said with a smirk on his face.

"I don't know. I wasn't here. I was somewhere else. I saw the man in the black coat again. I saw fire. I feel like I am going crazy." She looked worried.

"You will be okay; you're not the only one who has gone through this," Efron said. He started wondering again what The Society would do with her. Kill her, or keep her and make her do what they want, like they have with the others that have been in her place.

"What! There have been others?"

"Yes, but they're just stories. No one really knows the truth, because The Society keeps it pretty snug so as to not let anyone know."

They both glanced over at the door because they heard a noise. They saw an unknown person standing there staring. He had heard every word they had said. The man ran fast and disappeared before they could get to the door to grab him.

"Oh, what am I going to do? Who was that man and what was his business here?" Said Cecilia.

"I don't know. I've never seen him before. He is much quicker than any other I have seen.

Efron was trying to think whether he had ever seen that man before. He couldn't place him anywhere. While he was sitting there thinking, Vilhauer walked through the door. He looked at the busted-up door and wondered why they hadn't tried to leave. He walked through the door and looked at them both.

"Do you two have anything to say for yourselves?"He commented with a scowl.

"For what?" replied Efron.

"Are you kidding me? I'm babysitting two infant vampires who can't control themselves and just feast on anyone. One of you ate the receptionist, and I want to know who. She was the great-, great-, great-, granddaughter of the chief of immortality. He will have your head for it. You can forget stating your case; he will kill you on the spot himself."

"Who says we did it? And who is the chief of immortality?" Cecilia said.

"Efron, have you been teaching her anything? The Chief of Immortality is the guy who transforms you, and also kills you; he is our father, well, not yours. And who else would have done it?"

"Maybe it was that crazy man who ran out of here like a manic. Or maybe you did it? Why would you put her so close to humans knowing she can't control her urge to be satisfied?"Efron said accusingly.

"Listen here you little shit, you don't talk to me like that. I have done nothing but help you, and you defy me, doing as you please. That is not our way; you are going against protocol. You are supposed to do as your guardian says. I am your elder, and you will treat me with respect, or I swear I will request that you get terminated because you cannot be controlled and are a danger to everyone."

"You will do no such thing, Vilhauer. As I see it, everything is your fault. You put us too close to a human, and Efron is your responsibility. You were supposed to take action, and you didn't. So now you will suffer the consequences." said Cecilia.

"Excuse me, little girl? The only reason you're still alive is because of me. So, I would watch what you say next. Anything you say will be used against you during the examination in front of The Society. And personally, I don't care if they kill the both of you, and your bastard child," he said with a smile on his face.

Cecilia lost it. She rushed at him, putting her hand around his neck and throwing him against the wall. She pounced on him like a cat and bit a piece of his arm off. He couldn't fight back. She was too strong, and he couldn't figure out why.

Efron quickly grabbed the gloves sitting on the table next to the bed. He grabbed the silver-infused bane chain that was on the curtain and broke it off. He ran over to Cecilia in a flash and smacked her on the back with it. She fell to the ground moaning in pain. It was more agonizing than when the chunky man stomped on her, when she had nothing to eat, when she was first transformed.

"Why did you do that?"She was now curled up in a ball of pain.

"Why do you think I did it? You can't kill him. They would terminate you."

"What is going on here? You can't just attack me. You were stronger than me. No infant is ever stronger than their elder unless…Unless? Oh goodness, The Dark Guardian is dead! He now lives in you." Turning to Efron, "Efron, this might save you after all. You created her, but who killed The Dark Guardian? How is it possible for anyone to get close enough to him?"

"You know nothing, Vilhauer! I am not the Dark Guardian. He still lives. You fib and will say nothing about you knowing The Dark Guardian, and the guy who ran out of here — he is the one that killed the lady up front by the desk." she said. Cecilia looked straight into his eyes. He looked like he was lost.

"Now, run along."

"What am I doing in here?" asked Vilhauer.

"You were asking us if we were hungry, and we are not, but thank you anyway," said Cecilia.

Efron had never seen anything like it. She had changed Vilhauer's mind, made him forget.

He was a true believer now. She was starting to possess more abilities. He was getting excited, but frightened at the same time. What will they do with her? It had been years since the last Dark Guardian had escaped and was in hiding.

They will know how to use her powers against her and take her for everything she has. It all made sense now; why they didn't want just anyone transforming creatures into us. They wanted someone they knew everything about. So, when they transformed them, if they showed they were The Dark Guardian, they could take control immediately.

I now regret transforming her. I have put her in more danger than I could have imagined. What was I thinking, but she was chosen for this? Efron thought silently, shaking his head.

"I heard every word you were thinking. It puts a lot into perspective. What do we do now? What if they kill me to make someone else The Dark Guardian?"

"They know nothing about you. How powerful you already are. They don't know what to expect from you. The world is in your hands. The Dark Guardian is known to absorb abilities and use them for his own if he doesn't already possess them. But I believe you are the first woman to be The Dark Guardian."

"I want to leave, now!"She shrieked in fear. Not only of the unknown, but also of what she was, it scared her.

"It will be okay; there is no escaping this place." Efron barely got the words out of his mouth before she stood up and ran for the door, pushing Efron out of her way.

She was out of the room in a flash. She was met at the door she entered on the way into the house by two of the fastest guards. They got into a scuffle; she threw some fantastic punches and tore off one of their heads. It was nothing an ordinary vampire couldn't do in any fight. She couldn't over power the last guard. The guard knocked her off her feet and held her by the neck. She was scared, and her abilities were not working, and she couldn't understand why. Her neck was cold, and it felt like it was going to get snapped. She thought he was going to kill her.

By the time Efron had gotten there and jumped on his back, the guard had wrapped her in silver bane-dipped chains, so she couldn't move. The guard gave Efron one big hit in the gut that threw him across the room and against the stone wall. Efron was knocked out cold. The guard wrapped him in silver bane-dipped chains as well. The pain from the chains woke him up from his stupor. The guard was dragging them down a hallway to a different room that held cells with cages. She was screaming the entire way in excruciating pain, and not the good kind of pain. Her screams broke the glass picture frames one by one in the hallway. Efron had been trained to take the pain so he could control it to be bearable. The guard carelessly tossed them into separate cages.

"Thank you for the fight. I haven't had one in a long time. You both will answer for your crimes, with the appropriate punishment. You won't be able to escape this cage, so I wouldn't try."

"I thought the other room was a holding cell?" Said Efron.

"No, it was just a room. Vilhauer lied and was being nice. He thought you deserved better than being thrown in a cage for several days. He was supposed to have someone guarding your room but failed to do so. I won't be that nice. I couldn't care less about the two of you."

The guard left the room in a flash. They both sat on the concrete floor. It was worse now than before; she had killed a vampire without The Society making the final call. She wasn't scared. She was hopeful they would terminate her, so she wouldn't have to live this way. This wasn't living, she was a monster. She looked at her body; it had slashes from the silver chains being wrapped around her. She was bleeding, but not the normal color of red. It was the same black she saw from Efron when she clawed his stomach open during intercourse. Nothing was making sense to her. There had to be a reason she was chosen to be The Dark Guardian.

The Dark Guardian was normally passed through genetics, but the last Dark Guardian didn't father children before he was transformed into one of us. At least that's the myth that everyone is told, but no one really knows. Efron knew her parents while they were alive, and neither of them had been vampires. Efron just sat there and stared at her. He wasn't sure how much longer he would get to see her face, for he didn't know their fate. He wanted to spend the rest of his time looking at how beautiful she was.

"Cecilia, can't you use that ability to influence their minds and make them believe it didn't happen like you did with Vilhauer in the other room?" Efron asked, as if he had hoped they were going to make it out okay.

"I don't know. I am dangerous. I just don't know how to control what my body does. Just leave it, Efron. I don't want to live like this forever. You may enjoy being immortal, but I don't." She glared at him.

She lay down on the floor and closed her eyes. She imagined being in the middle of the field again. She could feel the wind on her body; it was blowing her hair. There was a flicker of firelight coming from beyond a hill.

She thought, it's a dream, it can't hurt me, I must see what it is. She was glowing from the rays of the fire as she got closer. It didn't hurt at first as she approached the hill, but the closer she got, the more pain it was inflicted upon her. She fell to her knees in excruciating pain, screaming like a little girl. It felt like a million knives were stabbing into every part of her body. She was getting burned all over her body. This is a dream; she didn't understand why it was hurting her. A hand reached down to her. It was the man in the black coat.

"You are stronger than you believe. Stop screaming and get up." She closed her mouth and tried to stand, but fell back down in pain.

"It seems you are not ready to believe. You are weak; no one can help you but yourself. You must find the way."

"Who are you? Why did you choose me? I don't want this."

"You will figure it out. You have no choice in the matter, and you are what you are. Accept it, and things will start to make sense to you." The pain was so unbearable she wanted out. She imagined being back in the cage on the floor. She kept this dream to herself. She thought it would be better not to involve Efron in them anymore than she had to. She thought it would be safer that way for him if he didn't know too much. But there was one problem in trying to keep him in the dark. She now had burns all over her body when she woke. Efron's eyes looked like they were going to bulge out of his sockets.

"What the hell happened? How is this possible? Do you hurt?" he said.

"Not now, I don't. And don't worry about it; I don't have to tell you everything. You have no idea what I am going through either. So why should I have to include you in it? It could be more dangerous the more you know."

"We are in this together, you go down, and I go down with you."

After a moment, Efron looked back at her. "I was thinking the reason you got the ability to mend the mind is because Bianca can erase people's memories and put a new image in their head, making them believe it is true. She is the most powerful leader in The Society. You have absorbed her ability. You are now a threat to them."

"How does that help me when I can't control it? Can you ever remember what she takes away?"

"I don't know if you can, but it's worth a shot in making her change her mind if you can. I mean, depending on what her choice will be, makes for our fate. You can hear thoughts. So if you can get in her mind before she does yours, it will help us."

Cecilia just sat there and said nothing. She didn't feel tired or worn out. She wasn't sure what to do. She stared at Efron, and then just looked around the room. She imagined what her life could have been like if vampires had never existed. Then she wondered if she was here because everything creates a balance. Things happen so that better things can fall into place. But this was not better; this was worse.

She wanted to be little again and see her parents. She remembered how her mother used to read to her and her younger brother before bed. It felt like just yesterday she had been hugging her father. He used to call her Cece. She loved playing with her brother on the floor. She could still hear his giggles when she tickled him. She wondered what happened to him daily. He was a chubby little boy with blonde hair and green eyes, but Mom and Dad, they had brown hair. She hated the vampires for taking her away from her family. She missed them every day. But there was nothing she could do about it, so no reason to dwell on it, she thought.

She started looking around the room again and caught Efron's eyes. She thought she would try to practice with him and change something he was thinking. He was thinking about death, and whether he had doomed them both. He cared whether he had put Vilhauer or Siren in any kind of danger.

She focused really hard and decided to change his thought of putting Siren in danger. He will care about her no longer, she thought. She decided to make him feel disgusted with her, and made him think of all the bad memories of her, especially seeing her with Adonis over and over again. Lastly, she would make him forget any good memories he had of her. She had no idea if it would work but only one way to find out.

"Efron, tell me about Siren?"She whispered.

"What about her? She was my mate and a complete bitch. She doesn't care about anyone but herself. She dresses like a whore. Usually, vampires ask the male mate for permission to have sex with our female mate. Not with her — she always came to me and asked to get around. Of course, I didn't care. Why should I? I don't love her. I believed she screwed all the vampire men and all the creature men that were our servants. I'm pretty sure there are some whom I don't even know about. If The Society finds out what she did without asking, she will be terminated for it."

"So you're telling me women vampires have no freedom?"

"No. You must obey your male mate."

"Wow! Things just got better for me, didn't they? You turned me into this freak, and now I have no say in what I want to do."

"This is a gift. You get to spend eternity with me. It's way better than getting eaten."

"Way better than getting eaten? What? We kill people. Have you forgotten what it's like to feel and be human? I was just transformed not even a week ago. I don't even know what day it is anymore. I don't know what my purpose is anymore." She started to tear up. She sat there for a second and remembered why she had started the conversation in the first place; to talk about Siren and see if her plan had worked. While she was sitting there, she heard footsteps coming from the hallway. She didn't have a good feeling. It was Vilhauer.

"It is time. Follow me." Vilhauer said.

Chapter Four

Cecilia and Efron stood up as Vilhauer unlocked the cages they were in, and then headed for the door that lead out into the hallway. Cecilia grabbed Efron's hand and squeezed it tight, following Vilhauer.

Efron was scared. He had the feeling he was going to lose the love of his life again for good. Maybe even see her terminated right in front of him, and he couldn't live with that. He would do anything he could to protect her. He would even go as far as being terminated himself if he could save her. Without her, life was not worth living. He hasn't been in front of The Society since he was transformed.

Would they understand? Or even care that he wanted her with everything he had? He had forgotten for a second that he had broken protocol and they would make the choice based on what she could do and if it was a good fit for the vampires to keep her. She already was the mate of Efron, so if they kill her, they kill him.

He knows there is more The Society is hiding but doesn't know what it is. He made a promise to himself to find out someday, and with Cecilia's powers it would make it easier in finding the information he needed to bring them down.

Cecilia looked pale. She was nervous they would find out who she was, or what she was becoming. Being terminated was kind of what she wanted, if it meant she could be free. Although she was probably already damned for eternity because she had already killed a human. Being a vampire, she had no soul, so her soul had already been taken to hell forever. She could smell human blood, so she knew there were some people here, maybe slaves or food. She was hungry again, and could feel the dryness of thirst in her throat, it was burning like needles poking her tonsils, and she hadn't felt it like that except when she was first transformed. Do I go for it? She thought, and kill these men so they know who I am?

The pull urging her to feed on blood was nothing like she had ever felt before. The last two times, the humans had been right next to her, so she didn't have to control it. Well, except for the receptionist out in the lobby, where she completely lost control. Just thinking about it made her eyes turn black.

She slammed two of the guards against the wall, almost sending them through it. The blow was hard enough to knock them off their feet, and have to regain their strength to go after her.

Just as she was about to take off and run for the blood, two guards standing next to Efron pulled out silver bane chains and roped her like a calf. She fell to the ground and screamed in pain. It felt like icicles burning her skin.

"Let her go! She's just hungry. What do you expect from an infant vampire who can't control herself with the urge to feed? That is your fault for not feeding her again before we left the room," said Efron.

"No, she is too dangerous. We are doing only what we are instructed to do by The Society, not by some little half-wit that breaks protocols," said one of the guards.

They dragged her close to them, stood her up, and replaced the chains on her wrists up to her elbows. She walked in pain, and could feel the silver bane dipped chains eating away at her skin. The only thing she could compare it to was like having acid put on your skin and it burning down to the bone.

She could smell her arms burning, the revolting rotting flesh smell. She thought she was going to die from the pain. Looking down at her arms, she could see the chains embedding themselves into her skin. She was walking slowly with one foot in front of the other, but didn't want to move much more than that because it hurt so badly. They had to pretty much pull her like they were walking a dog on a leash. It didn't faze her as much as she thought because her eyes were still dark-black and she could still smell the sweet human blood. She wanted a taste, and at that point, nothing else mattered to her as much as that. Her blood was dripping out from where the chains were embedded into her skin. She looked down, started to feel faint, and passed out.

She opened her eyes in the dream or reality. She wasn't sure what it was quite yet. She was on her knees next to the blazing fire in the middle of a field. She didn't have a craving for blood here. The fire didn't hurt like it did before, maybe because she wasn't thinking of getting burned by flames. She was getting pain from a different reality. The flesh on her arms was hanging off and she could see her veins and bones. But the chains were none existent in this place. She heard a familiar voice again. She looked through the fire. It was him the guy in the black coat with a mask covering his face.

"Stand up my girl. You're making yourself look so weak and pathetic."

"I don't care how I look; I am not here to impress you. Why have you brought me here again?"

"I didn't bring you, you projected yourself. I see you are still not in control of your powers. What a shame." He just shook his head.

"I don't know how to be in control. I'm not even sure if I want to be in control. Termination sounds so much better than this."

"Be careful what you wish, girl. There is one close by that can tell what you are, and that person will have no mercy on your soul."

"Who is it? Why do you keep calling me girl? I have a name you know."

He vanished once again. "Typical, just like any man, gone without a word." She snarled. She stood up and looked up at the sky it was black with stars all over, the moon was full. It was beautiful. She wasn't sure where she was.

She turned around, and there was a big opening to a cave just beyond the hillside. It looked like some hideout; there was a light shining out of the cave. She wanted to get a closer look. She turned to go toward the cave, and before she finished taking a step, she was suddenly on her knees in front of The Society.

She had no recollection of how she had got there. Her arms at this point were like bloody stubs with the chains hanging off them. The guards must have dragged me in here, she thought.

She looked over at Efron and saw that he was surrounded by guards. He was staring at her, longing to reach out and touch her, to keep her safe from this.

He didn't have chains on him; like she did. He just stood there, looking awkward. She could feel his fear and see how terrified he was by the look deep in his eyes. She could still smell the sweet human blood, and her eyes were still black as night with red veins on her face. There was no hiding that she was different.

She glanced quickly around the room. There was a beautiful blond, golden-haired woman sitting on a throne in front of her with men to the right side of her. On her left was a woman sitting in a chair, wearing a black cloak with gold trimmings. She also had a green talisman around her neck.

The blonde hair woman was sitting higher than the rest on a platform and protected. There was also a small table to the side with a lamp on it. She must be the main leader of The Society, Cecilia thought.

There was a walkway right behind her leading up to a staircase ending at a metal door. The area in front of her was filled with rows of wooden benches, similar to church pews, facing toward this woman. It appeared as if she were some kind of god or leader, she was obviously important.

The room was constructed of brick walls and completely painted white. There were only about ten guards in the room that she counted. She could take them, she thought.

Siren was also in the room, as well as Adonis. She didn't understand why they would be there. She could take them all if she could just free herself from the chains on her arms and heal. Even if she could free herself, she didn't know how to enforce termination. She also noticed a black glass window higher on the wall above the women. She wondered what it was; she had never seen glass like that before.

"Glad to see you're still with us," said the woman in a crisp, clear voice.

"And who would you be?" Cecilia said in a taunting voice.

"My name is Mistress Bianca." She hissed, giving Cecilia a dirty look.

"And who are you, the leader of these fine vampires?" She said sarcastically, while looking around the room at all the vampires present. She just shrugged her shoulders in disapproval, still with her eyes black as night.

"You might say that," she confessed. "I am so much more than you could ever imagine. Now be quiet, you're getting blood all over my floor." She sighed, looking at the bloody mess.

"I'm going to tell you what choices we have made and then ask you questions. How you answer could possibly change our minds about your fate. Efron, step forward and explain your actions." Mistress Bianca demanded.

Efron walked toward the middle of the room where Cecilia was kneeling. Before he got too close, Mistress Bianca put her hand up in a stopping motion to him, and he stopped in his place and stood still.

"There is not much to say other than I did what I did out of pure love for her. A connection, a bonding I have never had with another." He explained

"Love? There is no such feeling when you are a vampire; love is non-existent when you have no soul. And you were not to make that choice and transform anyone unless we give the condolences to do so. We transform creatures, not other vampires." She shouted.

"It wasn't his fault." Cecilia cried out. "Please, take these chains off; they hurt." She cried out in agony.

"Only speak when you're spoken to! Now shut your whining mouth! Give respect, and you shall receive respect. Vilhauer has already talked to us and told us the story about what happened, but I will want to hear your side of the story from your own mouth. Siren's as well, even though hers will be harder to trust because she is never forthcoming. Right now it is not your turn."

Looking back at Efron, "Now, Efron, explain." Demanded Bianca as she flicked her hair back out of her face with her hand. She was getting irritated and angry.

"Well, when she was a Human, her mate stabbed me with scissors in the neck and tried to kill me, so I had to take him out. I couldn't let him think he could try to terminate me without consequences. So, I killed him. It was quite enjoyable, I would like to add. The feeling of life and energy draining from his body was quite orgasmic. He was smiling just thinking about the memory.

"After I terminated him, I had to kill her, because she had no one to breed with. So, I sucked her dry until I could hear no heartbeat and left. When I came back to clean up the mess, I saw Cronus was latched onto her neck. Who knows what he really did in the heat of the moment? He's uncontrollable; I had to fix his mistake at his house. He would not let a mother creature give birth to her babies, or matches. I should note.

"He must have snuck away, got to Cecilia, and didn't realize he had released venom inside, which caused her to change."He said, with such a sincere look on his face. It was almost believable to Cecilia.

They all believed his lies. Because they all knew how explosive Cronus could be. There was something else Efron was hiding from Cecilia. His ability was a secret, and only a few knew it. Whatever he wants someone to believe, they will. Some of the story has to be the truth, but he can manipulate it a little bit with no one knowing the fully story. He was very good at it, even if someone was reading his mind. Although his ability didn't work on Cecilia or Vilhauer, and he didn't know why. It was the only disadvantage of his gift. Vilhauer said nothing, just stood there and nodded his head up and down in agreement with Efron's story. He didn't want the vampire he had mentored and treated like a son for the past nine months to be terminated. He knew Efron had a purpose and was supposed to be in his life for eternity. He didn't know why, just that he knew. Vilhauer would rather have Cronus take the blame for the mistakes that Efron had made, because they made them is take of transforming Cronus into a vampire.

"Guards, go fetch Cronus now and bring him to me!" screamed Mistress Bianca. There was whispering in every part of the room, so that the noise was echoing off the walls. Then the total feel of the room changed from nervous to tense and then got dead quiet. If someone had dropped a needle on the floor, you would have heard it ting. The light bulb that sat on the table next to Bianca started flickering. "Excuse me for a minute or two."

Bianca got up from her seat and walked up the stairs behind her, then opened the door that was next to the black glass window. While she was in there, two guards had brought Cronus into the room. He looked a bit confused about why he was there.

"What's the meaning of this? What is going on here? I'm not supposed to talk to you until tomorrow about the incident on the island," screeched Cronus.

"We are talking about how you turned Cecilia into a vampire without consent, and went against protocol. You knew the rules, Cronus, such a pity," said Efron, shaking his head.

"I did? I don't remember doing that. I mean, I forget sometimes what I do when I am in a blood frenzy, but I think I would have remembered doing that." Cronus said, still looking confused.

"Well, you did, and now you must face the consequence of turning me into this… thing," grumbled Cecilia. She knew what was going on because she could read Efron's thoughts. She didn't really care if Cronus died, because to her he was a useless vampire; he meant nothing to her. She then thought about her daughter. Would she be able to see her again? Maybe she should do what they want, and they won't hurt Efron, her baby, or her. What are they going to do to my baby once they realize who I am, if anything at all?

I need to focus and get some control before Bianca gets back. The chains on her arms were digging through flesh down to her bones. She felt as though she would pass out again every time she looked at them. But she kept conscious, breathed through it and managed the pain. Only a few minutes had gone before Bianca opened the door, walking back down the stairs and sitting down on her throne.

Everyone started whispering again. "Quiet. Down. Now. Everyone!" exclaimed Bianca. She snapped her fingers, and immediately the room fell silent.

Cronus was shaking because he was afraid. I have never seen a vampire shake from being scared. They're not afraid of anything. He was looking straight at Bianca, and she was looking straight back at him. She didn't look that scary to me. There was nothing about her that frightened me.

She looked like she was in her mid-thirties, with blond hair; her eyes were a deep blue. She had a perfect hourglass figure. In her demeanor, you could see that pain had changed her, and you could see it deep within her eyes. She was blunt with her words, a little sassy, and didn't have mercy for anyone. Was she the one about whom The Dark Guardian spoke about? Was she taking her pain out on others? Did it satisfy her? I noticed she didn't have a mate anywhere nearby.

"Step forward, Cronus. I will not give you time to explain yourself, since I am just now hearing of this. You should have come to us first thing when returning to our lands when the boat docked. You have broken protocol. You killed a creature in the middle of birth so she couldn't deliver. You could have damaged valuable creatures during that time. You also didn't do the research and check how many she was having. Most of all, you are being punished for transforming Cecilia into a vampire without our consent." She demanded.

"But wait, I can explain, please," he whined. "No, no, no," Cronus pleaded.

"No. There is no time for it now. We have given you a few chances. I told you, the next time you ended up in front of me, that would be it; I am done, no second chances. Cecilia was meant to die, not to be transformed into one of us. She already had that chosen for her, and you changed her path. Now we shall make a choice where you can no longer break protocols. What I say is final!" she demanded.

Cecilia's eyes widened. It was she, the one who gives no mercy. Focus, Cecilia told herself. Think of nothing else but what is going on here, in this moment, in this room.

"Guards, take him to the inferno," she ordered.

Cronus took off, running from the room. He was just getting into a sprint when a guard whipped a silver bane-dipped chain out and lassoed Cronus around his abdomen. He hit the ground, and the tile under him broke into pieces. He screamed as they dragged him away. His fingernails dug into the polished tile on the floor. There were scratches leading all the way across the room's floor where they were dragging him to. They stopped in front of a single steel door.

Cronus continued screeching and fought all the way, kicking and screaming, to the door. They stood him up, twirled him out of the chains, and flung him into the room. The door was slammed shut behind him. They had difficulty locking the door shut with the metal bar because it was rusty and hadn't been used in so long.

The walls went transparent as soon as they locked it. Cecilia was confused how it was transparent. She looked around, her eyes stopping on the woman standing next to Mistress Bianca, dressed in black. She had her hand open, with her palm facing up. It looked as if she were whispering some sort of language.

Cecilia chose not to stare long and looked back toward the room where Cronus was. She didn't want the woman to notice she was looking at her and draw attention to herself. She could see everything inside the square steel room.

Cronus was trying to find a way out. He was scared, pacing, running in circles, clawing the walls. Cecilia felt a bit scared; she had never seen anything like it. The guards hurried and backed away from the door. Mistress Bianca pulled a chain that was dangling behind her against the wall. As soon as she pulled it, the room Cronus was in started to become a raging inferno.

Cronus began screaming. He caught fire, started running around frantically, pleading and begging for his life. It was terrifying. All the vampires had the look of fear on their faces, except one…Mistress Bianca. She looked as if she were enjoying it. She had a hint of a smile on her face.

I wonder what happened to her to make her so evil. How could one be so heartless and cold? But then again, we don't have souls, but I felt miserable for him. We did this to him, but he possibly would have met this fate tomorrow anyway.

I am sure everyone outside in the village heard Cronus scream. He was still running around looking for an escape; he fell and started crawling on the ground. He started to make a crackling sound. His clothes had burned off, and then he exploded into nothing. Into complete ash, it looked like a firework show. He was gone just like that, as if he had never existed. Would anyone miss him? How could I have gone along with that? Do I have no humanity left inside me? But I had to do what had to be done to protect Efron and possibly my baby.

"Efron, step forward," demanded Mistress Bianca.

Efron stepped forward and stood in the middle of the room. Mistress Bianca looked angry. She was looking right into Efron's eyes. It looked as if she were searching for something. Maybe she was looking for the truth about what really happened in my room that night. Efron looked a little nervous. The light next to Bianca flickered again. "Excuse me for a minute," she said. Bianca headed up to the other door again. As the door closed behind her, Cecilia caught a whiff of human blood.

She began to squirm out of the silver bane-dipped chains.

Efron looked at Cecilia and thought, "Stop! Now is not the time; control yourself."

Cecilia looked at Efron and read his thoughts. "You must control yourself. You will give too much away. To be honest, I don't know what they will do with you if they find out what you are becoming. Rumor has it they locked up the others who had powers like you and kept them captive for years. So stop before it's too late." He pleaded with a warm look on his face.

Mistress Bianca walked quickly back down the stairs and returned to her throne again. She looked straight at Efron.

"So, here is what we have chosen. You will no longer be allowed to go out to the island and be an enforcer until you can prove to us that you are ready. You will not be with Cecilia; she is not your mate, Siren is. Your path was chosen for you before Cecilia was transformed." Cecilia was steaming mad.

Her eyes turned red. She had gotten one arm free from the chains. It healed immediately, and she swung her body around to Siren and wrapped her hand around Siren's throat.

The guard with the free chain tried to lasso Cecilia again, but missed. Cecilia picked her up and threw Siren across the room. Siren hit the wall. You could hear a loud crack from her back when she hit, broken bricks falling to the ground.

Cecilia had now pulled free from the other guard and levitated across the room and was now standing next to Siren.

She had one foot on the ground and one on her face. Suddenly, Siren was frozen still. Cecilia looked confused as she looked around; everyone in the room had stopped; like time just stood still. Everyone was now frozen in place. Cecilia turned around and looked at Mistress Bianca.

"Bravo," Mistress Bianca clapped her hands and had a smile on her face. "You have just revealed to me that you are The Dark Guardian. No vampire has been as strong as you are, and The Dark Guardian is not affected by Raven's ability to stop time, which you have not been affected by. Now, this is what is going to happen when I have her return time. You are going to stand there and take your punishment, or Efron will not be leaving this room alive. You will also never see your baby again. You will do whatever I ask, or you will be killed as well. Do you understand me?"

"Yes," Cecilia complied.

"Has The Dark Guardian revealed himself to you in your dreams yet?" Bianca murmured.

"How do you know about my dreams?"Cecilia asked.

"There are things you don't need to know, that I understand. You're confused; I will help you, but not here. So, has he revealed himself to you?" she demanded.

"I have seen him in my dreams, but haven't seen his actual face yet. He's hiding it from me." She said.

"So he's really dead, then." She looked as if she were sad and in mourning. "I wonder who had the courage to kill him. I just find it odd that he is dead, and yet you have been transformed at that same moment. Interesting," she said.

"I don't know, I was doing what I was supposed to, and then I was transformed into this thing. And cursed to live for eternity." She sighed.

"Oh, honey, this isn't a curse. This is a gift. You are the most powerful being on this earth, you should enjoy that. Also, you are absolutely stunning. Anyway, back to the plan. You are going to let my guards take you down and back off of Siren. It is not Siren's time to be terminated. Now, I am going to count to three, and you will go back to standing over Siren again as if you were going to kill her." Cecilia walked back over and stood over Siren again. "One, two, three," Mistress Bianca counted off.

Raven put her hand down. Time resumed; Siren could tell she didn't look as angry anymore. The guard again swung the silver bane-dipped chain around Cecilia. Cecilia fell to the floor in agonizing pain. The feeling of freezing shards in your skin was too much to bear.

They dragged her over and shoved her to her knees next to Efron. Efron could tell something had happened, but was not sure what. Mistress Bianca was giving a look toward Cecilia as if it were some kind of sign to obey.

"Now, before I was so rudely interrupted. Efron, you will stay in the colony from now on. You are to look after the infant creatures we just brought in; no exceptions. You will control yourself and not feed on them. You will only be looking after those who have been given the choice to be transformed into one of us."

"When they have become of age, and they are ready to be transformed, then we will see if you are ready to become the enforcer you were meant to be. We thank you for delivering Cronus' assignment. Again, I will say that Siren will be your mate. Cecilia is no longer your concern.

Efron looked confused. Why was Cecilia just kneeling there, not saying a word?

"You will do exactly as I say, or there will be more consequences. Do you understand?" Efron nodded his head in agreement.

"Efron, she is not saying anything because she is sparing your life. You don't think we know what really happened. I just collected it all out of your memory when you weren't paying attention. You may think you have everyone fooled, but not me," said Mistress Bianca.

"Then why did you terminate Cronus?" He retorted. "If you know what happened?"

"That wasn't my choice to make. I had to go to a higher authority for that choice. And it wasn't just that. He was annoying and out of control. He was like a lit fuse on a bomb that would go off at any moment. We don't have time to be a babysitter and clean up his messes anymore. We were waiting for him to mess up one more time, and he did as we expected, so he was taken care of. This is your first offence, hopefully you're last. Don't expect another chance from us.

"Your last punishment is to live with everything you have experienced. You are to tell no one of anything that has happened in this room. And if you do tell anyone of the events that you have seen, you will also be taken care of and terminated. So don't test me!" She screeched.

"Efron, you may now step back in line with the guards."

"Yes, ma'am." Efron walked back next to the guards and was shaking his head in disbelief.

"Siren, step forward."

Mistress Bianca looked straight into her eyes and collected the last 24 hours out of her head. She saw everything. From the encounter with Adonis to the fight with Cecilia in the guest room. She decided to dig further into her memories. She could see all the encounters with all the different vampires and all the creature servants. She saw she had no permission from Efron to do anything she had done. She had taken more meals than one is supposed to take. She had disgraced their ways.

"Well, you've been busy. You're a disrespectful little one, aren't you?"Mistress Bianca said, shaking her head, and clicked her tongue. "You can't just do what you want. You have made women vampires look preposterous. No wonder Efron doesn't want to touch you anymore; you have fucked half the island." Siren looked down as her cheeks blushed red with embarrassment. "What do you have to say for yourself?"Mistress Bianca demanded.

"In my defense, he never wanted me. He never truly mated himself to me. He didn't even like fucking me. He also made me beg for it, or seem like it was a chore every time. He had already chosen one to spend eternity with before he was transformed. He slept with her and has always loved her. How can I compete with that? I sought it elsewhere because at least I was wanted." She explained. It was quite sad, honestly.

"We know everything that has happened between Efron and Cecilia, more than anyone else knows. Their punishment for all the protocol breaks is that they will spend eternity alive, but never to be together again."

Efron looked at Cecilia, who was just looking down at the floor in shame. He felt like he was going to vomit. The thought of not seeing her again or feeling her touch made him dead inside, if he wasn't already. There was nothing he could do to stop this from happening.

"Siren, don't you worry. You'll forget all about her, and everything that has happened in this room today. You were made to be a beautiful creation of lust, and you will be the best at what you do."Mistress Bianca said shrilly.

Siren stood there in confusion, just staring at Mistress Bianca. She got up from her throne and walked up to her and placed her icy hands on her forehead. She looked deep into Siren's eyes and dissolved her memories. She took them for her own. She went all the way back to the night on the island when Cecilia was transformed.

"Now, Siren, you will not be sleeping around anymore unless your mate allows you to. So, keep your legs closed unless you have permission from Efron to fuck others. Guards! Get Siren something to eat and return her to her waking quarters. Efron will be there soon to take care of her heat."Mistress Bianca then took her hand off Siren's forehead, and she fell to the floor like a lifeless corpse. The guards nodded their heads to her, picking Siren up off the ground. They walked toward the door at the back of the room. Siren looked paler than usual, and she was bleeding from her eyes, ears, nose, and mouth. She was covered in her own blood.

Mistress Bianca pulled a handkerchief from the pocket of her green dress and wiped her hand that she had touched Siren's forehead with, then replaced it back into her pocket. Like she was some high-class lady touching filth. She then went back and sat down up on her throne.

When the guards got to the back of the room, the doors automatically opened, allowing them to leave without stopping and waiting. Cecilia then saw someone she had never seen before walk in through the wooden doors that opened with no visible assistance and watched as the doors closed behind him; she noticed Raven putting her hand down.

It was the Chief of Immortality. He was a tall man with broad shoulders, long, wavy red hair to the middle of his back, and was wearing a black suit of all things. He was one of the older, respectable vampires. Who always knew when to suit up. He walked up to the front of the room and stood in front of Mistress Bianca. He was fuming.

"What are you doing in my chair, Bianca?" He said angrily. "And why have you started the trials without me?" he demanded.

"I have been authorized to take our leadership in a different direction." She snapped.

"That's impossible! I have always been the one to make any final choices, and to transform creatures or terminate them," he said.

"Um, actually, there was a time before you," she said. Everyone in the room looked at one another and was confused as to what she was talking about.

"We are talking about the here and now, not the past," he exclaimed.

"Come forward, Chief. You need to accept what is; it would be a wise choice for you to do so. It's the right choice for us, and there will be no future actions taken." Said Bianca, as she let out a snarl to show her dominance.

"No, I refuse your request. I don't have to do anything you say. I am the Chief of Immortality, and no one tells me what to do," he stated. He was getting angry, and his fangs popped out for defense, while his eyes turned black. He was ready to fight anyone who came at him. A few more guards rushed into the room from the back door and surrounded him.

"Don't you get it? No one can defeat me. I am older and wiser than all of you here. I have transformed you all, and you really want to take my life? Don't you all feel the desire to save me? The sire bond? The way you are treating our kind is wrong, and soon there are going to be big choices to make, and I hope you are all ready for that. You will have to choose a side. I hope it's the right one." He shouted while turning in circles, declaring to all around him.

Mistress Bianca yelled, "Bring them in!" The door she had walked through earlier at the top of the stairs opened, and five men came out with silver bane-dipped chains in their hands. They were not wearing gloves, just like the guards on the surrounding floor. This meant they were creature servants.

They were dressed in black body armor from head to toe, but their hands were exposed. They had black helmets on so you couldn't see their face. Behind them was the human family of The Chief. Then another five guards entered the room behind them. The Chief knew what bringing his family there meant, he should have known Bianca would go this far.

He backed down released his fangs to normal, turned his eyes back to ordinary. He then got on his knees and put his arms straight out. He begged and pleaded with Mistress Bianca to not hurt them. But it was already too late to change her choice. He knew what was about to happen next. He looked at his family with pain behind his eyes. He started to cry and weep. They had never seen him cry before; he wasn't afraid of anything. He had burgundy color tears coming down out of his eyes.

"I'm sorry. I have failed you all," he screeched. Cecilia was going nuts in her mind with the smell of blood. It smelled like the sweet blood from the receptionist she had sucked dry. It was very difficult to keep herself under control and composed. But she could, to an extent. She just focused on the burning sensation from the chains on her arms.

There were about fifty creatures standing there related to The Chief, ranging from the ages of 80 years old to toddlers. Many of them had a lot of similar features as The Chief. You could tell they were related by blood. There were too many guards for The Chief to take on by himself, so whatever happened next he couldn't stop.

"Take the children under sixteen to the orphanage," Mistress Bianca shouted. There was no fight from their parents because they knew they would all be killed if anyone said a word or moved a muscle. Some of the creature guards took the children and walked out with them through the door that was on the side of the room. The children were screaming and crying out, trying to pull away from the guards and hang onto their parents. "Mommy! Daddy! No!"

The Chief was getting angry; that his fangs popped out again, but he just sat there on the ground rocking back and forth because he couldn't do anything.

"We have let you go on with this crazy notion of keeping your family alive for years to feel somewhat normal, as you call it. None of us has any living family, so why should you?" Bianca demanded.

"No one else's family survived the attack. And we all made the agreement." He shouted, barely able to keep his composure from crying. Tears were pouring down his face.

"We made the agreement for them to stay alive, not an agreement for you to keep them in your life and to know about our kind. It's been determined by higher powers already. You knew it was coming; you know what's going to happen now, and you can't do anything about it." Bianca stated.

The guards that were surrounding The Chief swung the chains around him but not to wrap around his body entirely. One chain wrapped around each of his arms, and one wrapped around each of his legs. There was even one wrapped around his neck. Each guard still had their silver chain in their hand, but now they were holding the ends of them tight. "Pull!" Yelled Bianca.

The Chief's skin was burning off, melting like butter, with steam rising above. They had only broken the first few layers of skin. Bianca was getting excited and a little angry because it was taking them so long. She grabbed a pair of gloves that were in the desk drawer next to her and put them on. She walked down before The Chief and took hold of the chain that was wrapped around his neck and gave it a monstrous tug.

His head fell to the ground and made a wet thumping noise. The chain whipped back and lashed her cheek.

"That's how you do it, you incompetent fools! Now, finish him. She dropped the chain and walked back to her throne and sat down.

The guards jerked the chains as hard as they could, and The Chief's body tumbled to the ground; well, parts of it went to the ground then turned to dust. It was as if he had never existed. His entire family was crying, but no one said a word or made a peep because the more they defied her, the more painful the death would be.

One of them fell to their knees praying. The creature guards walked back up the stairs and out of the room one by one. A woman belonging to the Chief's family tried to hold on to one of the guard's uniform, and said, "Help us."

Before she could get the plea for help out of her mouth, Bianca was right next to her and latched onto the woman's neck while she was screaming. The screaming stopped, and that's when they knew she was gone. She let go of her and dropped her to the ground. The women went limp and obviously dead. Bianca walked to the front of the room. Most of the guards had exited the room, but a few remained to block the doors so no one could exit.

"The rest of these creatures are for Cecilia to eat, because she is about to lose a lot of blood, and I don't want her passing out. Guards release her!"

The guards walked up to her and took the chains off her arms. Cecilia was excited by the lust she couldn't resist. She didn't want to kill all these innocent people. But the smell made her wild. She was sniffing the air, and red veins appeared on her face.

"Cecilia, you can't resist it; you know you want to. They smell so good, don't they? Oh, and the taste is marvelous. Stop fighting who you are and let it take over."

As Bianca finished talking, she wiped away the blood that was left on her mouth and chin with the handkerchief she pulled from her pocket. Cecilia couldn't fight it anymore. She darted at them, and they scattered like flies. She enjoyed chasing them down. They were her prey, and she was the almighty predator.

One of them ran in front of Bianca, and she put her leg out to trip him. He fell to the ground and hit his mouth first. He hit the ground so hard it busted his teeth out, and blood was oozing from his mouth.

Cecilia pounced on him. She turned around fast and didn't bother trying to get the vein from his throat; instead, she bit him right on his gums. He tried screaming for mercy, but with Cecilia's mouth wrapped over his, it was muffled. Cecilia felt brand new and powerful.

"Let's make this a little entertaining, shall we? Guards, throw some chains on the ground; let's see what she can do," said Bianca. A man picked up one chain and started whipping Cecilia on the back. She fell to the ground screaming, but quickly got back up. She moved faster than he could whip it against her. When she got to him, she sliced his neck open with her razor-sharp claws. His blood was squirting out of his wound; she was drinking his blood like it was a water fountain.

It took her less than five minutes to finish the rest of them off. Efron was watching her and not in any way turned on, because this was not her. There were dead bodies covering every inch of that room; it was a massacre. She could no longer control herself. The hunger took over, and she lost who she was. After she was done, she was so full she just lay there on the ground. She thought she was going to puke because she was so full.

"You were right. That was magnificent." She burped and tasted a little iron. The guards walked toward her, dropping to the ground to grab her. She attempted to push them away with her mind.

"Cecilia, don't defy. Remember our conversation?" The guards again attempted to pick her up and wrapped the chains around her and her hands.

Bianca walked toward Cecilia. "Stand her up." The guards stood Cecilia on her feet. Efron moved toward Cecilia and Bianca, but before he could even flinch, Raven looked at him and put her hand up, and stopped him in his place.

"No!" he screamed. Bianca placed her hand upon Cecilia's forehead and looked deep into her eyes.

As Bianca was doing this, Efron shouted, "I love you, Cecilia. I always have and will never stop searching for you until we are together again. I will always find you!"

"Is this going to hurt?"Cecilia asked.

"No, I am a mind grabber. You won't remember a thing." Bianca looked straight into her eyes and started dissolving every memory Cecilia had of Efron. She even dissolved all the events that had happened in the last 48 hours. She even took the memory of Luna being born.

Cecilia's whole body was shaking; she started convulsing. Blood was pouring out from her eyes, ears, nose, and mouth. She lost so much blood, it was everywhere. She passed out. Bianca slapped her across the face, and she came to. Bianca again wiped her hands off on her handkerchief and then went and sat back in her chair.

"Guards, you know what to do with her." Bianca demanded. Efron was trying to break away from the remaining guards that surrounded him but had no chance. He fell to the ground and started crying, which he hadn't done since he lost her nine months ago. The guards standing next to Cecilia picked her up off the ground. She was surrounded by her own blood, drenched in it. The guards got covered in her blood from lifting her up. They walked to the side door; it opened for them automatically when they reached it, and they walked through, then it closed behind them.

Efron didn't know where it led. They left a trail of her blood all the way to the door. The last thing Efron saw of Cecilia as they carried her away was her arm swinging back and forth in the air.

Chapter Five
Efron

Efron just sat there on his knees not knowing what to do. His face was now streaked with bloody tears. He felt helpless with all the surrounding guards. His body numb; he couldn't move, he didn't even want to try. He had lost Cecilia again.

He feared she would lose who she was and would eventually become the monster he made her to be; the monster they wanted her to become. He couldn't protect her. He felt sick to his stomach from the guilt. He wanted to terminate Bianca himself. He hated her; he had hated no one so much until her.

Oh no, he remembered he had to change his thoughts fast, because she would know what was thinking if she focused on him. Efron felt lost. He didn't know what they had done with Cecilia or where they had taken her. He was worried about her. He knew they wouldn't kill her; she was much too valuable to them. They needed her for whatever plans they had.

He was afraid because the possibilities were open for them to do whatever they wanted with her abilities. He was also concerned about the vampire race. What was in store for all of them now that they had another Dark Guardian?

Will they take us all out or make us be some kind of army against the human race? Efron wanted to use his ability to change the choices they made to take Cecilia and to kill off the Chief. For the first time since he had been transformed, he was afraid of the future. He promised himself that he would find Cecilia again and help her remember. But now he must follow what he is told, because he has no idea what Bianca has planned, or what the higher power has planned. Efron stood up on his feet and wiped the tears from his eyes, leaving blood smeared across his face.

"Am I free to go now?" Efron asked Bianca.

"I suppose. You need not worry about this mess here, or what happened in this room. I will not grab your memories.

You will live with all of this and go on as if nothing has happened. Right now, you need to go back to your waking quarters and take care of Siren, and no, I don't mean terminate her. I mean, have intercourse with her. Vilhauer will escort you to your waking quarters. And Vilhauer, not a word of what has happened here from either of you, or you both shall be terminated if any word gets out. I will do it myself with great joy. Guards, clean up this mess and throw their bodies into the inferno. That is all for now." Bianca demanded.

She looked quite satisfied with the events that had transpired in this room today. She stood up from her throne and walked out the door they took Cecilia through. Vilhauer grabbed Efron's arm by surprise. His eyes turned black, and he hissed at him and jumped from being startled.

"Calm down, there is nothing you can do but follow what you have been instructed by her. We should go," said Vilhauer.

"I know. I just can't believe they took her after everything."

They started walking toward the main wooden doors exiting the room. They turned right and began walking along a long corridor. There were no windows, only chandeliers, to light the way.

"Well, what do you think they are going to do with her?" Vilhauer said, shaking his head.

"I don't know. I was hoping they would let us be together. I didn't want them to find out what she was becoming."

"They already knew, at least Bianca did, or they wouldn't have taken her."

Vilhauer opened the door for Efron, and they exited the building together. They walked out onto the dirt street. There were street lamps along the road to light the way. No cars were on the island; they didn't need them to get around.

All the waking quarters looked the same, but they had different numbers on the buildings. The duplexes were three levels high with stairs and a door to enter the residence. They had tinted windows on them so you could see out but others couldn't see in.

The windows were made from the same material as the dome that covered the island. It stopped the deadly rays of the sun from getting into the quarters like the dome did. They were placed on the buildings just in case there was any issue with the dome being compromised.

Efron's new job was to raise the creatures they took from the island. One of them being the child of Cecilia. He had to protect her with everything he had, and would die for this little human. She was the only thing left of Cecilia, and he had to do right by her and hold on to her.

He now remembered the diary Cecilia gave him; it was still inside his coat pocket. Why didn't Bianca take it, he thought? Maybe she thought it was nothing. All Cecilia said was that she wanted Luna to know her real parents when she gave it to him.

He ruined everything Cecilia was supposed to become. There were things he didn't get to explain to her. He didn't want things to go wrong from changing her into a vampire. Hopefully, one day he could explain to her why he did it, who made him do it, and the plan that was set forth for her future. She is supposed to change everything; the future was in her hands. He couldn't let it be for nothing. There was not a single word exchanged between Efron and Vilhauer during the two blocks they walked to Efron's waking quarters.

"She won't be in charge forever Efron, remember that. There is a higher power over her. It won't last with how explosive she is. There are things I am aware of that you don't know. Only we older vampires know about the true history of The Society and how it got overthrown by the new leaders, but mostly Bianca and her greediness for power.

"We used to live in the shadows of the human world, but they wanted to change that, which I think was a mistake. It puts us all in danger. Maybe one day I will tell you the complete story," explained Vilhauer. Efron said nothing because he knew more than Vilhauer knew.

Vilhauer continued walking forward as Efron turned and started toward the bottom floor of the building to his waking quarters. He didn't want to go in, but he had no choice. He stepped one foot in front of the other, dreading the walk. He grabbed the handle and cautiously opened the door stepping across the threshold, then closed the door behind him with a click.

He had to fake the way he felt for Siren, which wasn't appealing. It gave him an awful knot in his stomach just thinking about her. He started to gag a little. He didn't want to be here with her.

He couldn't stop thinking about Cecilia. Now he knew why. It was because of the Sire bond when he changed her; it made his feelings intensify. Siren was lying on the bed, apparently daydreaming. He immediately walked over to a shelf in the corner of the room and removed the diary from his pocket. He placed it on the shelf next to his other books before Siren could see what he was doing.

He walked over to the bed slowly and looked into Siren's eyes with disgust; she still had dried blood all over her from the earlier events. She couldn't even bother cleaning herself up, he thought. Thoughts of terminating her crossed his mind, but knew he couldn't because of the consequences.

He removed her underwear from underneath her black dress, and told her to turn over onto her stomach. He then unzipped his pants, taking them off along with his underwear. For the first time it made him sick to his stomach to touch her.

He closed his eyes and banged her quick and hard with her face down in the pillow, his left hand pushing on her back into the bed and using his other hand to pull her hair, almost ripping it from her scalp. Her head was beginning to bleed.

"Ouch! A little rough," she said.

"Shut up and take it he replied." He released the heat from his body and climaxed. He then stopped when he finished and didn't care if she released hers or not. He got off her and stood up.

"Finish yourself off, Siren," he demanded. She looked back at him with disapproval.

"What? You heard me." He then removed his shirt and tossed it to the ground, walking off into the other room completely naked.

It was sort of like a bathroom, but with no toilet because vampires don't have bodily functions like creatures. All there was in the square stone room was a tall white pedestal sink, a shower nozzle, and for the handles, it had an on and off switch mounted on the wall. There was a drain in the middle of the floor for water to drain after a shower was taken, and a wall-sized mirror. He turned and looked into the mirror. He still had blood spatter on him from the human massacre. He walked over to the shower handles and turned them on. Hot, steaming water hit his hair, and blood started running down his body, and then down the drain it went.

<center>~~~~~~</center>

Cecilia

A million things were running through her mind. How did she get inside this cell? Where was she? She was confused and lost. She was frightened. She had blood all over her face, arms, hands, and clothes. She had no idea whose blood it was, which scared her more.

Her teal dress was torn in several spots. She began crying as she lay down on the bed in her cell. She closed her eyes to see if maybe she could get some sleep. As soon as she closed her eyes… Bang! Someone was hitting the bars on her cell. It was Bianca.Shehad taken a metal bar and hit the cell with it.

"Wake up my dear, vampires don't sleep."

"What? I'm not a vampire. I'm a human," she said. "You are though; I can smell death on you. Are you going to eat me? Why do you have me here? And whose blood is this on me?"She looked down and noticed a flat tummy.

"Where's my baby?" She screamed out.

"Yes, you are a vampire. I took your memories of the last few days away, and some other things that I saw fit that you shouldn't remember. They are now my memories. Maybe I will return them someday, or maybe I won't. Your baby is safe and will be okay." Bianca turned to Lance, a guard who was standing in the corner of the dark room next to the door, and told him to go get a creature and bring it for Cecilia. Lance exited the room.

"No! It can't be. I'm no vampire." She yelled frantically.

"You already said you can smell me, so that wouldn't be me you smell. That is your craving for creature blood. Your

73

requirement now, to stay alive, since you are a vampire." Bianca explained.

Lance returned. As he opened the door, Cecilia got a glimpse of the room around her cell. It was painted dark blue, with no windows. There were stone benches lining each wall. She felt like she were an animal at a zoo on display.

Lance walked toward the cell with the creature. He unlocked the door to her cell, opened it, and shoved the woman-creature inside, quickly relocking it behind him so Cecilia couldn't escape. Cecilia was sniffing the air like a hungry dog. She could smell her; it was the sweetest smell she had ever experienced. Her eyes turned red as her body shook; her fangs popped out.

Her gums hurt; she put her fingers to her mouth and felt them with disbelief. She tried to fight the urge by pushing herself up against the back of the cell. "No! I will not do it!"She yelled.

"Please don't kill me," the woman cried. She was shaking and terrified. Cecilia didn't resist the temptation for very long. She gave in and jolted at the woman. She knocked her to the floor and fell upon top of her. She wasn't sure where to eat from, but she remembered she had seen vampires eat from the neck before on the island when she was a human.

She took a bite from the vein in her neck. It was pulsating in her mouth, and she was in a daze. It was so good she couldn't stop. The woman was screaming, but it didn't seem to bother her. She eventually passed out. She felt a sensation come over her body that she had never felt before.

There was a sense of satisfaction; her core began to overheat. She was now extremely hot to the touch. When there was no more blood flowing to her mouth from the woman's body, she released her hold. She now stood over the cold, dead woman's corpse.

"What have I done? I'm a monster!" She sat on the concrete bed in disbelief, staring at the woman's crumpled body on the ground.

"You are only doing what is natural to our kind," said Bianca.

"Why did you turn me? What do you gain from me being a vampire? I thought The Society had to make the choice of who is changed, and who breeds. I was chosen to be a breeder. None of this makes sense." Cecilia questioned.

"We gain a lot from you, and someday you will find out, but now is too soon. You are not ready to take on what has been planned for you. You're very special; there is more to you than just a vampire." Bianca announced.

"What do you mean?" Cecilia looked confused.

"Do you have any idea where you come from?"

"No, unfortunately I don't. You vampires took me from my parents and my home when I was a child!" She yelled.

"Did it ever occur to you that those people were not your real family? They had brown hair and green eyes, and you have blonde hair and green eyes." Bianca explained.

Cecilia stood up and walked toward the bars where Bianca was standing. She was getting angry.

"Stop lying! You don't know a thing about me or my family. You parasites killed all of them in front of me. You're horrible; you are horrible creatures, not humans." She screeched.

"Cecilia, before you start pointing fingers, you just killed a creature or human, as you call them. Just know there are things you don't know about yourself that are significantly worse than what any creature has ever done. Now calm yourself and sit back down. You will not disrespect me or The Society this way."

Cecilia sat back down on the bed with a look of hate in her eyes. "That family you were placed with was supposed to hide you, so you couldn't come back to us, to me. The person who placed you there took you away from your true family. We destroyed that town to find you; it wasn't to take creatures. That's just a story to hide the truth." Bianca said.

"But I was told it was to take children away to raise them to become the new race. I guess that's what I am, the new race. Then why did you take Efron then?" asked Cecilia

"Don't believe all the rumors you hear. We took Efron because he was a friend to you, and we thought it would help you and make it easier. The person who took you and placed you there with that family didn't care what pain it caused to your true family. That man just thought about himself," said Bianca.

"Man? What man?" Cecilia demanded to know.

"Your true father, my husband at the time. He was locked in this very cell until he escaped." She said.

"My what? My father? He was your husband? So that makes you my..." Cecilia started to feel sick and looked light headed.

"Yes, Cecilia, I am your mother, your real mother. I mean look at me, look at our blonde hair and green eyes." Bianca murmured.

"How can this be? I am now more confused than I was before. And if you're my mother, then why do you have me locked up in this cage? Why did you lock my father up here?"She demanded.

"Because, like I said, you are special. You are more than just a vampire. I didn't think you would ever get your powers back, but you have. I didn't know they would be returned once you were transformed into a vampire. Apparently, you needed to die to get your Empusa powers returned to you. Not only that, but the fact that you can teleport in your sleep means your dragon isn't dormant anymore either.

"I thought you were just going to be a normal human like I once was, before I was transformed. You were meant to be a breeder. Not a choice that I made. Vampires must not have any true family. It clouds our judgment of the choices we have to make. I put it together and figured out that your father's family gene only comes to its full ability when you are transformed.

"You, apparently, carry the gene. Once I heard of the things you were doing to others, I knew you were just like him and his family. Your father was locked up because he took you away from us, well mostly me, and decided to go against what we had already put in motion years ago for the new rule. He had a change of heart and said it was too dangerous for his family and didn't want his daughter or any future children growing up in an open world where humans knew about us.

"He was right about some of it. He thought mostly of his family, the ones that had the gene, who are dead and the ones that are still alive and hiding if not dead too. We vampires are the more dominant race; we should not be hiding. It is the creatures that should be scared of us, not the other way around. If your father had just waited a few more years, he would have seen everything was fine.

"We needed your abilities or someone in his family to overtake the one who is stopping us and keeping us on this little island. We should be on the big land, in the big towns, with all the creatures, living how we want, not being confined to this place." Bianca explained...

"Just wait a minute. Do you hear yourself? You want a normal life and to live among humans? There is no such thing as normal when you are immortal and a blood-sucking parasite. Sounds like you all didn't think through what you wanted for this race. Sounds like to me it would have been better to stay in hiding. At least you wouldn't be rats in a cage. You sound crazy." Cecilia replied.

"That's where you come in, my dear." Bianca had a smile on her face.

"And what if I don't want to help?" Cecilia looked a little afraid.

"That's where you're wrong, dear. You don't have a choice. You would have if your father had cooperated. You would have been free." Bianca shrieked.

"No, you just said it yourself, I would have been killed. Vampires don't have true families." Cecilia replied.

"We were going to change that rule; we had you in hiding, my child. You were with your father's people. After I had you, we left you with his family to keep you safe. I never saw you again after I handed you over to your grandmother. His family took you and hid you from me, from us. I found out later that your father knew where they took you and that he had a hand in your disappearance. I locked him up and my love for him died because he wasn't the person I fell in love with and we wanted different things, and the fact he took my child away from me didn't help either." Bianca said.

"But you found me. You let me rot in an orphanage run by vampires. So don't act like you care about me, or my well-being, or my life, you crazy lunatic." Cecilia yelled.

"Watch your tongue or I will remove it for you. You're right, I no longer care. That motherly instinct I had is no longer in me. It has been a little over 18 years since I have held you in my arms, and soon after I was transformed. I have gone cold. I learned to let go of you a long time ago. To care about nothing, so I wouldn't get hurt. The only thing I care about is what I want to accomplish for myself and our race. Oh, and the taste of blood, can't forget that. I only need you to take down the leader so we can be freed. Then you can go on your way as long as you don't try to stop me. If you do, then I will take you down without hesitation, so don't get in my way." She demanded.

"Go on my way? Yeah right, I have a feeling about you; you don't keep your word. Your morals mean nothing to you. Why are you telling me all of this, anyway?" Cecilia asked.

"Because you need to know what you are and where you come from. I am being nice enough to tell you things. Things I am sure you have wanted to know for years. So be quiet and listen. The Dark Guardian is not running The Society. The Dark Guardian is just a story we came up with to cover up the real truth about your family and their gene. We didn't want all the vampires to know about the gene and what they are capable of. That they would have compassion for creature life. We don't want that. The only ones that know the true story are The Society, and now you."

"Lucky me," Cecilia muttered sarcastically.

"I was so disgusted when I found out what your father and his family had done to hide you from me. They had made a whole town believe the family had been pregnant and had a baby girl, and then later a little boy. They compelled them all so none of them knew the truth. I never knew it was possible to compel a whole town for the same lie. You were so young when we finally found you. You had no memory of anything, but the life you had been living. How could you have? You were just a toddler when you were placed there, Bianca said.

"Oh, I remember the terrible night you guys took me. Don't remind me." Cecilia was starting to tear up, remembering her family and her baby brother, Kane.

"I will never forget the night the vampires came into my home and pried me, and Efron, and many other children away from their families. I remembered my father trying to stop them from taking me. The vampires made me watch. While one in particular slaughtered my whole family.

"He killed my mother, my father, and my younger brother Kane. There was nothing I could do, they overpowered everyone. No one could stop them. That was the first time everyone found out about vampires. They killed anyone that saw anything, or took them captive to eat or to be mated like I was.

"They devoured the entire city as men had to watch while their wives were being raped, and screaming in pain and agony until they went silent, being fed on until they died. Something no child should have ever seen. And the children that they didn't take, they just sucked them dry of blood. Then to finish it off, they just snapped the men's necks after they were done feeding on them, threw them into a burning fire that was already engulfing the city.

"There were some elderly folks trying to get away, but they weren't fast enough. The vampires played with them, it was like watching a game of cat and mouse. It was a game of who could catch more than the other. I was traumatized. I still have nightmares about it. When we were leaving on the boat, I looked back at the city. My home was engulfed in flames and was burning to the ground. It smelled like a slaughterhouse. I'll never forget that smell. But what you all didn't know is you missed one. I saw a young boy who got away from it all. He was unharmed, untouched by your evil souls, and he still lives and deserves to be free." Cecilia said, her eyes filling with tears. Then they turned red; she was angry.

"I had no idea, Cecilia," Bianca replied.

"Spare me your pity, Bianca. You were probably there, and you don't care. You are not my mother and never will be. My mother died in that house, the only house that has ever been my home. Leave me alone and get out! I'm done talking." Cecilia shrieked, growling at her.

"I can take those memories away if you want me to." Bianca exclaimed.

"No! You just said you care about nothing, not even me. Besides, I want to keep their memory, because if not, I would have no memory of my TRUE FAMILY! Just leave me be. I am nothing to you anyway," said Cecilia. "Just go away," she cried.

Bianca got up from her seat and walked toward the cell where Cecilia was and said, "I was just trying to help, don't take my kindness for weakness. I won't offer again. We will talk later, but don't think about taking a nap because it won't happen. The Dark Guardian will not be contacting you again from beyond the grave as long as you're under my authority." She demanded.

"What do you mean? Vampires don't nap. What does napping have to do with him? And how do you know he's really dead?" Cecilia said.

"We don't know if he's dead; it's just speculation. Again, you're special like him; you have the ability to sleep. Unlike us normal vampires."

She ignored the other questions and then yelled for Lance. He jumped up off his seat and told him not to let me sleep. Then she exited the room, closing the door behind her.

I just sat there in confusion. I wondered if I were to fall asleep, would I get more answers? Would I be able to reach out to the Dark Guardian? And if I did reach him, what would he tell me? Should I trust him? I don't want to trust Bianca; she has me locked in a cell. I guess there is only one thing to do. She lay down on the bed that was in her cell. She started to close her eyes, and as soon as she did, there was a big bang on the cell bars, causing her to jump.

"Are you sure you want to be doing that?"She said, growling at him.

"Yes ma'am. No one disobeys Mistress Bianca, or there are consequences," replied Lance.

"Well, you don't know how long I will be in this cell. I could possibly get out, and I may come after you first. I don't know if you have done anything to me, but I am sure you have since you seem to be her little sidekick. I am apparently really powerful, and once I find out how powerful I am, I may not be able to control my rage. You better hope you are on the right side, because I am not sure what side is right and you will probably want to be on whichever side I am on. You look a little scared there, Lance. Does the cat have your tongue?" Cecilia stated, and started smiling wickedly.

"I have been working for your mother for 18 years. I am not about to betray her now, or ever. You will see that what we want to do is the right way, and better for our future." He said.

"Do not call her that! She is not my Mother! I am not helping any of you! Not now, not ever!" Cecilia yelled. She was staring Lance straight in the face. "Why do you look so familiar to me? I know you, don't I? How long do I have to wait to be cleaned and out of these filthy clothes?" Cecilia demanded. Lance turned away from her so she couldn't see his face.

"I will talk to Mistress Bianca and see if she can get someone in here to clean you up," he said.

Lance started walking toward the door. His posture wasn't as strong as it had been before. It was as if he was afraid to turn around and look at Cecilia. He wanted to turn around and peek, but resisted because she would know he was scared. Why would he be scared? Unless…there was something he had done to her previously that she couldn't remember.

While he was walking away, Cecilia had just a hint of a memory of the day that she was taken from her home. In it, she saw Lance. He was one of the vampires that had killed her family.

"It was you!" Cecilia roared. His walking turned into a sprint toward the door.

"I will terminate you for real if I ever see you again! When I get out of here, you're dead!" Cecilia screamed.

She paced back and forth in her cell, screaming with rage. Anger like she had never felt before. Her eyes turned bright red; they were burning.

She grabbed the bars of her cell and started to spread them apart. This caused gravel to fall from the cement they were embedded into from the ceiling. The bars started to shock her. Her hair standing on all ends, but it didn't bother her. The heat did nothing to her like it would a normal vampire.

Bianca came running in with a taser that had unlimited amounts of shock to it. It did nothing to Cecilia; it just made her more irate.

She grabbed Bianca's arm that was holding the taser and started twisting it toward Bianca. Bianca used every ounce of strength she had. Bianca yelled, "Get the serum, Lance!"

Lance ran into the room with a syringe and said, "Are you sure you want to use this on her? It will knock her out and put her to sleep," he said.

"We have no other option." She whined.

Lance was hesitant to be anywhere near Cecilia, but he followed his orders and plunged the needle into Cecilia's neck, administering the drug quickly.

Cecilia turned to look at him with pure hatred. She went to grab him. He knew one day she would deliver his final termination. Instantly she got dizzy and started stumbling. She became paralyzed and fell to the ground, hitting her head on the corner of the concrete bed.

She was out cold. For how long they couldn't know, because of her smacking her head on the bed, causing blunt force trauma. Now, she must heal before the waking serum can awaken her. It could be hours or even days.

Chapter Six
Cecilia

She opened her eyes and found herself on her knees somewhere else. It was the middle of a field, not her cell. There was a huge blazing fire pit in front of her; it made her jump back in fear. She was hyperventilating; she couldn't breathe.

She looked down at herself, realizing that her body wasn't exactly her body. What the hell, she thought? All she could remember was being in a cell and her so-called mother Bianca was screaming at her and her assistant Lance stabbing her in the neck with some kind of sleep serum that knocked her out and made her hit her head.

Her head was aching. She reached up to touch where it was hurting and found it sliced open and bleeding from the wound down her face. Her head was throbbing, she had an enormous headache.

That little asshole, she thought. Just wait unit I get my hands on him. She was so angry. The more she thought about him, the angrier she got. She knew Lance was the one who had killed her family so many years ago. She felt heat surge through her body and thought she was going to die.

Suddenly, she saw steam coming out of her nose, and she opened her mouth and screamed. "Aaaaaah!" Fire started shooting out of her mouth at a surging pace.

She stared around the massive fire pit, not noticing all the individuals in front of her until smoke filled the air and they began transforming into dragons. This startled her.

"What in the hell?" She exclaimed.

As she was looking around the pit, she realized it didn't look like an ordinary fire pit. It was as if they were expecting her to come, aware of her return. Something felt off; it feels like… a welcoming party? No… it feels more like some kind of initiation party. As she was looking around at everyone, one person in particular stood out. He was standing there in his dark trench coat. It was him. The Dark Guardian was here.

"You!" Cecilia shouted, fire blowing out of her mouth. "It's you, is it true you are dead? Am I dreaming? Why did you not change with the rest of them? Why are you still human?"

"There is a lot to explain Cecilia. Stop talking, and I will answer some of your questions. No, I am not dead. We had to make Bianca and The Society believe that I was. I didn't change because I am not afraid of you, although you are unpredictable at this point with your powers. I don't believe you will hurt me or us. They are afraid of you because they don't know you, and because we are in hiding. We are the last of our kind," he said.

"What is your name?" said Cecilia.

"Does it make a difference?" He replied.

"Well, I'm not calling you father, or Dark Guardian anymore." She exclaimed.

"So, you now know." He said, lowering his head down.

"Name!" She yelled.

"My name is irrelevant to what will take place, but I am not the Dark Guardian."

"Do you really think that with everything I have been through that I will never find out what your name is? Just tell me you ignorant man."

The fire within her was growing again. Why was he being so uncooperative? What is he scared of? Is he just as powerful as me?

"What is your problem? If I know you are alive, they will know. I am not working for them. Look at me. I have a gash on my forehead. I don't even know what is going on. Bianca has me in a cell. She has erased my memories from the last few days and has been shocking me so I can't sleep. I didn't understand the whole sleep thing, but she didn't realize that when she took my memories.

"She only took my waking memories. She didn't take my dreaming memories, if that's what these even are? She didn't take my memories of when I have met with you. I don't even understand where I am right now. Am I in some other dimension, am I dreaming, or am I just going crazy? My body is lying somewhere in a cage and who knows what she is doing to me."

"Son, may I speak?" Said Iris.

"Sure mother," he said.

Looking to her son, "You know what Bianca did when she was with you? She manipulated you. You know what she is capable of. You must save my granddaughter's body and bring it back here so we can properly do the ritual so she can be properly changed into the Empusa she is made to be. She needs to be here physically both mind and body. And once she understands who we are as dragon people, maybe she will understand us and want to stay. It is more peaceful here," said Iris, smiling at Cecilia.

"Yes, I know what I have to do. I just didn't think I would have to face Bianca again and things wouldn't have to escalate because I thought Efron would have done what he was supposed to do. That's what I get for putting my trust into a young kid." He said.

"What, did you ask Efron to do? And how do you know Efron in the first place? said Cecilia.

"I don't think I need to answer to you. You're just a child. You don't have any control over your powers. You're out of control; I mean look at you! You have blood dripping down your face from the wound on your head. You're in your dragon body and haven't even realized it. Also, you're scaring your people; ones you are one day supposed to lead. When you can compose yourself, then we can talk."

"Talk ha, you can't even tell me your name?" Cecilia laughed.

"My name is Tobias, now you know. Does it change anything?" he exclaimed.

"Tobias, what kind of name is that?"She said, in a sarcastic voice.

"It's the name of the King of Dragons, the father of the Empusa princess, Cecilia."

When he finished his sentence, he tore off his black trench coat, revealing himself to me for the first time. I imagined him to look… different. He was about 7 feet tall, had dirty-blonde hair with light blonde highlights, and broad shoulders. He wore no shirt and had a black loincloth to cover his most sensitive parts.

He had scars all over his chest, which meant he was a warrior. Along with them were some tribal-looking tattoos. He then shifted into an enormous, beautiful, dark-green dragon. He had green scales all over his body, and brown claws protruded where his finger nails where. Four brown horns appeared atop his head. His wings were twice the size of his body, and his tail was just the right length for his body with a pointed, sharp end.

After he changed, everyone else followed suit and changed as well. All of them were different in age, size, and color. They lie low, bowing toward the ground. All of them were much smaller than him, and I. Maybe because I was a mixture of now three different creatures: a bloodsucking Vampire, a Dragon, and an Empusa, whatever that is.

Maybe I did need him to help me understand whatever I am. Obviously it wasn't going to be Bianca that would help me. She just has my body locked in a cage. These people seem like they want to help me, maybe get to know me. My grandmother is even here, she was a beautiful purple dragon. Maybe I have more family than I realize. Maybe that is what should be important. And maybe they can help me get Luna back as well. I wonder if they even know about her. I wonder if they will help rescue Efron as well.

Cecilia was waiting patiently for them to finish whatever kind of ritual they were doing. Maybe they were all excited because the princess had returned to their lands and they thought they were saved.

She didn't know how to be a leader. She didn't even know what was going on with herself or how to control it. She wanted to talk to Tobias alone so she could get some answers. She wasn't even sure how long she had left before she would be awakened and be back in the cage; back on the Vampire's land.

"Not to interrupt, but Tobias, can we please speak alone? I don't know how much time I even have here; once I wake up, I will back be in my body. I am not even sure how this out-of-body experience works! You all seem to be enjoying yourselves here, as if nothing is happening. I am not sure what

Bianca is planning to use me for, and I really don't want to find out. I am scared, okay! So please help me. Help me find out how to stop her, and help me find out where I come from, and who I am."Cecilia yelled over all the chanting and crackling fire.

Everyone stopped visiting and chanting. Staring at Cecilia, one by one a popping sound would happen. Smoke burst in the air as they started changing back into their human selves. Most of them were men who looked like skilled warriors; a few of them were women. They all looked bigger and scarier than I looked as a human. I don't know why they would be afraid of little me, or even afraid of my mother.

My body began to cool suddenly since I had first arrived here. It had been a while since I had my explosive outburst of anger. Now, I just stayed heated inside all over. All of a sudden I heard another pop with smoke around me, and this time the pop was inside my ears and I was human again.

It was weird, because I didn't force it, I didn't even know how I changed back. After I changed back, I realized I had no clothes on, and I grabbed my bare breasts with my hands.

All kinds of gawking and staring coming from the men, and women too. More power to them, I suppose. Apparently my clothes were burned off with the fire breathing out of my mouth, at least so I thought.

All the men had chain loin covers on, and the women had their breasts covered by a different type of loin cover, it was one that wrapped around their neck at the top and covered their breasts, then tied at the middle around their back then hung off their hips and covered the lower part of their bodies.

They all seemed to have something to cover up with. It was like being half naked was nothing to them. Apparently something I will have to attain. Most of them were covered in what looked like tribal tattoos.

Iris, who was Cecilia's grandmother, started walking toward her really quickly at a fast pace and was holding something brown.

"Cecilia, when you are ready, you can have my spare loin cover. I have been carrying it for you just in case you needed something to wear." She then pointed. "You can head into that cave over there to the right of the lighted cave. Tobias will be in soon to talk to you. There is a lot to discuss," said Iris.

"Thank you, I appreciate your kindness," said Cecilia.

Cecilia took the cover from her, put it on and headed up to the caves on the hills and entered the small opening to the right, where Iris told her to go. She was met by a few guards when she got to the cave opening, which Iris hadn't warned her about. They already knew to send her to Tobias' chambers. Everyone there knew it was Cecilia, the Empusa Princess. Plus, who couldn't tell — with her extremely blonde, almost white hair, like her father's.

She was then escorted into Tobias' chambers. The inside looked nothing like she imagined. There were dirt walkways heading left and right, and one went straight up the middle, and that was the one they went up. As they got further into the caves, the dirt walls turned into rock, and there were candles lit to light their way. There was a door at the end of the hallway. When they reached the door, a guard opened it for Cecilia and ushered her inside.

The caves were carved out and made into glorious rooms. The chambers belonging to Tobias were huge. When you first walked in, there was a round table which was made from a blackish/brown rock. It was polished and shined to a marbled finish, and had about 7 chairs all matching and pushed in except one.

It was magnificent inside; she had never seen anything like it before. She was then instructed to sit in the chair at the round table and wait for him. So sit she did.

A leather rug lay beneath the table; she had no idea what kind of animal it came from to be so large. She hoped never to find out at this point. There was a chandelier lit with candles hanging over the table. She glanced around the room and noticed to the right there was a flight of stairs that headed up to another room. It looked as if that room led to the balcony that looked out over the room.

She couldn't see far up there, but could see about 3 huge shelves lined with books and what looked like a small library, with a sitting area.

There was also a bigger than normal king size bed to the left of some couches with a fire pit next to the bed on the left side.

She could only imagine what sort of books were contained on those shelves. Those books could be anything; from reading for enjoyment or could be the history of my family. Among the books were some trinkets and boxes that looked pretty old.

How it took everything in her power to not go around his room and snoop. Looking above the king-size bed, you could see what looked like bars in the roof. Maybe an escape route in case he had to get out in an emergency? That would make total sense, because who would want no way out of these tight quarters, especially if you are king? Plus, the smoke from the fire pit had to go somewhere.

Looking to the left of the table, she noticed that on the ground there were large claw marks. He must have changed into his dragon form in here. It looks to have happened several times, or maybe even had a fight in here a few times.

Looking beyond the claw marks, the cave was beautiful. There was a small freshwater stream running into what looked like a hot spring that then ran out another double door to the backside of his chambers.

She wondered what it looked like beyond those doors. Maybe he would show me if I asked. I hadn't seen much in my short life that I could remember. It was all taken from me by Bianca. These last few hours, and this place, brought a calming sense of home to her. It felt as if she belonged here.

Just then, Tobias walked in.

"You do belong here, with your family Cecilia," said Tobias

"If that is what I choose to do. I'm not technically here," said Cecilia.

"Well, you are, but you're not. It's complicated, but we are going to fix that. You are astral projecting," said Tobias.

"And what about Efron?" said Cecilia.

"We will get him later, right now my concern is getting you," said Tobias.

"How do you even know Efron in the first place? What did you ask him to do?" Cecilia questioned him.

"There is much to discuss, but first we will go back to when you were a child. You were here before. You just don't remember. Your mother Bianca removed those memories from you when you were a child. She planned on taking you and hiding you away, much like she is trying to do now.

"She is trying to use you to find the Dragons. That's why everyone is so scared right now. She can't find these lands alone, and she has been banished. You are of three mixed creatures, which is rare. You are extremely powerful when all three are activated. Once you had been changed by Efron, you became more powerful, and now all three are activated. She thought you were just like me, but you're not. Her plan was to take you away from me and your family. We would never see you again and you would rule and become evil just like her."

"What! Why would she do that? Especially if she loved me. I'm her daughter!" she was disgusted and looked like she wanted to vomit.

"If you haven't noticed, Bianca doesn't have any motherly instincts. She lost them long ago when you were a baby, when she became a vampire. There was someone else with whom she fell in love while we were together. Well, it was more that he manipulated her, is what you call it. Now I believe this person to be controlling her behind the scenes and no one knows. But I know, all because of his jealously and all because he wasn't next in line to be King. He had to ruin my family and try to take what is mine," said Tobias. He was visibly getting angry. You could see the veins popping out of his neck; he was so angry.

"I am assuming I have an uncle? What is his name?" Said Cecilia.

"His name is Thane," said Tobias.

"How do you know she is with Thane or that he has done these things?"She said.

"Because the night she came for you he was with her, they came in here and we fought right here, you can see the claw marks on the floor. The table was thrown across the room, and he changed into his dragon form, which is the number one rule to never do except against an enemy.

"So I changed because I felt threatened and he demanded to know where my daughter was. I then overpowered him."He then pointed above his bed. "He flew out my window up there over my bed, and as you have noticed there are now bars. They are there to keep anyone from attacking me and escaping. I haven't heard from him or seen him since. And as for your mother, she was unwilling to admit that she was with him, or that she was taking you to use you against us or the human race. Knowing that, I couldn't trust her. So, I had to hide you," said Tobias.

"If I am only powerful when I am fully changed, then how would she know what I am capable of?" Said Cecilia.

"Because someone would have told her how powerful you are once transformed. Which would have been... Thane. I believe she was put under a loyalty spell; I never put her under any spell. I loved her for who she was; that was enough for me. The only time it can ever be broken is if the one that put it on her is dead, or the Empusa takes it off of her. Once your body is here and we do the ritual, you'll become the full Tri-bred you were meant to be.

"You may be able to change your mother Bianca back, but it also maybe too late because she has been set in her ways for far too long and actually be in love with whoever has cast the spell on her. I believe it to be Thane," said Tobias.

"Look, I am sorry about your brother, my uncle I guess I could call him, but what made him do those things? Why would he turn against you?" Cecilia was confused.

"When we were kids we were close, but he was the younger one. You don't know this, but if you are the younger one in-line ofthe noble family, you don't get to become king or queen of the Dragons. I was first in-line after your grandfather passed. So I became king. He passed when you were about two years young. Around then is when I took you into hiding.

"You don't remember any of this because Bianca took your memories. You even knew all those people out there! (As he pointed toward the door) You know every single one of them. You just don't remember. And I hate her for that, and Thane for taking away my family, my life, to put us in hiding. They know where we are. They are waiting to strike. But we are going to strike first with no mercy. We are going to hit hard. We are going to get you home. They think they can just use my daughter." Said Tobias.

"I need to know. What does Efron have to do with all of this? Efron is an old friend of mine. I grew up with him. I need to know that he will be safe, and that he will be brought here as well." Said Cecilia.

"Efron was a pawn that your mother used against you to awaken your powers to see if you were an Empusa. It worked. He is actually one of my guards. He is a high Noble from another dragon Clan. Someone you are arranged to be with, which I doubt would be a problem since you both love each other already.

"Efron grew up with you, yes. Does he care for you? Yes. Some would say he even loves you. He also can astral project and was trained while here. They also changed him into a vampire as well. Which he and us were not fond of, but he was assigned to protect you, and he couldn't blow his cover.

"He can also walk in the sun, but they don't know that. The reason he has to have the heat removed from his body is that he will transform into a dragon. The Society can't know that. Where heat kills vampires. Heat and anger cause us to change. Efron didn't want you to change, so he told you to engage in intercourse, which was the right thing to do. Plus, you guys did it as young adults already. So, was it really a problem?" Cecilia smirked at his question.

"I thought so. He was told to change you into a vampire and bring you back to me… He failed. Now I have to find another way to get your body back to us. Yes, I will rescue you and him. I just have to figure out how," said Tobias.

"You don't know about Luna, do you?" said Cecilia. It was difficult to swallow. She had a huge lump in her throat.

"Who is Luna?" said Tobias

"She is my daughter. Well, mine and Efron's daughter. Efron doesn't know he's her father. He thinks she is the daughter of the mate I had back on the Breeders Island," she confessed.

"You mean to tell me there is another baby that has Nobel blood, and possibly Empusa blood on the Vampire lands! Shit! This is getting to be more complicated. Now I have to bring more warriors with me. Does Bianca know that baby is yours?" Yelled Tobias, combing his hand through his hair with frustration on his face.

"Yes, I believe she does," said Cecilia.

"Fantastic, then that means he knows," said Tobias.

"I don't know what kind of condition your body will be in, but you may have to fight with us and change when we get there. Because now we have three rescues, we have to do. We are done talking about the past for now. I must get my team in here. We have to talk about a rescue effort now," said Tobias.

Tobias got up from his chair, flinging it across the room and grabbed his head. (You could tell he was pissed.) He then headed toward the back door, pushing it open, and then yelled.

"Wiley, Dante, Zeke, Una, Brogan, and Ivy! Front and center to my command. We need to discuss a mission immediately."

From what she could see out the door, it looked like the sun was starting to rise. It was beautiful. She watched as these gorgeous and handsome warriors came in one by one through the door. For some reason Zeke looked very familiar to her; his very blonde hair, his walk, even his smile when he caught her eye.

There's no way that could be him, she thought. I saw him die. They made me believe he had died. Why would they do that, and then to have him be right here, in front of me? His name was different. Or maybe that was his name all along and Bianca made me forget. Am I going crazy?

She grabbed her head and noticed the wound had started to heal. It didn't hurt anymore, which means she had little time left here. Soon, she's going to wake me soon.

"Help!" I screamed. "I don't have long. I'm healing. She will bring me back soon and wake me. Make a plan and help me. Get me away from her! Help Efron and our child Luna escape."

I had more questions as I pointed at Zeke. "Why does he look like my younger brother that died in front of me years ago? The younger brother of the family I was hidden with years ago. Someone answer me? Is he really my brother?" Cecilia demanded! She felt as though she couldn't breathe. She was starting to hyperventilate.

"Cecilia, there is a lot to talk about, but yes, this is my son Zeke, your brother. He didn't die. They thought they had killed him. A man named Lance was told to take care of everyone in your home and grab you. They got you, and Efron was to go along with because of his age. Everyone in your home was to be terminated.

"Like I told you before; the grab was a cover-up to get you. When I came back, I found my son barely breathing. If you look on Zeke's neck, you will see a big scar where they thought they killed him, but he was relentless and he held on until I got there. We were able to save him. You see, Zeke is not your mother's child, and that is why she wanted him dead. That's why I also put him into hiding with you, so that you would both be safe. You and Zeke are only half-siblings."

"Who is Zeke's mother?" said Cecilia.

"Her name is Vika, she is my wife, and at the moment your queen. She is in her homeland and being kept safe before this war starts. You've met her before; you just don't remember. We were a happy family. We still are, and would like to make you, Efron, and Luna a part of it. Look Cecilia, I know you have a lot of questions, but right now we have to discuss how we are going to make a plan to get you, Efron, and Luna safely out of the Vampire Lands," Tobias said, sternly.

Just as those words came out of Tobias' mouth, the wound on Cecilia's head was healed, and she started to fade away into nothing, as if she had never been there to begin with.

"Look, why do we need to make a plan? We need to get them before that crazy bitch does to them what she tried to do to me!" Zeke yelled.

"Because if we don't, some of us will die. Calm down, everyone, and sit. This is what we're going to do."

Everyone in the room sat around the table waiting for Tobias to lay out his plan.

"We attack at night because they will expect us to attack at daylight because we can. Also, they will have the sunshield down, which will make it easier to break through. I know where they are keeping Cecilia. It is in the same cage she had me in. Cecilia confirmed it," said Tobias.

Iris walked in, "Why didn't you call me to this meeting? I am your advisor. And what about the baby, Luna? Where are they keeping her? She exclaimed.

"Mother? How did you know?" Tobias said and looked shocked.

You don't think I wouldn't know or be able to feel the soul of my great-grandchild out there? Especially when she is an Empusa. There's something else about her you all must know. She has the transitioning blood, so we have to get her out. Now! I just didn't want to say anything with Cecilia herein case they pulled it from her mind. We also can't let Efron know until he fully returns in both body and mind.

"It seems he is the only one that knows where they are keeping the child. Next time, call me in here when the meeting starts." Said Iris, as she rolled her eyes at Tobias.

"Zeke, Ivy, Brogan and I will go after Cecilia. I know where she is located within The Society's cage chambers. If they haven't changed it much, it should be easy to navigate through. If they put up the daylight dome, it will be harder to escape. I doubt they'll have it up at night.

"Efron has told us a bit about the child orphanage where they keep the children. They should have Luna tagged already with a name barcode on the back of her neck. I am assuming she will have jet black hair like Efron. Once Efron hears the sirens go off on the island, he should know it is time to leave and the plan has been set into place. Hopefully, he doesn't do anything stupid and try to save everyone." Said Tobias.

"He can't do it alone. He needs to just get out and come home. Hopefully, that's what he does, because he never does what he is told." Said Dante.

"Who are you to speak down of him? He is in another land and has had to hide his identity from blood suckers. They even changed him into one. You don't know if you could do better.

Plus, he will be our King someday so don't talk down of him." Said Una.

"Una is right Dante. Someday he will be married to my daughter, so don't speak poorly of him. He still has to learn our ways. Back to the plan, stop getting off topic, it is time sensitive and we have to work this out. So Una, Dante, and Wiley will go get Luna," said Tobias.

"What about me, my son? I am not sitting this out. Not with my grandchild and my great grandchild. Plus I am the strongest eldest here." Said Iris.

"You are my advisor, not a fighter or warrior," said Tobias.

"Hold your tongue, my son. You maybe my king, but I am still your mother queen, and I have fought way more wars and have done more rescues than you. I am an asset in a fight, and I will be helping to get the Empusa dragon princess and her daughter back to where they belong on our Dragon lands, their homeland. That is final!"Iris said with determination.

"Ok mother, fine, you can go. Just be careful. I don't want to lose another family member or have to do another rescue. You can go with Una, Dante, and Wiley," said Tobias.

"It will be my honor to do a rescue with such beauty and talent," said Dante.

"Don't push your luck Dante. Just because my husband the king died years ago, doesn't mean I am ready to move on, and you can have me. You are half my age boy." said Iris, with a chuckle.

"We'll see about that, and I assure you I am no boy, all man down there." said Dante, with a smirk on his face.

"Oh goodness, can you woo my mother some other time? Preferably when I am not in your presence." said Tobias, rolling his eyes is disgust.

"Sorry my king, I got caught up in her beauty," said Dante.

Just as they were finishing up talking about how the plan would go, the door to Tobias's chamber swung open. They all jumped to their feet, the chairs they sat in flung backwards, ready to fight. But it was no one they needed to worry about fighting. It was Efron, in his astral projected body, so he wasn't fully there.

"Efron what are you doing here? You were told not to come back in any form, until the rescues are being done, it could jeopardize everything." Said Tobias.

"I am sorry, I had to come back one last time, and they have Cecilia. They figured out she has Dark Guardian powers." said Efron.

"Efron, slow down. We know all of this. Cecilia was just here. She has explained everything to us. I also had along one-on-one talk with her and told her something's too. Once we get you all back, we will explain all of this," said Tobias.

"So, she knows my identity now?" said Efron. He swallowed hard, like he had something stuck in his throat.

"You knew this day would come. Now, there is a lot more at stake. Unfortunately, you have also been turned into a vampire; you can choose to eat human blood or food like us. I would choose wisely when you return. I am also King, so don't think I can't take away your seat to the throne in the future or your hand to my daughter away. I am capable of a lot many things, but if you hurt my family… I will come after you.

"Cecilia seems to have no problem with the information that I have told her. So, when we invade, you need to just return, no rescues, no side jobs, no goodbyes. Just return home. We will take care of the rest. If they find out that you have betrayed them and who you are, I am sure Bianca will kill you without hesitating. If you have to kill anyone just do it, don't make a big scene, but do it quickly. Understood?" said Tobias.

"Understood, My King!" said Efron.

"Now, go back and wake, before your mate realizes you were sleeping. Because, as you very well know, vampires don't sleep. This time let the heat stay in your body like we practiced, so you can fly with us home when we come. You have changed several times here, but never in person, it may hurt the first time. You will need to push through the pain. We need you to be here, and she needs you. Now, go back, don't return, we'll see you soon. Oh, and Efron, don't die!"said Tobias.

And just as he appeared, Efron was gone. Where he once stood was now empty. He too had vanished into thin air, like he was never there.

Chapter Seven
Cecilia

She opened her eyes; she was back in the cell. Rock debris had fallen, some of the bars were bent, and she was covered in blood, most likely from the gash caused when splitting her head open. She was trying to piece together what had happened while she was gone, and what they had done to her body if anything at all. They obviously didn't seem too bright to know what they were doing. She noticed they had her facing the wall, so they wouldn't be able to tell if she opened her eyes and was fully awake. What idiots she thought? She then realized she couldn't move. She couldn't understand why.

"I know you're awake, Cecilia. You're thinking, why can't I move? Well, let me tell you. There is a paralyzing serum we have, and after we gave you the waking serum, we gave you that one as well. We felt it necessary so you couldn't attack us when you came to." said Bianca.

"How necessary for you? You want me to listen and be on your side, but you keep locking me up and poisoning me with serums. Yeah sounds like you are the good guys to me."Said Cecilia.

"Look, you think I wanted it this way? I am not fit to be a mother, I am a ruler. I want you to help me, he wants you to help us, he needs you to help us. He loves me and he will love you too." Said Bianca.

"By him, you mean Thane. The back stabber who took my father's wife, put a spell on you while I was young, and took you away. He controls you and you are bound to him. You don't even know what you want because you are controlled by him." said Cecilia.

Cecilia was starting to move her body. The serum that Bianca gave her didn't work for long. The heat in Cecilia's body burned it off faster than Bianca thought it would. She was more powerful than her father ever was. She rolled over and started to get up slowly.

"You know, you are sick and demented vampire? You use people to your advantage to get what you want, well no more, not with me." said Cecilia.

"Honey, I am a vampire. None of us are good. You will come to realize that once you let the vampire in you come out. Don't forget those other creatures too. You've got a lot going for you, and I'm sure you don't want anyone bossing you around, especially since you know you are a Noble now. Nobles do what they want," said Bianca.

"I am choosing my own path. Unlike you, no one has made me do anything that I don't want to do. I am choosing myself, no one controls me." Yelled Cecilia.

"Give it time my dear; you are not free. Someone will snatch you up, plus you are The Dark Master, so you have more power than you could ever imagine. It's sad you don't know what to do with it yet. I can help you with it, Thane could too." Said Bianca.

"No!" Cecilia yelled, turning away and then said, "I'll figure it out on my own."

"Well, you won't be leaving like you think you will. Feel the back of your neck. (Cecilia put her hand to the back of her neck as quickly as she could.) You feel that ripple; we placed a brace inside your neck while you were asleep. It's healed over and under your skin, so you can't take it out. It physically won't allow you off the island. It won't even let you sleep and escape to the Dragon Lands. So my dear, you are stuck here. It also takes away your powers temporarily. So you won't be able to hurt anyone."Said Bianca.

Bianca started to move her hands around and try to pull memories from Cecilia from the Dragon Lands. Unfortunately the brace stopped any power from working including hers.

"Well, that's unfortunate. The brace works too well, and I can't see what was talked about during your visit to the Dragon Lands," said Bianca.

"Maybe that, or maybe I am fighting you off now, I guess you won't know." said Cecilia, with a smirk.

"Ugh, you're lucky we need you or you would be terminated by now." Said Bianca. Then she stormed off and yelled at the two guards to keep watch.

As Cecilia was sitting in the cage, she was freaking out. How am I going to get off this Island? Maybe the brace won't work. I should try to dig it out. They are going to come for me and I can't leave. This could also just be a hoax, and those could be my scales that I feel back there, since I didn't feel them before because I never turned until I went to the Dragon Lands in my dreams, I really don't know. Only one way to find out, she thought. She focused on one of the guards and pushed him back against the wall. He was moving, but not as fast as she would have thought. I have to get out of here; it's not safe.

The guards ran toward the door to get Bianca and just as they reached the door, the doors flung open and she walked in with a man; it was Thane. If I wasn't scared before, I sure was now. She brought him in to show, she had me captive and locked in a cell like an animal.

He walked toward the cage all dressed in black. He wore a black coat, and black pants, and had short hair that was slicked back. He stood about 6 feet tall with tan skin. He walked like my father. You could tell it was his brother, my uncle the traitor.

"Cecilia you don't remember me, but I am Thane."

"Oh I know who you are; you can save the introduction," as she hissed at him. Embarrassed, she stepped back; she didn't know where that came from.

"I see you haven't really talked to her yet; you're not very convincing, and I am sure my brother got to her first. Do I have to do everything myself?" Said Thane

"No sir," said Bianca

"I am assuming you must be hungry since you have returned. I know you can smell the blood of the humans, as you call them. We are all just creatures of the land. I'll have Lance get you one if you would like?" Said Thane.

"Quit trying to act like I am not a prisoner here. I'm in a cage, and my so called mother and her associate put a brace on me so I can't use my powers. Like you really care what happens to me, other than to use me for your own gains to take control of the vampire race and to rule the dragons." said Cecilia.

"Oh honey, I already rule the vampires, I don't need you for that. I have had the vampires under my thumb for years, or I guess I should say claws," he said. His fingers extended into claws as if to demonstrate. Thane's claws had grown to about five inches long.

Lance returned bringing in a creature for Cecilia to eat. She was hungry, but didn't want to say so. She also didn't want to feed on people anymore. Tobias had told her she had the choice of eating food instead, and if she was going to be on the Dragon Island, she wouldn't be allowed to eat humans anymore. She would need to control the urge for the blood.

Lance brought the poor human over to Thane and left him there in front of him and then left the room abruptly.

"Please don't kill me, I have a family, a wife and she's with child," pleaded the man.

"Oh, it won't be me that kills you, my dear fellow. I am not a vampire," said Thane.

Thane brought his hand up to the man's throat and made a slight cut across it with a fingered claw. Blood started flowing down to the man's chest. Thane grabbed the door to the cage that Cecilia was in and opened it. It wasn't even locked, liked she had thought. Thane tossed the man in there with her like he was live bait. Cecilia could smell the fresh blood coming from his fresh wound. She wanted it bad, but she knew it was a trap. She tried to hold back for as long as she could. The craving became too much and she pounced on his neck sucking him dry. Once she was done she backed into the corner and just sat there looking embarrassed.

"You feel different don't you, more powerful? What my brother didn't tell you or explain to you is, you may not want to feed, but you need human blood. You need it for your powers. You need it for the Empusa part of you. I may have been exiled, but I know what you are and how to help you. Empusa's have been around my family for thousands of years," said Thane.

"But you told me she was The Dark Guardian? Is Tobias still alive?" said Bianca.

"Only speak when you are spoken to. This doesn't involve you," threatened Thane. He shook his head and rolled his eyes at Bianca.

"Why wouldn't you lock my cage, I could easily leave. I don't want to be here. I didn't even want to be a vampire, or the Empusa Dragon Princess. I didn't choose any of this," said Cecilia.

"I can take the Empusa part from you if you would like? Then all of this could go away. Everyone would stop trying to trap you and need you. But, you would have to give it to me willingly," said Thane.

"I don't know," said Cecilia.

"Well, you have plenty of time to think about it. We have a powerful enchantress that can pass it onto me through a ritual," said Thane.

"Something to think about," said Cecilia.

"There is a room next to this one outside those doors from where we came in. It's to the right and there's a shower in there you can clean yourself up. Change your clothes from the wardrobe, take advantage of it. Your cage isn't locked anymore; it hasn't been since you returned. You are free to roam, but don't think about leaving Vampire Island, that neck brace is also a tracker." said Thane.

Thane turned away from the cage she was being held in and walked out the door he had entered through earlier with Bianca. Alone, Cecilia thought now was the time to get out, to escape. She couldn't feel Bianca in her head anymore which was strange. Maybe she was strong enough that she could push her out. Maybe it was the blood; maybe she did need it to be stronger like Thane said. She just had to figure out how to get the brace out of her neck.

She got off the concrete bed she was sitting on and maneuvered over the body that was still on the floor in the cage with her. She pushed the cage door open, as it creaked it startled her, it was surprisingly unlocked like he said. There wasn't anyone in the prison quarters like before watching her. She still felt like she was being watched with every move she made. She walked slowly and headed toward the brown double doors that they had left from. She pushed them open and walked through them.

She now stood in a hallway that was gray, layered with brinks, and no windows. There were candle sticks burning on the walls to illuminate the way. She had no recollection of this hallway on the way into the prison cages. But how would she when she had been unconscious?

As she peered around the hallway she looked down both ways and no one was present either way. She could try and leave, but she had to figure out how to get this thing out of her neck first. She looked down at herself and figured she might as well clean up. The blood was starting to smell as well.

She walked to the right as fast as she could and there was a gray door; she opened it really fast and then closed it, locking it behind her. She pressed her body against the door and began crying as she slumped to the floor.

After a few moments, she composed herself and stood up. She looked around the room; another beautiful room. A chestnut brown, queen-size bed with poster head boards, sat in the center of the room. The room was decorated in different shades of reds, and black. Again, there were no windows. Something that was typical on Vampire Island. That way no sunlight could stream in to fry them. The floor was concrete and the walls were of the same brick as the hallways. Hanging above the bed was a candle chandelier for light. There was also a small wardrobe in the left corner of the room. On the other side of the room was a piece of thick glass, almost like a separating wall, with a shower nozzle behind it and a floor drain.

Well, there's the shower, with no separate room, all in the same area, she thought. She stripped her clothes off where she stood. They had become sticky from the blood. She let them fall to the floor as she walked out of them and into the shower area. She leaned over and grabbed the shower nozzle, turning it on to its hottest setting. She could feel bits of steam coming off her body from the water, it felt good. The blood was rushing off her body with the water; she felt fresh and new again.

She stepped out of the shower, grabbing a towel that was hanging next to the shower area to dry herself. After she was dry, she headed over to the wardrobe. The wardrobe was quite old; one of the doors was falling off. She carefully opened it as it creaked. Within she found very elegant clothes fit for royalty.

Looking through the clothing, she found nothing that fitted her liking. She noticed there were two drawers inside the closet. She opened one of them. There she found a simple, hooded, plaid, dark red and black dress. It had long sleeves and buttons along the side. She grabbed the dress and put it on. It fit perfectly.

She braided her long blonde hair and placed it back into a ponytail. After she put the dress on, she went back into the wardrobe and opened the other drawer. There were several black boots in there. She tried on three pairs before she found a pair that fit. They were knee high but they would work, she thought. Just as she was finishing lacing the boots she heard the lock on her door starting to jiggle. She stood back and hid behind the open door of the wardrobe so no one could see what she was wearing because she was going to make an escape for it. The door opened and two guards had flung Efron through the door and shut if behind them.

"What's the meaning of this?" said Efron.

"Lock that door!" said Cecilia.

"Cecilia?" said Efron, not believing his eyes.

"Yes, and you have a lot of explaining to do. I know who you are now. I am so upset. This entire time you have known me, you have been lying to me. Why didn't you tell me? Apparently you and I are to be wed? And I am a Princess, oh and don't forget the Dragon and the Empusa part. And the Blood sucker part. And you're also Tobias's guard, and from another Clan. And sent here to keep an eye on me feel free to stop me anytime and fill me in here Efron." said Cecilia, almost in a single breath.

"Yes, it's all true. I'm sorry. I couldn't break my cover. I wanted to tell you when we were kids, but your father told me it would be putting you and everyone in danger," said Efron.

"Well, my father is still alive. Which you knew the whole time. Also, you knew about the Empusa part of me and how it couldn't come out and be active until I was turned into a

Vampire. But you did what you were told and changed me because he wanted you to. Or maybe it was for your own selfish reasons," said Cecilia, scolding Efron.

"There is so much to explain. Just know, I couldn't stand by and watch you die, I had to get home to your father. There is another plan in place with Thane and Bianca. If you don't get out of here soon when they come all hell will break loose and people are going to die," said Efron.

"I know. They are already trying to get on my good side. By putting you in here with me. I don't know if they are watching you. I don't know if you turned on Tobias. But my plan is to get out of here. I need to let you know, I have a brace on my neck that prevents me from leaving the Vampire Island. It's also a tracker. I can feel it pulsating at the back of my neck. I couldn't feel it before, but I can feel the ripples from the device now. I haven't had a moment to think how to get it out," said Cecilia.

"Have you thought about when you change into dragon form, just to rip it out? Maybe the heat from your dragon will destroy the device? It might not be able to handle it. They probably didn't think about if the heat from your body would overwhelm it," said Efron.

"Huh, I didn't think of that. They really haven't figured out about you yet, have they? I guess they wouldn't have, because I don't think you would be talking the way you are right now, so I don't think they are watching us. They told me I was free to roam the Island, but not to leave," said Cecilia.

"That's weird. I thought you were to be kept in here and watched so you didn't escape, but that would make sense if they have something planned for you and they want you on their side. Tobias told me not to return until after the rescue. Things are going to get messy, and they will be confused, maybe ambushed if they show. I should contact them one more time and warn them," said Efron.

"Yes, you should tell my father I told you to do so. I can't with this brace; it won't allow me to astral project. It allows me the use of my powers, but they are very weak. I'm not even sure it will allow me to change into dragon form," said Cecilia.

Efron did what he was told by Cecilia and went over to the bed to lie down. He closed his eyes and within minutes he was out. She stood guard by the door in case someone came by. Every once in a while she could hear someone walk in the hallway. It left her on edge and her heart beat faster. Efron was barely asleep for less than 5 minutes. He woke in a frantic state. He could barely breathe when coming too.

"It's too late. They must have already departed. I couldn't locate them. They should be on their way here now. I told Owen, who is one of the King's guards, what was going on, and he said he'd attempt to catch up with them. They had barely departed approximately 15 minutes before I arrived. Owen is one of the quickest flyers. Hopefully, he makes it in time before they reach us," said Efron.

"Well, it's time to go. There's no sense in staying in this room. We are free to walk the Island. Although we must be careful, I feel we are being watched. They are on their way; we might as well be out in the open and help if we can. Also we need to get Luna. Do you remember where the Orphanage is?" said Cecilia.

"Yes, I do. It's all the way at the end of this hallway to the left. I'm surprised you can't smell it. The fresh blood of the children is a very potent smell," said Efron.

"I smell nothing, actually. Is that weird?" said Cecilia.

"Now that you mention it, yes it is. I actually can't smell it either. Something isn't right. Let's move," said Efron.

Efron grabbed Cecilia by the hand and they proceeded to leave the room they were in. Carefully, Efron opened the door slightly; it creaked a little. The hallway was as black as the night sky. That was unusual; there were always lit candlesticks. He couldn't smell any human blood. He just smelled the kids less than an hour ago. He hadn't been in there that long with Cecilia and the hallway had been lit. He couldn't sense anyone in the hallway in either direction.

"It's clear, let's go," said Efron.

Cecilia put the hood from her dress over her head, and out the door they went into the hallway. Cecilia was holding Efron's hand as tightly as she could as they were running down the corridor. Still, there was no sign of the children the entire way down the hallway to the double doors. When they arrived in front of the doors, Efron tried to open them. He noticed there was a chain on the door and that it was locked. The door was always locked but never had a chain on it. He pushed the door open. The doors broke off their hinges and fell to the ground, the wood shattering because the doors were so old. There were no kids, no babies, and no beds for anyone to sleep in. The windows were open and the room was freezing. The room was completely empty.

"They were just here, I don't understand. I could smell their blood. Unless, this was all just a trick to make us believe they were here. I don't believe it's you they need Cecilia, I think its Luna. We need to leave, now. Let me see the back of your neck, they could be tracking you," said Efron.

Efron looked at the back of her neck, and felt around.

"I don't believe you have a brace. I believe those are just your scales from your dragon form. Have you changed yet? Once you change, scales start to show on the back of your neck and down your arms. It will happen regardless if you change here into dragon form, or during astral projection. They could have manipulated you to believe they were controlling you, because you didn't know. I have never changed into my form because it would give away who I really am," said Efron.

"If that's true, then why can't I use my powers?"Said Cecilia.

"You said they gave you sleep serum, right? Burn it off. It makes you lethargic and powerless," said Efron.

The more Efron talked, the more Cecilia got angry. What if it was Luna they were going to use and not her, and Thane just manipulated her into believing that he had wanted her Empusa powers? She wondered where they would have taken the children; they didn't just take Luna they took them all.

"Efron, there is something I have to tell you," said Cecilia.

"Yes, you can tell me anything," said Efron.

Just as she was about to tell Efron who Luna's real father was they heard footsteps coming down the corridor. They both got ready to attack whoever it was; Efron could tell it was another Vampire. Efron jumped and pushed them against the wall. There was a scuffle. Efron overpowered them easily. He finally got them to the ground and in a hold facedown.

"Efron, stop, it's me, Vilhauer. I'm not going to hurt you," said Vilhauer.

Efron got off him and was still in defense mode, because he didn't know why the hallway was all dark, and why no one was around, or why the orphanage was empty.

"Things have changed. The Society never existed, and everyone has gone wild. Bianca has lost control. This new leader, Thane, said he has been ruling the whole time over her, and wants us to be free and there are no rules and we can do whatever we want, and said he won't be controlling us anymore. It's madness. There is no order and no structure. They had to move the orphanage to keep the children safe," said Vilhauer.

"This is crazy, why now?" said Efron.

"Where did they move the children too? I want my daughter," demanded Cecilia.

"I don't know. I have never been so much in the unknown before. Follow me, we shall find them together," said Vilhauer.

Vilhauer started walking toward the exit, with Efron and Cecilia right behind him. Cecilia was afraid of what they were going to be walking into once they reached the exit and walked out into the open. If everyone were going wild and doing what they want who knows what's going to happen.

Cecilia grabbed Efron's hand, gripping it tight. They finally reach the exit to the outside. Efron opened the doors and paused at the view in front of them. Everyone was crowding near the stage at the center of the common area. Bianca and Thane were standing on the stage. Thane was still talking; he was festering up all the vampires and making them mad. Telling all of them, shifters are on their way and coming for them. This wasn't true at all. They were coming to rescue me. They were all angry and shouting; some even started fighting each other.

"Don't fight each other. Save your energy for the real threat...My brother Tobias, and his men. As a token of trust in me, I am going to give you something back, something that should never have been taken from you," said Thane.

Thane grabbed Bianca by the arm and tossed her down on the stage and said, "Give them all back their memories."

"I can't do it all at once," said Bianca, trembling.

"It wasn't me asking. I demand that you do it now," threatened Thane.

Bianca knew this would be the end of her. She stood to her feet. She froze everyone in time and returned their memories as fast as she could. It was overloading her with power and exhausting her.

"More! Do everyone, even your daughter," said Thane

She burst with power and shot out memories as fast as she could. She collapsed onto the stage floor. Blood was running out of her eyes, nose, and coming out of her mouth. She couldn't move. She just lay there, shaking and convulsing. She now realized she had only been a pawn, that he never needed her or even loved her. He just wanted her powers to control the vampires. She didn't see it until now.

Cecilia watched from afar when suddenly a piercing pain coursed through her head. The pain was so overwhelming that she dropped to her knees. Her memories came rushing back. All of them, all at once… all the way back to her childhood. She remembered everything and everyone. Her home, and her mother who she now saw dying in front of her, in front of all the vampires, and she couldn't do anything about it. As everyone was coming to and recovering from their excruciating headaches, memories were flowing back into them. The hatred for Bianca was building; all because of the choices she was made to do… by Thane. She now had a target on her back, and it wasn't just one. The crowd was getting restless.

"Let's kill her!" exclaimed one.

"She doesn't care for us. We can care for ourselves!" yelled another.

"She killed my family, now I will kill her!" said another.

Thane seemed quite pleased with himself. As he stepped back, walking away from her. He didn't put another hand on her; he didn't need to. Bianca just lay there; she had no energy to move. She couldn't fight anyone if she tried. Suddenly the crowd charged the stage. They jumped up on stage and started tearing her apart limb by limb. You could hear her screams; but the crowd got so loud her screams died out. There was so much hatred; it was all over before we even knew it had started. In a matter of minutes the mob left the stage; she was gone. All that was left was a bloodstained stage. And just like that, I no longer had a mother. Maybe it was for the best, for she was a heartless vampire.

Chapter Eight
Cecilia

I stood there in complete disbelief; I could see the world around me falling apart. I didn't understand what I was supposed to do. People were relying on me, and I was stumped. I looked to Efron for guidance, and he looked just as lost as I felt.

Vilhauer was leading us down a dark alley away from the crowd. My stomach was in knots. I wondered how much longer it would take for my father to get here. I thought we had been quiet, that we could sneak away without getting seen or heard from until. We turned the corner by a little black shack and there, three vampires were feasting on a human. We hurried past them as fast as we could, trying not to be noticed. We were almost out of sight when I heard her. We stopped in our tracks.

"Where do you think you're going, Cecilia? We have unfinished business!" screamed Siren.

"You really want to do this now Siren? I will terminate you," replied Cecilia.

"Why yes, I do. You stole my mate, and just as we have it he is with you now, how nice," said Siren.

Cecilia pulled her hood back and said, "Fine, I will take care of this now!" Her body was so heated from all the running and the adrenaline rush. She looked down at her hands and her claws were coming through her fingers. She could feel a fire burning in her throat. Siren looked down and saw Cecilia's hands and stepped back. Siren had fear in her eyes. She knew if she were to take on Cecilia, she would not survive.

"What are you? You're a demon!" exclaimed Siren, with a terrified look on her face.

"Something like that or whatever you want me to be," said Cecilia with a grin.

"Wait, I don't want to do this," squeaked Siren.

Siren turned and sprinted away from Cecilia.

Cecilia opened her mouth, and out came a stream of fire in Siren's direction. Efron grabbed Siren just in time and pulled her out of the way.

"Why did you do that, Efron?" Cecilia screamed in an angry voice.

"Because, she said she didn't want to fight you in her last breath before you blew a fire stream at her. You really just want to kill everyone? That's not who you are, or who you want to become. We need all the help we can get, to get off this island.

"Help from her, are you kidding me?" Cecilia said sarcastically.

"Please, I'll help you. Just don't terminate me. I know of a few ways off the island," said Siren.

As they were all standing there having an argument they felt a rumble from the ground. They all looked up and the dome was opening. It was still night, so it wasn't such a big deal. But it had never been opened before, so it made everyone feel uneasy.

"Do they normally open the dome at night?" Asked Cecilia.

"No, they don't. It's against the rules and all the vampires would be terminated by the sun when it comes up. There is only three ways off this island; one by boat, by plane, and by a train," said Siren.

"By train? That sounds ridiculous. Where would a train go?" Efron questioned.

"There are tracks on one of the beaches that lead into the water. The train is completely sealed off from water getting in, and the train stays on the tracks to wherever it leads." Replied Siren.

"Why haven't I heard of this train?" said Efron.

"Because, you were too close to The Society. It is a secretive escape path. Only certain vampires know about it. I heard about it through Knox, he was talking about taking a group to get off the island," said Siren.

"Vilhauer, is this true? Is there another way? To be protected from the sun?" said Efron.

"Yes it is, but it hasn't been used in years. No one knows if it still works," said Vilhauer.

"Well there is only one way to find out, but we need to find the children first. I am not leaving this island without my daughter," said Cecilia.

"We can't take Thane on without your father and his crew helping. I'm not even sure how far away they are right now," said Efron.

"They said they were coming. They'll be here," Cecilia announced with certainty.

"Who is coming?" said Siren.

"The less you know, the better," replied Efron.

"I figured he was going to come for her. So what do we do until then? We can't get the child without help, and I need to get off this island before he instructs everyone to kill each other," said Vilhauer.

"I might know where the children are, I smelled something sweet a while ago, by the women's barracks. It was a smell that wasn't there before," said Siren.

"Well, what are we waiting for? Let's go. And Siren, if you lead us astray, or if anything bizarre happens, there will be consequences," said Cecilia.

Siren led them down the dirt alley. There were brick buildings with no windows on both sides of the street the entire length. It was about a mile away from where they had started. Cecilia kept wondering if it was a trap. That would be something Siren would do since she hated her so much. Cecilia was ready for anything that came her way. She just watched her mother die. She wasn't about to lose anyone else. As they got closer to the quarters, something didn't feel right to Cecilia.

"Stop, something is wrong." said Cecilia. They all stopped in their tracks. Cecilia was feeling dizzy, and nauseated. Suddenly, Cecilia fell to the ground and passed out. They could hear screaming coming from inside the women's barracks that sounded like a baby crying. Efron picked Cecilia up from the ground and held her in his arms. The back of her neck was glowing red, and as hot as a fire. A woman busted opened the door to the barracks. It was Iris.

"Tell her to stop, she can't come any closer. It will kill them both," said Iris. She had Luna in her arms. Luna's neck was also red and as hot as an inferno. Luna was still so little with jet black hair and she was screaming in pain.

"It seems they have used a device so they can't get close to each other," said Iris.

"No, this is not possible. I thought it was just her scales coming through, and they put it on Luna as well. Why would they do that?"Efron asked with concern.

They heard a creaking noise coming from behind them. "I did it so they couldn't get close to each other and so that Cecilia wouldn't leave the island because she can't leave without Luna. Now where is Tobias, mother?" said Thane.

"You bastard! Cecilia is destined for great things, and to be your queen one day!"Efron proclaimed.

"Don't worry, he is here, and he's coming for you," said Iris.

"Mother, you're always on the righteous side of Tobias. You know what I am doing is better for the Clan. We can be free instead of being stuck on that island hiding. All Cecilia has to do is give me her powers in a ritual and it will all be done," said Thane.

"My boy, you are so wrong! She would never give you that part of her, she'll eventually accept who she is, and destroy you," said Iris.

They all looked at each other confused. A popping sound came out of nowhere and suddenly smoked filled the air as Iris changed into her dragon form. She was a purple dragon with a line of gold scales, and claws. Her claws were almost a foot long. On top of her head were two large brown horns. Iris leaped into the air spreading her wings and flew away with Luna into the sky.

As soon as Iris was no longer within sight, Cecilia's neck turned back to normal, and began coming to. Thane was in disbelief that his mother just took off with Luna. More popping sound was echoing within the area and Thane had transformed into his dragon form. He was as black as the night, with a line of red scales down his torso, red claws, and six horns atop his head.

He was enormous and scary. He jumped up and spread opened his wings and was lifted into the air after Iris with the flapping of his enormous wingspan. As soon as he cleared the buildings, another dragon came out of nowhere. It was Tobias. He engaged Thane, attacking him in the sky. There was a scuffle in the air between them; they both came crashing down to the ground at lightning speed. Once on the ground, all you could see from afar was the bright light from the blazing fire they were blowing at one another.

"What do we do now? Should we go help him?" Asked Cecilia.

"No, he can handle him alone, plus he has his crew standing by. It's time to get you off this island. Do you think you can change to your dragon form and fly?" Efron commented.

"I don't know if I will be able to, why did I pass out, and where is Luna?"Cecilia replied.

"Iris was here. She has Luna, and she is safe. Thane put some kind of device on you where you can't get close to Luna. It would kill you both if you were to come within feet of her," said Efron.

"What! Then what's the point of going to the Dragon Lands if I can't be close to my daughter. I don't want to kill her," said Cecilia in agony.

"They will figure out how to get the brace off, they have to. You and Luna are the number one concern to the Clan. You both will change everything." said Efron.

"What about us? Will we just get left here to rot on this island? Said Siren.

"You two can get off the island using the train I was thinking, if it works. I'm not even sure if I can change into my dragon form. I have my claws though, which I can't control. I can breathe fire out of my mouth. Unfortunately, I just don't feel the dragon part in me," said Cecilia.

"Quit being a baby and try. If I were able to have a daughter, I would do anything to get to her. Unfortunately, that will never happen for me," said Siren.

"Vilhauer, why are you so quite?" said Efron.

"I'm just in shock I suppose. I knew there was something about you Efron, that didn't sit right with me, or this life. I didn't know it would be you to find the princess, and save us from this life," said Vilhauer.

"Well I didn't know it would be this complicated. Well, with your help, you are now a part of this. I will make sure to protect you from termination, and from anything that comes our way," declared Efron.

As they were all talking, Cecilia tried to change into her dragon form. She could feel the heat in her body growing but nothing was happening. There came the popping sound in her ear but no change. She couldn't transform, and she didn't know why. The back of her neck starting to glow red and was stinging in pain, and hurt. She was getting angry, and with all that was happening there was a fire burning in her throat. She was stuck on the island. There was nothing she could do. As she was trying to transform a shadow came out of dark. It was her brother Zeke.

"We have to go now! Father has knocked out Thane and he'll be unconscious for a while," said Zeke.

"I can't transform. I think it's the brace in my neck," Cecilia said with frustration in her voice.

"You have to feel it in your gut. You have to believe and become one with your dragon," said Zeke.

The popping sounded again, the back of her neck started to glow red. Cecilia would start changing then revert back again to her human body. This time with her claws retracting back in.

"I can't do it, it hurts," cried Cecilia.

"Well I hate to do this to you, but we must leave. I can't carry you, and we can't wait. Once Thane wakes up, he will be much stronger and we won't be able to stop him. We will come back for you I promise, find a way out of here, and hide," said Zeke.

"What kind of rescue is this? You're leaving me? He'll kill me. He killed Bianca." Fear began to consume Cecilia.

"We know he killed Bianca. Father almost terminated Thane because of it, but couldn't do it at the last minute. We have no choice. We have Luna and need to leave. We'll figure out how to get her brace off, and once hers is off, yours should deactivate. Efron, watch out for her. Fight to the death if you have to. Vilhauer, Siren, I will tell the king of the honesty and nobleness you are showing to help our princess, my sister. That will always give you a place in our homeland. I am sorry, Cecilia. I must go. Be strong, Cece," Zeke looked at her with sorrow in his eyes.

Zeke took a step back from Cecilia and the popping sound began to ring in their ears. He changed into a beautiful blue dragon. Colors of purple sparkled within his scales as he turned throughout his entire body. He had four black horns atop his head, and black claws. He gave one last glance to Cecilia. "I promise I'll find you," he said. He spread his wings and jumped, flying off into the night's sky.

Cecilia looked up watching the other dragons join him. It was like a fairy tale; they were all so beautiful. She knew their names but didn't know who was who in their dragon appearance. She only knew Zeke and her father's. None of them were big enough to carry her for that long, to travel back home. They would most likely get tired and drop her. They would fall, or she would, from the sky and plunge into the freezing ocean where they would accept their death and drown. The safest place was home for them. She felt as if she was watching her life go by as they flew away. The nervous feeling in her gut about how she would get off the island or if she would even make it out alive. She understood why they had to leave, and she accepted that fact.

Looking around at Efron, Vilhauer and Siren; they were her best bet to making it off this island. Efron looked scared to his core; he was supposed to go with them, to return home. Now he was stuck with heron this dreadful island.

"I am not sure what is coming next, but it won't be easy," she mumbled to herself.

Chapter Nine
Cecilia

I had to come to the realization that my daughter was no longer here with us on this island and that she was safe. She was with the clan, my family, I guess I could call them. It was weird going from having only Efron by my side to having an entire group of people. I wasn't sure I could trust Vilhauer or Siren. Efron trusts Vilhauer, he was like a father to him. I'm just not sure how he would do in a fight that escalated to the death.

He was quite lengthy and thin with hardly any meat on his body. You think they would have made him build up before he was changed into a vampire. Maybe I'm wrong and he could be really strong underneath that scrawny body. Right now, Vilhauer was risking his life in helping me. It's possible he knows more than what he says. He doesn't seem very scared. His demeanor is to take on the world and whatever comes his way, like a snake attacking its prey.

Siren was a different story. I don't know if I would turn my back to her. Who knows if she would terminate me to the final death or not. I hated her; Efron had felt and looked for comfort in her arms when I was taken away to the mating lands. Siren was beautiful from head to toe. She reminded me of a perfect angel with long brown hair. She had a v shaped face, with an empty expression. She looked like she could kill someone with the bat of an eye. She wasn't very tall, but she was very flexible, and could move faster than a prancing tiger trying to attack for their meal.

She was always angry every time I had seen her. I couldn't blame her, Efron made her life better, and I did take him back from her. Not that it was my fault. She didn't make Efron a priority anyway. Efron made the choice when he transformed me. I didn't want this life, but I was stuck in it now.

I wonder what would happen to the human lands if they got word of what has happened here. This place was falling apart. The dome was down; everyone was frantic, not knowing what to do when the sun comes up. There were dead humans everywhere. It was apparent that the vampires couldn't control their hunger urges. It was sad knowing that I used to be one not long ago, and I don't have any remorse when I kill someone.

Being a vampire felt natural to me now. I was faster, and unstoppable. Out of all the creatures I am, I think vampire is my favorite. The only problem is once I go back to the Dragon Lands, my vampire self will have to lie dormant, because I can't feed on people. It's not only that, but Vampires have no conscience and couldn't care less about the destruction they cause. Being part dragon I have some humanity left and it would be different for me.

As we were walking down the alley way, we took a right onto a main street. Shortly, we came along to a tavern.

"We are trying not to get noticed, don't go that way," said Efron.

"I have to talk to Knox and get info for the train, do you want to get off the island or not?" Said Siren.

"I'll wait outside for I don't need to run into Knox, we have history," said Vilhauer.

As we stepped inside the floor squeaked with every step we took. The place looked like an old run down hole in the wall. Many of the pictures on the walls were hung haphazardly and crooked. The green-colored walls didn't do the place any justice either. Looking around, many of the patrons wore blood stained clothing.

Many of them were also enjoying alcoholic drinks like it was their last one. There was a group of vampires huddled in a back corner booth; they were feeding on two humans. And of course that's where we were headed to.

One of the humans at the table appeared to be dead. The smell of fresh blood was driving me crazy; I could feel the burning hunger in my throat. I hadn't eaten since Thane offered me food while I was in the holding cell. All this running around had made me ravenous.

"Would it be too much to get a bite to eat, Efron? I know I have to give it up, but since we are still here... All this running around has drained much of my energy," said Cecilia.

"Hold yourself Cecilia, Knox allows who gets to eat, and who doesn't in his tavern," warned Siren.

A man that was sitting on the edge of the booth spoke up, "I am Knox."

He held out his hand to shake mine. I extended my hand to greet his, and he ended up pulling me closer to his face to sniff my hand. It startled me, and I pulled back a bit, which made him angry. So he tugged again and pulled me closer to him.

"You're new here; I've never seen you around. And you don't just smell like a normal vampire, you smell of power, something evil, and sinful and I like that. What are you? Did you come in with those dragons?" Said Knox.

Everyone in the tavern had now turned their heads toward Knox's table and was staring at Cecilia. Knox was one of the original vampires that overtook The Society, he was quite old, but young at heart. He had red hair, was both chubby and a bit stocky. Not my taste.

"No, I didn't come in with them. I was already here. To answer your question, I don't know what I am, other than a vampire. Aren't we all a little something more than just a bloodsucker?" Said Cecilia, with a stern look on her face and pulling her hand away from him.

"I like this girl, she has spunk," Knox said, and started to chuckle, with a smile on his face. "Efron, I haven't seen you in a while. I thought you were done banging Siren. Why are you here with her?"Said Knox

"Okay, enough of the introductions, Knox I need to speak with you in private," said Siren.

"I suppose so Siren, you're lucky your one of my previous loyalties, or you would get smacked for interrupting me. He scooted out from the booth and stood from the table.

With a flat voice Knox commanded, "Come," looking to the three other vampires feeding. They all headed toward a black door located in the middle of the back wall. Everyone in the room was still staring at Cecilia, watching her every move.

The three vampires that had gotten up with Knox stayed by the door to guard it. No one was getting in there. Once the door was open, wooden stairs could be seen leading up to a solid brick room with one sliding glass door to a balcony. There was a brownish table in the middle of the room with four chairs, and a king-size bed in the corner with no blankets or sheets on it. There were bloodstains all over the mattress. Siren knew this room too well; it was the mating and feeding room. It was where Knox made his bargains.

"What do you need Siren? You know once I give you information you need to give me something in return, I don't do favors anymore. Those days are behind me," said Knox.

"I need info on the train. Where is it, and does it still run?"She said, in a silent whisper.

"The train, are you kidding me? It may not work, and it's over on the east bayside. You're not planning on leaving are you? You'll never make it out alive. There are guards all over the bayside. Also, the train hasn't been used in years." Knox explained.

"Yes, we need it to leave, because certain circumstances have arisen. I would also appreciate if this conversation stayed just between us," said Siren.

"Well it maybe leaked, or if someone offers me the right price for the information," said Knox.

"What would you like in return from me, for it not to get leaked?" Asked Siren.

Just as Siren was able to get those words out of her mouth, Cecilia had her hand up and her claws out slashing them across Knox's neck. Her claws were like sharp swords. The slice was so quick and precise it took his head straight off his shoulders. He had a look of disbelief with his eyes still open. Just to get hit by one of them was enough to take you out. Knox's head fell to the floor, and his body followed. There was blood squirting everywhere. He was obviously dead.

"What the hell Cecilia?" said Efron in disbelief.

"I had no choice; if he told anyone our escape plan Thane would find out and come after us and we would be dead. I did what I had to do to keep us safe," said Cecilia.

"True princess, but how do we get out of here now? Knox's men are down at the door," remarked Siren.

"I would like it if you wouldn't address me by that! Look over there, there is a door and a balcony up here," snapped Cecilia.

"It's locked smarty pants; you don't think creatures have tried to leave that way before. It's unbreakable glass. And if you make any noise, the guards would be up those stairs within seconds," said Siren, shaking her head and rolling her eyes at Cecilia.

Cecilia walked over to the door; she still had her claws extended, dripping with Knox's fresh blood. She retracted them a little bit. They were like the pricks from a cactus, sharper than any knife. She picked the lock on the sliding glass door. She put one of her claws in; first moving it counter-clockwise. The lock popped immediately, and she slid the door open. Suddenly, the alarm started screeching. "Time to go!" shouted Cecilia. They all ran toward the door. Cecilia was the first one out, followed by Efron, then Siren. Cecilia scuffled down the balcony, and they all followed. When they made it to the ground, Vilhauer met them.

"What happened? Did you get what we needed at least? Why did the alarm go off?" Asked Vilhauer.

"We got the details, now we need to get out of here," said Cecilia.

"Well, not only will Thane be after us, now we have Knox's whole crew. Fantastic," said Efron, sarcastically.

They all ran as fast as they could to get off the main road and into the dark alleyway. As soon as they turned the corner Knox's men had reached the balcony. They looked around and couldn't see anyone or anything. Cecilia watched from afar and was proud of her demise. Killing came natural to her now. She knew it all too well, like the back of her hand. It's what she was transformed for.

Siren led the way, and they started going east to the bayside beach. Personally she was afraid of what was to come next. Cecilia seemed unstable and unhinged; she didn't want to meet final termination because of her. She was really afraid of her now; she wouldn't pick a fight with her now after what she had just seen.

Vilhauer followed quietly, he knew in his chest they had killed his old friend Knox. Since they took over The Society years ago, Knox had changed into a power hungry vampire and was never the same. With the new world Vilhauer had to pick a side and he hoped he was on the right one. He trusted Efron, even though he found out he was a totally different person than who he claimed to be.

They continued on their journey. They made it into the woods, where it was wet from raining. The trees were dripping water, and the ground was soggy and muddy. They didn't want to take the traditional pathway, because they may get spotted by Thane's guards. While they were hiking through the woods, they saw a black shadow dart across the sky. It must have been Thane. They were almost to the beachside and could see the sand. Thane had landed on the beach and transformed back into human form.

"How did he find us?" said Efron.

"Oh, I have a pretty good idea. It's that thing in her neck," said Vilhauer.

"Now what do we do?" Siren asked, trembling down to her feet. "I don't want to be terminated."

"Don't be afraid to come out, I know you're here. This is inevitable, you have nowhere to go!" Yelled Thane. He was sitting on a log picking at his claws that he had released.

Cecilia walked out from the woods and onto the beach. She looked at Thane with disgust. He had cuts all over him from the fight with Tobias. He looked beaten down and angry.

"I don't want to hurt you Cecilia, I need you. I need you to give me what is rightfully mine. I don't need to hurt you to get it," remarked Thane.

"Then how will you get it, because I am not willingly going to give it to you," she replied.

She heard the bushes moving behind her, it startled her; it was Efron, Siren, and Vilhauer. They were now being held captive with stakes to their chests by Thane's men. Now he had her, she didn't want them to get hurt. She would do anything he asked of her now.

"Let them go and I'll do anything you want," she pleaded.

"I know you like to kill, it's becoming part of who you are. I know you are the one who killed Knox. Only dragon claws could cut clean like that. Just so you know, before you took his life I had made a deal with him to have eyes and ears everywhere in his tavern, even in the mating room. Your journey was over before it even started." Thane said with a grin.

Cecilia stood speechless, not knowing what was to come next. Thane came close to grab her; he extended his hand out to her. She slowly reached her hand out and took his. She knew this was it; he was going to kill her. "Let them go. I'll do what you ask," she said.

"I'll let them go," he replied. "Bring the train out of the shed!" He yelled to his men. "Once they are inside the cabin, it won't open until they reach their destination," he told her.

Thane swept his foot across the sand. You could see the tracks coming forth from each swipe of his foot. They lead straight into the chilly water. Some of his men came up and started digging with their hands to get all the tracks uncovered. The train was exposed and out of the covered area, it looked more like a submarine with wheels.

Everything on it was sealed. There was one window and one door on the backside. It was rusted over in several spots. Thane walked up to the train and opened the door. Flies busted out the door, it smelled of mold and dead rotting bodies inside. Once opened there were two skeletons that were inside. Apparently the last ones to use it forgot to remove the humans that were their food inside. How gruesome to succumb to a death of starvation, that they had no choice and no way out.

Thane's men pushed Efron, Vilhauer, and Siren inside. Would this be the last time I see Efron, she thought? I gazed at him, my heart yearning for him to do anything, to save me. The train didn't even look like it would hold water out; it was so old and damaged. They crawled inside and took seats, trying not to vomit from the overwhelming smell of death.

The fuel odometer was at full capacity. Thane's men shut the door, and sealed it shut with the lock handle. Thane released my hand and went behind the train and gave it one big push with his leg and that was all it needed to move, it went slowly into the water on the tracks and down it went. Submerged into the water, it was now gone, they were gone, and I was alone now with him.

"So what happens now?" Said Cecilia, glaring at Thane.

"Now you give me what I want. You can come out now Raven, it's time," he said.

Just across the way I could see a small woman coming out of the shadows. She was dressed in what looked like a black hooded cloak with a black dress and a gold beaded trim. I couldn't see her face, because it was covered. I don't know if that was for my protection or hers. She came close to me and grabbed my hands placing them into Thanes. She then drew a circle around us with a stick in the sand while chanting some words. She was a magic yielding being. An enchantress is what you would call her. It was the same woman who was sitting next to Bianca the first time I saw her sitting on that throne in the termination room.

I felt a warm sensation overcome me. All of a sudden, I got light-headed and fell to my knees. I didn't want this Empusa part of me, but I hadn't had the chance to figure out what it was or what it could do. As we were in the circle, a blue light surrounded us, covering our heads and bodies like a dome. My hair was becoming brown in strips; I was feeling weaker by the minute. I was angry and sad. It was painful; my claws came out and went straight through Thane's hands. It brought him to his knees as well. "Aahhhhh!" he screamed. "You have to give it to me! It's mine! Let go, and things will be so much easier for you!" he yelled.

"No, it's mine!" I said. My hair started to turn back to blonde and the brace that was in my neck protruded out and shot into the air out of my neck. It hit Raven in the head and knocked her out instantly. As soon as Raven fell to the ground, the blue light that had surrounded us disappeared. I heard popping, which only meant one thing. I looked at myself and I could see my dragon form. I transformed into a dark green, beautiful beast. It didn't hurt; it was almost pleasurable. I kicked sand over the circle Raven made around us and broke the connection to her power.

Thane looked at me in despair, he knew he had lost. He wasn't getting my birthright today. I yanked my claws out of his hands. I took a step back, opened my wings, and jumped off into the sky. I went up so fast I almost lost control, falling back down. I had no idea where I was headed, but I knew it was going to be far away from here, far from him.

Chapter Ten
Efron

We could barely breathe in here. The smell from the rotting corpses was revolting. We were crammed into this small cabin with nothing to satisfy our hunger. Without the taste of blood, it was only a matter of time before we become wild, because of our natural instincts to kill one another. I couldn't stop thinking about Cecilia. Would I ever see her again? Is she dead? The thought crossed my mind a million times. I couldn't think of anything else. Now I will have to deal with Tobias. Lord knows what he will do to me. Maybe he will understand that I couldn't take on Thane alone.

The train was going super slow, and who knows where it was headed. I looked out the one window that was located at the front of the train and all I could see was water surrounding us and seaweed floating around about. I ached for Cecilia. I wish I could have helped her, but one move and I would have been terminated with the final death. I wonder what would hurt more. Getting staked in the chest to death by wood? Or us killing one another over hunger? I really didn't want to find out.

It seemed like forever that we were in the train. There were small drips of water coming from the ceiling. Hopefully, this thing would hold until we got to our destination. I could easily transform into my dragon form and bust out of here and fly away. But that would leave Vilhauer and Siren to their demise. It must be daylight by now. Good thing we are underwater and nowhere near the sun's surface.

I took that time to look around the train and see what I could find. There was a lever with wording on it, but I couldn't make it out. All I could read was "lands." I couldn't see the first part of it. So I figured, might as well push it up and go toward the lands. The handle was a bit rusted and stuck, but with a little force, I was able to move it up where it said lands. When I moved it up, the handle broke off. Well, there's no turning back now. The train jolted and started to move faster. It frightened us and caught us off guard. It felt like the train was heading down a hill. I looked out the window, and I was right.

"Where do you think we're headed?" said Siren wearily.

"I'm not sure, the only other place I would think this train would go is to the land with the creatures. I am not sure if they got word of what happened on the vampire lands," said Efron.

"They could be in just as much chaos as the vampire lands," said Siren.

"I highly doubt it; the transfer boat hadn't left for the land so how would they know?"Said Vilhauer.

"That's true, I suppose," said Siren.

As the train was going down, I looked out the window. I saw something that I couldn't explain. It looked like a sea snake. Instead of one long fin like a fish, it had two, one for each leg. It also had scales and horns atop its head. The train kept chugging along. I got a weird feeling in my gut. I then saw more of them go by, some of them were small and others were bigger, and they were everywhere, surrounding us. I caught the eyes of one of them, they were bright blue and they looked angry. They didn't seem happy we were traveling through their domain.

"We might have a problem," said Efron. Siren and Vilhauer both looked at him confused.

"What do you mean?" said Vilhauer.

"No problem for us, we're vampires." Remarked Siren with confidence.

The train came to an abrupt stop as if it had hit something; it flung them all forward and they all hit the front of the cabin. They all looked out the window but couldn't see anything. All of a sudden the train started going straight up toward the surface like something was pulling on it. They could tell they were heading toward the surface now because they could see the water getting clearer as they were going up.

"If whatever is out there opens that door, we are dead from the sun," remarked Siren.

"Not necessarily. I'll transform and you both can hide behind my wings," said Efron.

"You'll change, change into what? You're one of them? A dragon?" questioned Vilhauer.

"Yes, I am both a vampire and a dragon. You both will be shielded from the sun if I transform," he said.

"What if your wings are not big enough? What if you can't change like Cecilia?" Siren said with worry.

"This whole time you have been lying? I can't believe this," said Vilhauer.

"We don't have time for this right now, Vilhauer. Do you both trust me?" yelled Efron.

"Yes, just do it!" yelled Vilhauer angrily.

Using what I learned in training with Tobias, I began to change. I felt as one with my dragon. We all heard a popping noise which echoed in the train. It was so loud it was making their ears ring. Efron looked at his hands and saw brown claws protruding from where his nails had been. He looked further down and saw the dragon he had become. He had yellow scales everywhere with a white chest, and four brown horns on his head. They were the same color as his claws. His wings had veins running through them; they were gigantic.

The cabin of the train got much smaller with his body taking up more than half of it. He was bigger than the other dragons. He was also from a different clan, the Ayrs, but was given to be wedded to Cecilia and protector of the Ashore's clan, so he was told.

They heard a creaking noise coming from the door, it started to swing open. Efron was just behind the door with his wings open. "Get behind me!" Efron yelled.

Vilhauer and Siren tucked themselves behind his wings. As the sun hit Efron, it burned for just a moment, but then it felt enjoyable. He was untouchable in the light. He looked around; they were all staring at him. It was the hidden Anchors Clan. He had only heard stories of them. Everyone thought they were a myth.

They were all huge, some bigger than the others. They were different shades of blue and teal, with white bellies. They all had sharp claws and horns on their heads. Their teeth looked like deadly daggers. They were moving in on us slowly.

"Don't move! We'll kill you if you do. Who are you? Where do you come from?" said the largest one in a taunting voice.

"We are not here to hurt anyone. We're just passing through," said Efron. You could hear the nervousness and shakiness in his voice.

"No one has just passed through here in years. Someone always wants something, and how many are there in the cart with you?" He demanded.

"There are three of us, the other two can't be in the sun, and I see you guys are sea serpents. I am from the Ashore's clan. My name is Efron. We got into some mishaps in the vampire lands."

"Vampire land, those things are not welcome here. They fed off some of us last time we opened our land to visitors. I take it there are two of them in there with you. I wouldn't trust them. They will feed on whomever they see is able to meet their hunger needs," he said in a stone voice.

"I am sorry you have had issues with vampires, but the two in here are not like that. Also, I am sworn to protect them by the princess, since they helped her escape," replied Efron in a rigid voice.

"What? The lost royal has been found. We heard, but didn't believe," he said with surprise.

"Yes, she has been found, and I am to wed her. She is to be my wife," said Efron.

"If you are her protector, where is she? Not sure I believe you. You are alone with vampires and are in our forbidden waters," he yelled. They were all getting angry and shouting. One of the serpents blew a cold frost out of its mouth into the air.

"Well, she isn't with us. We got separated. How can I prove it to you?" asked Efron.

"Well, you will have to come to our village as prisoners, and I'll have my Sorcerer read your mind. Then, if you are who you say you are, I'll let you go, but the other two will have to stay locked up until you leave. I don't want them running free around my people," he demanded.

"Fine, we'll go with you. Not that we have a choice in the matter." Said Efron, as he huffed.

The clan swam closer to the train, putting their hands on the cab and began pushing it. They started swimming so fast, that they were moving like a speedboat. Efron turned his head around and looked behind him. Behind his back he saw an island overgrown with tall trees, so tall and bushy that he couldn't see under them. There was barely any shoreline to speak of where they could land. The island looked like a big bushy shrub.

Once they got closer, he could see water caves located on the right half of the island. This was where they headed, toward the one with the largest opening. It was the biggest water cave he had ever seen. There were holes throughout the ceiling of the cave, with sunlight shining through. There was a small shoreline in here where the train came to a sudden stop. They had hit land.

"If you are who you say you are, you have no reason to fear me or my clan, so you can change back into human form. If you don't, I will take it as a threat and have to attack," he threatened.

"Understood," said Efron. Popping sounded and echoed in the cave, and Efron was back in his human form. Some of the clan had turned into humans as well. The enormous serpent had changed back as well. He was an older man with tan skin. He had long, gray, braided hair, with facial hair just as long. He was covered in scale markings on both arms and his torso. Battle scars covered most areas of his body. The other clan members that had changed were covered in similar scale markings as well. They all seemed to be a bit older than any of the Anchors Clan members. This clan had been hiding for decades, so no one really knew how old they were, or how long they had been here.

Efron, Vilhauer, and Siren got out of the train and stood on the shoreline. The one teal serpent that blew smoke out earlier didn't change back into human form. She was eyeing Siren. You could see the hatred in her eyes. She got closer to Siren and then blew steam and shards of ice toward her, barely missing her.

"What the fuck!" yelled Siren. She jumped out of the way.

"Enough! Mae, they were not the ones that fed on your child!" yelled the older man.

"They are all the same to me. They should all be terminated, and they are already dead anyway," said Mae.

"Mae, we are not going to start a battle with them here. We will see what Ace says and determine what to do with them. No exceptions, now back down," he said.

"Fine, she said and blew frost out of her mouth again and up into the air. She then sank into the water and disappeared from sight.

They all began walking and following the man. He had men at his sides and guards all around us. He headed for an opening in the cave walls. Beyond it was like nothing I had ever seen. There were trees and moss everywhere you turned. It was dark inside from all the shaded trees above. But no direct sunlight made it clear through the branches. Children were giggling, running, and playing as if nothing in this world mattered. They stopped to glance at us walking through their home. Some looked nervous and ran inside their bunkers. We made our way down a sand walkway; we had walked for a good mile into the shrubs. From the walkway, we could see a castle in the distance. It wasn't that big, but I could tell it was made of stone. Old stone that had moss growing on it between the cracks. We came to a metal gate adorning the huge building. A woman dressed in a light blue dress opened the gate and let us in.

Within the walls there was a chandelier for lighting and more people dressed in different shades of blue. There was a stairway right as you walked in that led to both the left and the right as you reached the top. We stood there waiting at the bottom of the stairs while a man dressed in a white cloak and gold trim arrived at the top of the stairway. This man was white, had long brown hair with a beard and a matching mustache. He also wore a green pendant around his neck.

"I knew you were coming. What is it you need from me, Anton?" said the man.

"Well, if you saw us coming, you should know what I require from you, Ace," said Anton.

"You're right, I was just messing with you, my friend," said Ace, with a smirk on his face.

"Come this way," the man said. We all followed him and ascended the stairs. The stairs creaked with each step we took. Once we reached the top of the stairs, we walked through a door along the right hallway. The door was wooden and opened with ease, but it squeaked when it was pushed open. The room was dark, and there were shelves on every wall. The shelves each had what seemed to be potions on them. In the middle of the room there was a huge glass orb that sat on a rounded table and underneath that a gray area rug. There were no windows in this room. The room was eerie and had a musky smell.

Ace walked over to the shelf and grabbed one of the potions. It was green with hints of yellow in the jar. He grabbed me and told me to drink every last drop from the container. I drank as I was told to do. It burned my throat a bit going down. He placed my hands on the orb, which I was hesitant at first, but stood still. Then he placed his on the other side.

The orb lit up green, and Ace's pendant around his neck started to glow. He asked the ball to show him everything from the last seven days. The orb started to show Efron's memories, and it started all the way back from when he had turned Cecilia. It showed the proof Anton needed to know he was telling the truth. The orb could also tell his future. It showed Efron reunited with Cecilia and Luna.

Efron was holding Luna, who was a lot bigger, her jet-black hair just like his. Not blonde like her mother and father. She then called him Daddy. Efron's eyes grew big in disbelief, and he pulled his hands away from the orb. He was in shock.

"No, that's not possible; I can't father children in this condition." Efron looked concerned.

"Well, apparently you did, and now Luna is the new princess. You said you are to wed Cecilia. I also see you are a hybrid as well, which I am not sure if I should worry or not if you would feed on my people," questioned Anton.

"You don't have to worry about me; I can push out the hunger using the dragon heat. It helps to diminish it," replied Efron.

"I don't like that you fed on our queen. But I see she is more powerful as a Tri-bred and it seems to have kept her alive. Hopefully, she can control her urges as well. Feeding on people is against the dragon way," Anton said with a grimace.

"She will learn," Efron was certain.

"Cecilia's isn't the one they need to make dragons; it is Luna. She is in danger from everyone." Ace revealed.

"What do you mean? The Society doesn't want her, and it was Thane controlling Bianca, and she controlled all of us. Didn't you see all of that in the orb? It is he that is a danger to Cecilia and Luna, not some fake society like everyone thought," said Efron.

"I have felt a shift in the magic for the royal Empusa and it is no longer Cecilia. It has been passed down to Luna. Luna can make more dragons with her blood during a spellbound rise with vampires. Which I am sure Thane knows about. That is why he is trying to take the Empusa powers from her."

"Then you have to let us leave, let us warn her. If not, then we are all in danger of a war between brothers; possibly between clans. I need to protect my daughter from her uncle!" he exclaimed.

"Then you must leave my island immediately. Get to the Ashore lands as fast as possible. As for these two, they must stay here. They will only slow you down. You must fly. That is the quickest way there. Siren and Vilhauer will stay here in a secure area, where they can be supervised," said Anton.

"How do I know you will keep your word and not terminate them?"

"Because they have helped our queen, and so they shall be safe from any harm that comes from my hand or my people, you have my word." Anton vowed.

Efron walked toward the door and started to leave the room. He looked back at Vilhauer and Siren. "I will come back for you both. Stay safe, and don't get into any trouble." He was looking at Siren when those words came out of his mouth. Then he walked out the door and was gone.

Chapter Eleven
Efron

Efron was flying through the sky as fast as he could over the blustering sea. It was dark and there was a storm brewing. There were lightning strikes in every direction, lighting up the clouds in the sky. He felt like he had been flying for days. He wasn't sure if he was even going in the right direction anymore. He was cold and wet. The water was just sliding off his scales. This was his first time, and the longest he had been in his dragon body; hopefully he could change back without any issues. Although this was the freest he had ever felt.

He wondered what he would say to Tobias when he arrived at the island. Did Tobias know this whole time that Luna was his daughter? Did he know that she was now the powerful one and that she could change the future? Is that why they didn't rescue them all from the vampire lands and they only took her? They all had to know. He felt betrayed by his own clan. All he knew was that he had to get back to her and protect Luna and Cecilia with his life, even if it meant dying for them.

As Efron was flying, he felt that something was nearby. He couldn't see anything because it was so dark. But as the lights flashed from the lightning, he saw it. It was a big, dark blob coming his way about a mile back. With every lightning strike, he could see that it kept getting closer and closer to him. It was flying faster than he could. There was nowhere to hide. This was it, his time to be brave and put his training to use. Cecilia wasn't here to be a distraction this time. He knew what he had to do, but didn't know if he had the strength to do it. He was going to kill Thane all by himself.

Thane finally arrived next to Efron in a matter of minutes. The flashes of light from the lightning reflected on Thane's scales, making him shine like a black pearl. He was beaten up and had wounds all over him; he was even a bit bloody. He was not at his best, and anyone could see he was weak. Now was the time, Efron thought.

"If you're thinking about terminating me, I wouldn't. I am still stronger than you, boy!" said Thane.

"I am just thinking of the possibility of what could happen with you next to me so frail. It looks like a cat got a hold of you," said Efron.

"Oh, that was your girlfriend. She is stronger than any of you know. Once she gives me what I want, I will rule the clans. Then you two can live happily ever after, and I'll leave you alone," Thane said.

"She will never give it to you. She has more to fight for now! And that's family. That's all she's ever wanted and she won't let it go. You'll never have what you crave, Thane! She's going to be queen and more powerful than you will ever be," Efron yelled over the booming thunder.

Efron glanced over at Thane and saw smoke coming from his mouth and nostrils. He was getting ready to spit a fire blaze at him. Efron didn't move in time to dodge it. He was hit right smack in the face with steaming hot fire. It caught him off guard. His face was burning and hot. He could feel his vampire fangs melting in his mouth and his blood boiling in his veins. He didn't know if that was a good or bad thing. He shook it off and regained his attention toward Thane.

He grew aggressively mad, smoke coming from his mouth, and he spit raging fire back at Thane, hitting him in the chest. After the fire disappeared, Efron tackled him in the air. He dug one of his claws into his side. Blood shot out from the wounds and gushed down his torso. Efron's other claws were in one side of his wings and ripped it completely down the center all the way to his spine. Thane screamed in pain, and his body went limp.

Just when Efron thought he had won and finally killed him, Efron looked down at him and Thane took his left hand with his claws and shoved them up through the bottom of Efrons chin straight up through his head into his brain. Efron was lifeless. That was it; he was gone.

They began plummeting fast down to the water below. Thane took Efron's claws out of his side and then let him fall to the sea below. There was a big splash as his body hit the water. What Thane didn't know is that there were Anchor dragons below in the water. They were traveling with Efron below to make sure he made it to his destination. They grabbed his body as fast as they could without being seen and disappeared.

Thane could still fly, but not as well with a torn wing and an injured side. He flew off into the dark sky with blood dripping off him into the sky.

Cecilia

Cecilia had been flying for days. She had been through a storm with lightning strikes. She was exhausted and tired, but knew she had to keep going. Today she felt different. She had an un-well feeling in her gut telling her something wasn't right. She could feel it in her bones. She just wanted to see Efron and Luna. She was hoping this was all just a bad dream and she would wake up in bed and have her daughter and Efron by her side.

She still didn't know what it meant to be a princess or soon to be queen. She didn't know what the Empusa powers she had were capable of, but she wanted to find out. She still had so much to learn about herself and her family. But it was hard to figure anything out with a psycho uncle after you. Worst of all, she was a vampire who kills things, and that she didn't want.

I wonder if there was a way to get rid of the vampire side, to snuff it out, like it never existed. I haven't fed in a while. I wonder why I am not hungry? I thought I had to eat to stay alive. I know since I am injured my wounds would heal faster if I had some blood. Her thinking about blood made her fangs start to protrude from her gums. They popped out, and they were huge in dragon form. She wasn't aware they could come out when she was in dragon form; now she knew.

After days of flying, she finally made it to Ashores Island; she could see in the distance that something was wrong. Everyone was gathered on the beach shoreline.

Chapter Twelve
Cecilia

As she landed on the beach they all were surrounding something and had long faces. She couldn't make it out. All she saw was a lot of yellow. There were dragons in the water that she didn't recognize either or had heard of. They were light green and light blue. She was confused. Then she saw the lifeless dragon on the ground. She couldn't think of any dragon that was yellow. They were all looking at her. She was confused. She started to look at everyone and caught Tobias's eyes.

"Where is Efron? Did he make it back?" Cecilia said with a shaking in her voice as she looked at the body on the ground. Tobias didn't answer; he just kept his head down. Cecilia never saw Efron in his dragon form, so she didn't know what he looked like. She also couldn't remember any other yellow dragons.

"No!" she screamed. "This isn't him!" Her knees buckled, and she fell to the ground next to his head. She looked into his lifeless eyes. She knew it was indeed her dear Efron. She just lay across him, sobbing. She couldn't move; she couldn't breathe. It felt like she was dying from the inside out. She knew something was wrong all day, but didn't know what.

Efron was her sire mate; without him she couldn't go on. She didn't want to live; she didn't know what to do. He changed her and they were supposed to be together forever. This can't be the end, this can't be real, she thought.

"What the hell happened to him?" She said with tears rolling down her face.

"It was Thane," a voice said, coming from the water.

"Who said that?" She turned around toward the water and was face to face with a water dragon.

"I am extremely sorry to meet you under these tragic circumstances, but my name is Kallen. I was with Efron when Thane attacked him over the sea on the way here. Efron wounded him pretty badly. We couldn't do anything from the water below, so we had to stay quiet. He should have arrived here way before us, but somehow we arrived first. I am truly sorry for your loss."

"So you did nothing, you just let him die? You cowards." Cecilia screamed and threw her arms in the air.

"You don't understand, miss, the only power we have is to shoot water, and that wouldn't have helped." Kallen murmured.

"So your claws and your big teeth would have done nothing? You could have grabbed Thane and drowned him," she shook her head.

"Again, I am sorry things turned out this way." Kallen moved away from Cecilia and sank back down into the water.

"Has anyone tried blood to bring him back? He's also a vampire; he could heal. Why is he not healing?" She pleaded. She looked around at everyone, and they all looked away with disgust on their faces.

"We have no mortal blood to give him, and it's against our rules to feed on people, you know that, and it's a rule that must be followed if you want to stay here. He is not healing because he was in dragon form when he died," replied Iris.

"You can't bend the rules to save him; you have no stores of blood? Not even a single vial?" She said. She looked around and realized that there were no young dragons and that the young children didn't turn into dragons until the gene was activated when they became teenagers or young adults.

"You're lying. The children can help him, and you don't have to force them. Ask them, I am sure they would help their future king."Cecilia said, desperation in her voice. She was begging on her knees crying. She could barely get the words to come out.

"That's a hard no, we don't feed on people," again said Iris.

"Well, you're not the queen, and you don't make the rules. I am asking my father, please Tobias, I need him. I just became what I am, and I can't do this without him. My daughter will need him.

"That's it! My daughter! It's my decision, and I will use her blood to bring back her father, no discussion. When she gets older, she will be glad I did it." Her voice cracked as she spoke. Cecilia looked relived, she had figured it out.

"Cecilia, we can't bring him back. When you bring a dragon back from the beyond, they become mad and are never the same. It hasn't been done in years and we promised we wouldn't do it again, regardless of who it was," said Tobias.

"That's news to me. Who did you bring back?" Cecilia looked at Tobias, but he wouldn't make eye contact with her.

"It was him, wasn't it? That's why he's so mean and crazy. That's why he betrayed everyone? That's why he believes he is the rightful ruler, and why he believes you all wronged him. Why wouldn't you tell me, Tobias?"

"It was for your safety. Because of what you are, you are connected to him. You are the one who brought him back, and you are the only one who can destroy him," said Tobias.

"My safety? It's a little late for that now. And I brought him back, why me, and how?" She demanded an answer. She was in shock.

"We used your Empusa powers. We didn't know he would turn mad, but he did, and he tried to take you. He turned your mother against me and destroyed our family. We had to put you into hiding for years. I won't risk that madness on Efron. With him already having a killer side, you never know which side will be dominant when he returns," said Tobias.

"How do I know I can trust you? You never told me this," Cecilia was more confused now than ever. Who do I trust? What should I do next? She didn't care. She just wanted Efron alive. She just got reunited with him. Her heart sank, and she knew what she had to do. She had to accept that he was gone for the moment. She leaned down and whispered in his ear, you will return to me. I promise I'll find a way. I will always find you. She acted as if she agreed with everyone and decided not to bring Efron back. Deep down, she already knew what she was going to do, with or without their approval.

The crowd gathered around and leaned down, picking up Efron's body. He was heavy in his dragon form. It took 10 of them to carry him. They carried him to the underground caves. They laid him on a bed of rocks. He would stay there until his body changed back into his human form, which normally happened when dragon's died. For some reason though, he stayed in transformation. Cecilia stayed with him until it got dark outside. She gave him a kiss on his forehead and left the cave.

She made her way up to the main cave's entrance. The two guards let her through the doorway. She walked down a corridor until she could smell her daughter's blood. She made up her mind. No one was going to stop her, and if anyone got in her way, they would regret it. She stopped at a brown door. The smell was so intense it almost knocked her off her feet. This is the place. She opened the door as slowly as she could without making a sound. She walked inside; the light inside was dim. Cecilia glanced over in the corner and saw Iris sitting in a chair.

"I knew you couldn't be trusted. What are you doing here?" Said Iris.

"I came to see my daughter; I haven't seen her since she was ripped from my arms. And I don't have to explain myself to you," she said.

"You think with your bloodlust, it would be a smart thing to see her? You can't control yourself?"Said Iris.

"Neither you nor anyone else can tell me what I can and cannot do. And who are you to act like you know what is best for my child? Your children are at each other's throats trying to kill each other," she said.

"You are in my room. You need to leave now, before you do something you'll regret," said Iris.

"Tell me something, Iris. How am I supposed to trust anyone here… when secrets keep coming out? Maybe I don't want to be here. Maybe I don't want to be a leader," said Cecilia.

Iris stood up out of the chair she was sitting in. Cecilia started to get angry and lunged at her. She caught her by the throat with her hand and pushed her up against the wall. Iris couldn't move, she could barely breathe, and she couldn't get any words out. Cecilia didn't know what to do next; she didn't want to kill her grandmother or physically hurt her in anyway. But she needed Efron back.

She started to dig deep into her mind and called forth her Empusa power. She could feel it, the darkness. It was like nothing she had ever felt. It was rising within her, and she liked it. Iris then started shaking uncontrollably. Cecilia whispered in her ear to go to sleep and that she wouldn't remember any of this altercation, and that she was never there. All she would remember is that Luna was a little fussy and then went to sleep and that she got tired and crawled into bed. Cecilia walked her over, laid her down, then covered her up.

She walked toward her daughter in the wood bowl shaped bassinet. This bassinet used to be mine, she thought. Luna was just lying there with her eyes open, staring back at her mother. Luna had jet-black hair just like Efron, but had Cecilia's green eyes. She was tiny, with ten tiny fingers and ten tiny toes.

"I won't hurt you," she whispered. "I promise, but we have to save your Daddy, little one. I am sorry I have to do this." She pulled a vial from her pocket and poked Luna in the arm. She took only a little bit of blood. It took everything Cecilia had to fight the urge not to drink from her. But she held her composure. After she was done, she pressed her arm with her finger. She then went to wrap the puncture wound with a bandage and noticed it had healed and was gone. It was like it was never there to begin with.

I can heal people, she thought. What else can I do? Cecilia placed the vial in her pocket and then stared at Luna until she fell asleep. She then walked out of the room like she was never there.

Cecilia walked back down the corridor toward the exit of the caves. She knew what she was doing was wrong, but she didn't care. Everyone had lied to her, and she didn't know who to trust. She kept walking with her head held high. This was her decision, and no one was going to stop her. She got back to the underground caves where Efron's body was.

His body was gone. She was confused and frantic; she didn't understand where he could have gone. She looked around the cave, and then someone pushed her from the shadows. She hissed.

"You do this, and he belongs to me." A voice said from the shadows.

Cecilia jumped. Who is that? She stuttered. She tried to act like she wasn't scared.

Thane stepped out of the shadows. He was healed, not a scratch on him. He was holding Efron's human body in his arms. He was back in his human form.

"Put him down, don't touch him, you did this to him!" she yelled.

"Be quiet. Do you want an audience?" Thane proclaimed.

"What do you want?" She said.

"I want to make a deal with you." He grinned.

"Well, get on with it, what do you want?" She said.

"I will take Efron and make sure he doesn't go mad. I will teach him how to control it, and I'll return him to you. There is only one condition. You give me what I want."

"Let me guess my powers?" She rolled her eyes.

"No, yours are not what I want anymore. I want Luna's powers," he said.

"She doesn't have any," she said.

"But she will, and they will be more powerful than yours," he said.

"How so?" she answered.

"Luna comes from the family bloodline. There is something you don't know about Efron that no one has told you. Not even he himself knew. Look at him for a moment and then look at me, the dark hair we both have, and the tan skin. He's from a different clan; he doesn't know who his father is. Put it together, princess. When the genes mix, the powers are stronger," he explained.

"Oh god, you're his father." She started to dry heave and felt sick to her stomach. She was backing away from him.

"Why do you think they are keeping me away? They can't handle the truth, the truth that they banished me for something I couldn't control, something they did to me. If you bring Efron back he will be connected to me because we both have been to the other side, he will be tethered to me and have to follow my every command." he said.

"Why would you kill him if he is your son?" she said.

"Because I know you would bring him back regardless of the precautions, and I need him by my side at my every beck and call." He smirked.

"And if I don't bring him back, that ruins your plan," she said.

"We both know you're going to do it, so just do it. You are not strong enough to fight your passion and love for him. How do you even know you're on the right side of things anyways? No one is telling you anything, and keeping you in the dark."

"Don't worry about who I am choosing to believe. I make my own choices. Just lay him down on the rocks."

Thane walked over to the rocks and gently placed Efron's body down. Cecilia walked over to Efron and grabbed the vile of blood out of her pocket. She placed it up to Efron's mouth and poured in Luna's blood. Next, she put her hands on his chest and started believing that he was breathing and shocked his heart over and over again. She felt the energy of life go through her, she started shaking, and felt weak. Thane put his hand on Cecilia's back and power came surging out of him and into her and then blasted into Efron. She never felt this much power before. She liked it, she felt unstoppable.

Efron jolted awake. He wasn't talking. He was aware, but had a haunted look in his eyes. He was just staring at Cecilia. Cecilia looked to her left; Thane was gone. Efron's chin was completely healed. Cecilia was so happy; she kissed Efron as hard as she could. He kissed back, but it didn't seem like him. He sat up and said, "Where have you been? I have been waiting for you to return me here." She said, "I'm sorry, I had something's to do, but you're back now."

"Efron stood up and was heated; he grabbed Cecilia by the arm and spun her around to where she was facing him. He kissed her like his life depended on it. He then picked her up with her legs around his waist and started ripping off her clothes. Her dress dropped to the floor and he put his hand between her legs and started rubbing her clit back and forth. She went wild, and just as she was about ready to climax he took his hand away.

"Not yet," he said. "I have been waiting for this, and for you to go off so easily, I don't think so." He turned her around and bent her over the dirty rock wall, pressing himself deep into her until she moaned. Thrusting in and out of her, harder with each thrust. She was completely naked and at his mercy. Her breasts were bouncing back and forth with each jerk. He grasped her breasts and rubbed her nipples, slamming into her repeatedly. He finally met his release while she was climaxing. They were both lost in each other.

"Not to interrupt, but what the hell, Cecilia?" yelled Tobias.

They both stood there naked not embarrassed at all. Cecilia stood straight up and grabbed her clothes off the ground and put them on.

"What do you want me to say, you would have done the same thing for someone you love. Oh wait, you did, your brother. I don't want to hear it, I will help him through this, and everything will be just fine." She retorted.

"I don't want you talking to her like that, she is to be your queen and needs respect," said Efron. He started to space out and just stood there staring.

"Put some clothes on before you address me. You two, have no idea what you have just done," Tobias said, with a look of shame on his face.

Efron grabbed his clothes off the ground and put them on. He was still in a sort of out of body experience. "I have to go, I don't know why, but I must leave now."

"What? Why now? I just got you back," said Cecilia. She went to grab Efron to hold him, to stop him from leaving. He smacked her hand away. "Efron where are you going, you can't just leave, I need you, we need you," she called out.

Not another word came from Efron. He was like a ghost… the popping came and he transformed. He stepped outside of the cave and took off into the air.

And he was gone again.

Chapter Thirteen
Cecilia

What have I done? Have I made a monster? He has never put his hands on me before. Maybe I am thinking too much into it. I mean he did just die and come back. I don't know what happened to him. Thane talked about the other side. What is it? Can only the dead go there? Is there another dimension, another world that none of us know about? Maybe it is somewhere I can go to harness my inner power. Maybe it's where my inner power comes from. I need to find out; I must know. Maybe once I find out I can break the tether from Efron and free him from Thane, he can't be his servant for life. Cecilia felt defeated; she wasn't sure where to go or what to do next. Tobias was just staring at her with disappointment on his face.

"I don't think you realize what you have done," he said.

"Neither do you. You don't know if he will be good or bad," she sounded like she was trying to convince herself.

"I am pretty sure he will be bad, especially with the vampire part he has in him. He won't need to choose. It has been chosen for him, and if you didn't notice, he didn't even look like himself. It was as if someone else or something else was occupying his body. You know nothing about the magic of the Empusa you have used."

"Well then, enlighten me or else I will just find out on my own." She persisted.

"You are just like your mother, so demanding. Don't you want to get used to being a vampire and a dragon first, before you let the magic in?"

"Seems like I don't have a choice, with everyone after me, and now my daughter. How else am I supposed to protect myself and her? I mean you're the one that wanted me changed into a vampire so my Empusa powers could be used. Why? What was the purpose?"

"You know we just got you back; there is still a lot you don't know. We will tell you in time. I'm not just going to dump it all on you at once. That is the worst way to welcome you back home."

"Why not? Do you think I can't handle it?" Waiting for a response. When none came, she commented. "I thought so; I am done talking to you tonight."

Cecilia walked out of the cave, away from Tobias. She walked out into the field where the bonfire had been held when she had first arrived on the island in her astral projected form. It was cold and windy. Her hair was blowing in the wind when she walked; it gave her goose bumps down her arm.

She noticed Zeke was sitting on a log getting warm by a small fire, he was alone. She walked over and sat beside him, looking at him with apprehension. She had flashbacks of his murder fresh in her mind. She couldn't believe she was staring right at him and he was alive.

"What do you want to know?" Zeke said

"I'm just trying to wrap my head around how you are still alive, and the fact that you take orders from that stubborn asshole, who is full of secrets. He tells me nothing." Cecilia said she was completely frustrated.

"Like I said, what do you want to know, Cece?" he replied.

Her heart fluttered a beat. "You remember what you used to call me? That was the last thing I heard you screaming the night they came." She had tears in her eyes.

"Of course I remember my big sister's name," he gave her a slight punch on the shoulder. "I remember we used to color, ride our bikes in the street, and you used to read me stories until I fell asleep. You were my hero when we had a normal life," he said.

"Do you even remember that night when they came for us?"She asked.

"Not really, I was so young. It was a blur, and I almost died. I woke up here on the island after being in a coma for a few months. Apparently Tobias had gotten word that Bianca's men were on their way to collect you. They had to take some of the other kids so it didn't look obvious they were only coming for you. They ended up scaring the town folks and made this silly story about The Dark One, who comes in the night and steals children for his feast. Of course, don't forget that Efron was always linked to you so he had to stay by your side, no matter what it took. Even as a boy, he was strong. I saw him just take off out of the caves a few minutes ago, and what I saw was his body, but it wasn't him. If that makes any since. I don't think he is strong enough to fight the evil deep down inside him that is going to be arising." He shook his head.

"So if vampires didn't take the children to raise them and feed off them..." She swallowed slowly and took a moment while thinking of the sweet taste of blood. "Then why did they keep the children and raise them in an orphanage?" she asked.

"That is what the vampires do with humans. We are trying to abolish it and free them. We want them to go back into hiding and free the people. They don't deserve to be kept on that island and bred like animals to be slaughtered like cows. Now that Thane has come out of hiding, no one is ruling them anymore. So who knows what they will do next," said Zeke.

"What does Thane want with me and my daughter?" Cecilia said.

"It's not so much what he wants from you; it's what he wants from her. Her blood," he said.

"What? Why would he want that?" she demanded.

"Her blood is a mixture of all the Clans, and it has special abilities... It can make new dragon shifters."

"How is that even possible? How do you know it's a mixture of all the clans?"

"From what I have heard dad and Iris talk about it, and have seen in the books in his room, he has it all written out page by page. I guess there are four clans, maybe more, and we are at the top of them, which makes us their rulers.

"We have been here the longest, and you with the Empusa powers, I am pretty sure that makes you the queen of them all. I know I sure wouldn't want to challenge you in any way to try to take that title." He chuckled.

"These books that you speak of, are they the ones on his shelf?"

"Yes, if they are all there. Sometimes, he removes them and takes them on his adventures off the land." He replied and then sighed.

"You know if Thane gets Luna's blood, it will work on all species, even the vampires. They could become like you, but with no powers. You draw your powers from the Empusa," taking a breath.

"You could still control everyone; it would just be a bit more difficult."

"Well, let's hope it doesn't come to that."

"Well, just promise me you will be careful. I don't feel like mourning you again." He said with a smirk.

"You won't have to. I am indestructible!"

The fire was turning to embers. "Well, we should probably head to bed," she said.

"I will," said Zeke. "It's been a long day."

"I don't believe vampires sleep; I'll just rest my eyes."

Cecilia and Zeke got up from the log they were sitting on, and he smothered the fire until it was out. They began walking back toward the cave entrance when a gust of wind hit them from behind. It knocked them off their feet, stumbling to the ground. It was Anton. He was in his full dragon form, and had Siren and Vilhauer on his back. Cecilia and Zeke struggled to get back up and stand on their feet. Anton dropped them to the ground and said, "Here, take them. They can't stay on my land anymore. I can't protect them anymore from my people, who are constantly trying to kill them. It's too much for me to handle in my position. I was asked to protect them for Efron, because they protected you, my highness. I have done my duty and my job is fulfilled. Please release me from this burden."

"You may leave them here. We'll find a place for them to stay," she said.

"Thank you."

"Father will not like this at all. What will they eat?" said Zeke.

"I don't know? I'll figure it out. Are there any animals on the island somewhere?" She asked.

"We'll have to put them down in the underground dungeon chambers for now; they can't stay out with the normal population. I don't trust them not to feed off the children. There should be wild animals around somewhere; catching them in dragon form is fun. You should try it sometime." He said and chuckled.

"I am glad to see you are okay, Cecilia," said Vilhauer.

"Yeah, this has been one crazy fucking ride," said Siren.

"If that's what you call it, so much has happened since I saw you all last," remarked Cecilia.

"Well, we better get you guys down to the chambers. We'll get something for you to eat tomorrow; hopefully you're not too hungry. We don't want to make our guests starve," said Zeke.

"Well, I had a dolphin on the way over, so I'll be held over for a while, I suppose. It had a weird fish taste I thought I would never have," said Siren.

"Like the taste of a woman's undercarriage! I can never get enough of that!"Zeke smirked while looking at Siren.

"Zeke, enough! You're my younger brother. Eww," Cecilia smacked him on the arm.

"So. I am a handsome young man, I have been told, and one that holds his own between the sheets." He winked at Siren. She smiled back at him, but didn't let Cecilia see how interested in him she might be.

"Where are the dungeon chambers, anyway? I don't think I have seen them before?" Said Cecilia.

"They are back farther in the underground caves where you resurrected Efron and had your bang fest before he left." Said Zeke.

"Could you be any blunter?" She replied.

"Well, I believe the entire island could hear you," he said.

She was a bit embarrassed. They all got to the underground caves and entered one by one. Cecilia kept hearing a voice. It was faint and quiet at first. The further they walked into the caves the louder it got. They passed a lot of rock walls. They seemed to go on forever, and the darkness seemed to consume everything.

They finally came to a big, locked gate; Zeke unlocked it and let us through. There before them was a long hallway, with a floor and walls made of red and brown bricks. The walls contained cell doors spaced every 12 feet apart or so. There were three cells on each side of the hallway and one large one right where the hallway ended. There was a string of lights in the middle of the hallway to brighten our path, but most of them were broken or didn't work. Small, still puddles of water were on the floor; it smelled musky and old in there, maybe even like moldy cheese.

Cecilia kept hearing a voice, and it was ringing in her ears at this point. As she got closer, she could finally make it out. It was saying. E-F-R-O-N. She looked down the hallway and was drawn toward it. She turned down toward the big cell door at the end. She started to walk toward it. She felt a connection to it. E-F-R-O-N, it kept repeating over and over again. She got to the cell door it was cracked opened. She grabbed the handle to pull it open the rest of the way.

It wasn't heavy, but the door squeaked when pulled open. It was different from all the other cells. There was a brick fireplace at the back wall of the cell with a window and bars to the right of it. There was straw scattered all over the ground, with a bed made of straw. There also seemed to be a much smaller bed made of straw next to it. Oh, don't forget the piss bucket in the corner.

On the wall directly next to the bed, there were line markings carved into the wall. I started to count them and once I added them all up it equaled two hundred and eighty days, which is forty weeks. That's as long as a gestational pregnancy for a baby. They had kept a pregnant woman in here, she thought. That explains the smaller bed, and why this cell seems a bit cozier than the other ones.

It would explain why it had a fireplace, because she would have needed to be kept warm. She noticed on the wall next to the line markings that there was another carving. It looked like someone had tried to scratch it off. She got closer to the wall to get a better look at it. She could read it clear as day.

In capital letters it said, "EFRON!" Her heart skipped a beat. She started to get angry; she couldn't believe what she was seeing. She couldn't breathe. She started to hyperventilate. Why was his name on the wall down in the cell? What were her father and grandmother hiding from her? Did Zeke know about this, too? Were Luna and she even safe here? Are they just using her?

Zeke noticed Cecilia looked uneasy, and as he walked toward her."Don't come near me," she said.

"What's wrong?" He retorted.

"Don't tell me you didn't know!" She yelled. She felt sick to her stomach like she was going to vomit.

"What are you talking about?" giving her a questioning glance.

She pointed to the markings on the wall and then touched it where Efron's name was carved into it. A shockwave went through her whole body, and the room lit up like the 4th of July with light that blinded them all. A blast of powerful wind knocked them all off their feet onto their asses, and they all hit the floor at once. It knocked Cecilia unconscious onto the straw bed.

Chapter Fourteen
Cecilia

Cecilia opened her eyes, she didn't recognize where she was. She was standing in a room that didn't look familiar to her. When she looked out the window, she could tell she was inside one of the cave chambers on the Anchors Island. This is a room she had never been in before.

Looking around, she saw a small entry table with flowers near the door to the room. In the left corner of the room was a large canopy king bed, with luscious black and red sheets and matching curtains. There was also a black claw foot tub to the right side of the room in front of the window with a black rug. In the middle of the room was a big fireplace with a red velvet couch directly facing it. On the wall was a tall Victorian elongated upright mirror sitting by itself, probably for whom ever had this room to jock and be full of themselves.

She noticed that the headboard of the bed had chains attached to it and claw marks in the bedposts. Well, at least they have fun, she thought. Looking around the room, it gave off a vibe of uncertainty, a feeling of darkness. She didn't know if she was it danger or was safe. At least it smelled clean. She couldn't tell whose room it was.

Suddenly, the door swung open and slammed into the wall. It made a big crashing sound while slamming open. She jumped as she saw Thane walk in. He was fuming and following right behind him was a woman she had never seen before. Thane looked straight at Cecilia, but didn't seem to see her. He looked straight through her. She stood still and didn't say a word. Thane grabbed the vase of flowers off the table next to him and threw it against the wall in Cecelia's direction. It shattered into pieces, startling her.

"I can't believe this! Why didn't they tell me earlier? Why didn't he tell me, I wasn't his real son?" He yelled. Thane was so frustrated pacing back and forth.

"I mean, I don't know, but you can kind of tell. You look different from them all." She said forcefully.

"Really, Scarlett? I never really thought about it that deep," he snapped.

"Well, your hair is dark, almost black. They have blonde hair, you are tan, and they are not. They have blue eyes, you have brown. You never thought about it?" She stuttered.

"No, it never crossed my mind." Thane said.

"Well, it did for me. I never brought it up because I thought we would rule anyway. I thought maybe you were still the king's original heir, and that maybe she wasn't your real mother. I thought maybe you would bring it up, but you never did." Scarlett said, with an unsteady voice.

"Really, is that all you want from me is to rule, to be queen?" He said.

"Isn't that what all of us Royals want? To rule all the family clans, have riches, and be taken care of with the king's heirs when pregnant?" she said.

"Wow, you gold digger," he said. "Wait, what?" Thane looked at Scarlett confused, and then looked down at her stomach. "You're pregnant? You haven't been taking the birth elixir to prevent it? We're not wedded yet!" he replied hoarsely.

"Does it really matter? You said you wanted heirs right away, so I didn't take it. We are arranged to be married anyway, so it would have just prolonged the inevitable," she said. All this while trying to look him in the eyes, but he wouldn't make eye contact with her. He was too angry to look at her.

"Really? You couldn't wait? It seems to me that you used me to make sure you had a secure life by any means ahead of you, with whatever offspring you had," he admitted, with a stone cold face that matched his body language of being stiff.

"How dare you!" She stepped close to him and smacked him across the face.

"If anything, it was you who used me!" Tears began rolling down her face. "I am of Royal blood from the Ayers Clan. What are you? A bastard child! You don't even know, do you? You led me on, believing this would be all ours. Why didn't you tell me?" She yelled.

He grabbed her by the wrist, tugging her, saying, "Obviously I was abandoned on this island after I was born, and The Ashore's found me and raised me like one of their own. So, that's all I need to know. If that's not enough for you, then maybe you should go back home and find a suitable husband. One that can take care of you and your unborn child."

He looked deep into her eyes. "Also, that will be the first and last time you ever put your hands on me. Do you understand?" he growled at her, his upper lip twitching.

"If that's how you truly feel, then maybe I will go home." Taking a breath of air, she found it cold in her lungs. She could hardly breathe; she couldn't believe this was happening.

"By the way, if you thought there was any possibility of me not being the true heir to the Ashore's, why would you want to get pregnant by me and have my baby?" He demanded.

"Because I loved you," she said. She looked like she was trying to convince herself when she said it.

"Loved, past tense. Yeah, sure that's what it was," he said in a flat voice. "You made that choice all on your own to bring a life into this world, which we were not ready for. You're selfish!"

Cecilia just stood there in the corner of the room and couldn't believe how she was able to see all of this and be unnoticed. Had she traveled back to the past? Was she dreaming? She looked out the window and the sun was setting outside, and she feared she didn't know how long she would be here for.

Scarlett and Thane were getting settled in for the night. Thane had sat down on the red velvet couch, watching the fire burn in the chimney. He turned his attention to watch Scarlett. Watching her every move, she decided to run a bath. She walked over to the tub, put the plug in and turned on the warm water, then started to undress. She dropped her dress to the floor. She was braless and panty less. The tub was filling pretty fast as you could see the hot steam coming out of the tub. Scarlett was now naked, standing in front of the tub. Her perky breasts out and all, Thane couldn't take his eyes off her. He was unknowingly biting his lower lip.

"Do you like what you see? It's yours if you still want it?" she proclaimed. "Why don't you join me and give me one final mind blow before I go home? Since that is what you want, isn't it?" She said, while licking her plump red lips, while looking at his groin area. He kept looking at her and he noticed he could see a little bulge on her lower belly. She slipped into the tub one leg at a time and sat down getting fully wet from head to toe with the water.

She quickly put her hair in pigtails. Just how he liked them. He stood up and walked toward the tub, unzipping the front of his pants on the way there. When he got to the tub, he pulled his pants down to where you could see his perfectly shaped ass from behind.

"Are we going to talk about our fight?" She proclaimed. He looked at her, pointing at her belly. "That bump should be a lot smaller if you are just finding out you are pregnant. So as of right now, I am furious. All I want you to do is shut up and don't say a word. Just open your mouth and show me how sorry you are." She nodded her head, agreeing, and cocked her head back, opening her mouth. He rubbed her mouth with his fingers. "Good girl."

He took a breath, and then grabbed her by the pig tails with his hands. Placing the tip of his member against her lips, he rubbed it around. She licked just the tip with her wet tongue and then opened her mouth.

He put it in slowly at first and then he slammed the whole thing until it touched the back of her throat and made her gag a little. You could see his ass flexing, moving back and forth with every thrust. He was moving his dick in and out of her mouth as fast as he could, pulling her hair and moving her head to his swaying motion. He was moaning uncontrollably. "Faster, use your hands," he murmured. She reached her hands up out of the water to cup and massage his testicles. He was close, ready to explode. Just when he was about to release, he pulled out of her mouth, grabbed his cock, and released all over her face and chest. He got it all over her hair and in her eyes. They were burning in pain.

"What the hell?" She pulled back in utter shock. She looked away from him and down at the water.

"I told you I was mad at you. You will get yours when I want to give it to you, and when you tell me the truth about that baby. Until then you will get no release, is that clear?" He then leaned down even closer to her; he released his claws from his right hand and grabbed her ponytail with his left hand. Pulling her close to him, he put his sharp claws to her throat. "And you will tell no one, and I mean no one, about that baby until I am ready. Do you understand?" She looked at him with complete fear in her eyes, swallowing hard; she knew he meant what he said.

"Yes, I understand," she replied. He let go of her and grabbed the bar soap that was between her legs at the bottom of the tub. He made sure while picking it up, he rubbed the soap against her clit while pulling it out of the water. He started washing his hands clean, and then dropped the bar back into the tub. He then reached for the black rigid towel on the side of the tub. Grabbing it, he dried his hands off and threw it at her, hitting her smack dab in the face.

"Now clean yourself up and get to bed," he said.

Cecilia was standing in the corner in utter and complete shock. She wished she hadn't just seen what she had, she wished she could speak up and say something; she was traumatized by watching the sexual encounter, but knew if something changed in this moment it could change the future in how things were supposed to pan out so she kept quiet.

Thane walked himself over to the bed. He undressed himself quite quickly and put on a black robe. He lay down and went straight to sleep as if nothing had happened. Scarlett just sat in the tub washing her face with the wash rag that he tossed at her. She was quietly crying with tears rolling down her face. She next pulled her ponytails out and washed her long, brown, curly hair. She was so beautiful, of average height, kind of muscular, skinny; she was fit for a royal's wife.

She finally pulled the plug in the bath and stood up. You could see the bulge on her tummy; she had to be at least three months along. She stepped out of the tub, grabbed the nearest towel, and dried herself off. Then she stood in front of the mirror looking at her naked self and put her hand on her lower abdomen.

"Efron," she said. And she rubbed her tummy. She got closer to the mirror to look at her neck. She saw a scratch mark. It wasn't a big one, but there was one. She looked almost frightened but angry; Cecilia could see it in her eyes. Thane was stirring and flopping around in his sleep. She flinched and was scared for a moment.

Scarlett backed away from the mirror and went to her armoire on her side of the bed and got a robe out. It was green cotton with white flowers on it, almost see-through. I saw the look in Scarlett's eyes while she was looking at Thane. She had thought he was a monster she could tame. She thought she could save him. But she couldn't, and now he was threatening her and maybe their baby too.

Quietly she said to herself, "What was the purpose of my coming here?" Cecilia thought. "So I could see Thane was still an asshole before he went mad? How can I get out of here?" Then an echo said, "You won't. Not until you see what I have brought you here to see."

"What the hell? Who was that?" She looked around, confused.

"Be quiet and watch," the echo said.

Scarlett walked over to the weapons closet Thane kept in his room. It was actually behind the mirror, so only a select few knew about it. She pulled on the mirror very slowly. The door squeaked as she pulled it open, but not loud enough to wake him.

She pulled out a small dagger that had dragon's bane mixed into the blade and the handle wrapped in green cord. She slid it off the side of the door, placing it in the palm of her hand. She gripped it tightly, and with her other hand, she pushed on the mirror. She closed the weapons closet ever so slowly, like it had never been touched. She was watching Thane sleep, his breathing going in and out of his body. Her mind was made up; she had enough of his games. If this is the beginning, what will the future be like? She walked over to his side of the bed and gently crawled on top of him. He was lying on his back. He awoke, surprised to find her sitting on top of him.

"Time for round two, is it?" He whispered.

"Yeah, something like that," she whispered in his ear.

"Glad you can see now you have been wrong, and so must be punished and do all the work," he murmured. She grabbed his member, getting a handful, she then squeezed. "Close your eyes and let me take care of you."

She had the knife right at her side on the bed. He closed his eyes and was ready for the ride of his life, so he thought. She kissed him ever so gently on his lips.

"Stay still," she said. "Trust me. You have never felt anything like this before." He never saw it coming, never suspected her of doing that to him. He had shared his life with her; his bed, his most private moments, his most vulnerable places and thoughts he never shared with anyone.

She grabbed the knife at her side and gripped it as hard as she could in her hand and stabbed him in his heart repeatedly. At least five times. That's what Cecilia counted.

The last and final time she stabbed him, he was able to get a scream out, and a single tear slipped out of his eye and slid down his face. She looked him straight in the face and whispered in his ear.

"You shouldn't have threatened me and my baby."His eyes rolled to the back of his head. He was gone. Scarlett covered herself in Thane's blood and then stabbed herself in the arm a few times, then started screaming for help.

"What the fuck! She killed him, she actually killed him." Cecilia was in shock. This was unbelievable! It was his lover who killed him. The soon to be mother of his child, Efron's mom.

The chamber door swung open, almost flying off its hinges. Thane's head guard, Stella, came running in with weapons blazing, ready to kill in her dragon form.

"What was that? Is everything okay?" she demanded.

"Unbelievable! They came in through the window and attacked us in our sleep! They killed him! They attacked me, but I screamed and they got scared, leaving the way they came in. Thane's there on the bed."She pointed to him as she was shaking uncontrollably and crying.

"Thane was limp, not moving, so it just happened within minutes, and he was still warm to the touch," said Stella.

There was blood all over the bed, dripping on the floor and collecting into a puddle. The wall was splattered in it. It was a murder scene. Even Scarlett was covered in his blood. How evil and conniving she was to say someone broke in and did this to him, when she herself did it.

Stella was in fight-or-flight mode. She was looking around the room and saw no sign of struggle. Saw no furniture unturned. There wasn't any blood on the wall, except by Thane. If they had left out the window they came in, it should be covered in it, or it should have left a trail.

"You're sure they left out the window?"Stella asked Scarlett.

"Yes! I know what I saw, Stella!"Scarlett exclaimed.

Stella was looking around the room more to see if there was still a threat at large. She had noticed there was a smudge on the mirror and it had a fingerprint on it. She walked toward it and opened it. She could tell Scarlett was getting twitchy, while she was looking about. She noticed that a knife was missing. Not just any knife either, the knife that had dragon's bane, the knife Thane was gifted from his father. The knife that Thane said was Scarlett's favorite because of the color and because it was easy for her to handle.

The fact was, only a few people knew about this weapon's cabinet, and Scarlett was one of them. In her eyes, she was the prime suspect. Stella's heart felt like it dropped to her stomach. She felt nauseous. She already knew what happened. She left the cabinet door open. As she was turning around, Scarlett charged at her, tackling her to the ground. Stella screamed for help.

"You couldn't just leave it alone, could you, Stella? You had to keep digging?"She yelled. There was a scuffle on the ground. Scarlett had gotten the upper hand. She was now behind Stella. She had her legs wrapped around her torso, with her pinned to the ground. Her left hand holding the knife, her other arm holding Stella's shoulders in place. Shit! She had the Royal Dragon's guard submitted on the ground at her mercy. She put the knife to her throat and was putting pressure on it.

"He was my best friend; I was supposed to protect him, you were to marry him, you loved him! How could you?" You could hear the pain in Stella's voice as she spoke of him.

"He threatened me, used me. I am not to be the future queen now; I have nothing. I have nothing to help raise this bastard baby of his now," she retorted.

"You really think he would have made you do it alone? After he was abandoned the way he was as a baby?" Stella pleaded.

"You don't know all the horrid things he said to me, and things he did to me!" she murmured.

"Oh, I know it all. He did it to keep you in line. Because your eyes were wandering to other men. It's probably not even his baby!" she said in a hoarse voice.

"Maybe I should kill you, too," she whispered in her ear. Scarlett pressed the knife tighter to her throat, and Stella started to bleed. Two guards finally arrived at the door, but stopped fast in their tracks. They couldn't believe what they were seeing. Not just anyone could take down Stella.

"Thank goodness you guys arrived. Stella here has gone crazy and attacked Thane and me. She killed him and then attacked me, but I caught her off guard."

"You can go to hell; they know I would never do that."She said shrilly, trying to break free. Scarlett started to press harder on her throat with the knife. It was starting to really drip blood now.

"Let her go, Scarlett," said Slade. He could see the desperation in Stella's eyes; she knew this was it for her.

"Never yield and get this bitch!" Stella cried out. Those were her last words.,

Scarlett's eyes were empty inside. They almost looked black, straight down to the pupil. She was ruthless; she didn't care at this moment who she hurt. She snapped there was no bringing her back, bringing her to reason. She took the knife and sliced as hard as she could and slit Stella's throat. She dropped her to the floor as if she was nothing.

She was limp, dead; she was gone. I couldn't hear any heartbeat from her. Scarlet dropped the knife and took a step back, putting her hands up. Slade and Brock jumped at Scarlett, grabbing her by the arms and wrists. They smacked her hard against the wall.

Cecilia never met Stella, so they must not have been able to save her from that termination that day. I think I have seen enough, time to go.

"Not yet," said the echo, coming through the walls.

"Who are you?"

"You haven't gotten any idea? Of who would want you to see this to save someone you love, that I love before it's too late?"

Cecilia looked around for Scarlett after realizing it was her, that sent her here. It was her cell they had been in, and she had been the one to carve the name Efron on the wall, but how was she able to project her here?

"I had an enchantress do it, you know her as Raven."

"We are not getting into that now, and I am not getting into an argument with some echo I can't see. Let's get on with whatever it is you have to show me."

Cecilia went over to the chair sitting in the corner and sat down to watch the next events play out.

Slade put Scarlett's arms behind her back and pulled out wrist locks from his pocket; he placed them onto her wrists and over her hands. He was shaking from all the adrenaline just moments before. He wanted to kill her, but he knew the King wouldn't have it, not after she killed his son. She needed to face punishment. Brock pulled out a knitted black sack from his pocket and placed it over Scarlett's head.

"What's with the foreplay, guys?" she said.

"This isn't foreplay, bitch! This is so you can't escape and can't see where we are taking you," said Brock. Everyone got quiet when they heard footsteps coming from the hallway. When they got to the door, a man entered the room. It was Klaus the Dragon King, my grandfather, who appeared in the doorway. He was holding me in his arms. I was just an infant and had no recollection of this event.

He looked at Scarlett with disgust. "You killed my son! I rescued you from your withering island with scarcely any food, and this is how you repay me," he said bitterly.

"To be fair, he wasn't blood, which you withheld from everyone," she screeched.

"Shut up! I don't care what your excuses are, you no longer get to say anything else, or I will chop your head off where you stand!" he shot back at her.

She immediately shut up and didn't say another word. "You will be sentenced to death by fire immediately, in front of the house for the death of my son," he demanded.

"I am pregnant," she blurted out.

"I thought you were looking plump," he replied. "It won't save you from termination though, so here's what I am going to do, since you are carrying my grandchild. You will be locked up in a cell for 9 months until the baby arrives, and then you will be executed, terminated from this earth. And just to make sure you are not lying about this baby being my grandchild." He walked closer to her and held Cecilia next to Scarlett's tummy, and she placed her hands on her tummy to confirm. She looked at her grandpa and said, "Efron!" And shook her head yes.

"Brock and Slade, make sure to have Raven glamorize the cell. I want no one to know she is there, not even my wife. Not even Thane when he returns from the other side, no mention at all, for all you know she was killed by Stella. Scarlett, if you make one peep on the way down to the cells, I will kill you now and no one will know you are with child." He ordered.

They exited the room with her and took her down to the locked chambers in the underground caves. It's where she would stay for the next few months until Efron was born. Maybe less depending on if she was lying on when she conceived.

After they left the room, Klaus squatted down and picked up the knife she had used to take Thane's and Stella's lives with. He then took me and walked over to Thane lying lifeless on his bed. I had never seen my grandpa before, at least that I could remember, but the way he looked, I could tell it was him from the stories I was told from what I had just seen. I got up out of the chair to get a closer look at him. I stood at the end of Thane's bed, but glanced at him.

Klaus had blonde wavy hair, almost white like the rest of us, a v-shaped chin, broad shoulders, and he was tall. I'm sure when his feet hit the floor every morning the devil shivered. He wore a button-up blue shirt with black pants.

I seemed to be happy and giggling while he was holding me. I wasn't afraid, but then I looked over at Thane and saw he was gone, tears starting rolling down my eyes. I am not sure how I comprehended at that age what was going on, but it looked like I understood.

"It's time, Cece, to do what we talked about. We have to bring uncle back," he said. Little me smiled at him a she placed her hands on Thane's chest. Her hands started to glow, and then she started to shake. "Back, back," she said.

Thane opened his eyes and looked around, while taking a deep breath in. He was alive.

"Who am I to you? And what is your name?" said Klaus.

"Does it matter?" He hissed and his eyes were glowing red! Klaus immediately stabbed him in the chest with the same knife, twisting it, and immediately killed him again.

"What the hell!" Cecilia jumped back and was frightened.

"Let's try again, Cece." Klaus placed Cecilia's hands on Thane's chest again and again. It took her three tries to bring him back. Little Cecilia had passed out at that point and had blood running down her nose. Klaus kept pushing her to use her Empusa powers but she was at her max and burned out; the final resurrection was too much for her.

"Whom am I boy?"Demanded Klaus, and grabbed Thane by his robe.

"You're my asshole father!" Thane said. He pushed Klaus' hands off him.

"Glad to have you back," Klaus said. He wiped the knife off with the sheets from the bed and then placed it into his pocket.

"Where is she? I am going to kill her! Thane shouted.

Chapter Fifteen
Cecilia

Cecilia was in utter shock, she was trembling all the way down to her bones. She couldn't stand still; she felt nauseated leaning over the end of the bed. She barfed all over the floor. The room was chaos. How could her family hide this huge secret from her? She was holding onto the bed and was finally able to compose herself. Just when she thought she had seen the worst of it, her parents walked in. She could smell the sweetness of blood. It was human blood, and her mother wasn't transformed yet. She was still human.

She saw little me and knew something was wrong. She grabbed me out of Klaus' arms, tears running down her face. "Cece!" She screamed. I was limp and wasn't moving. I had blood coming out of my nose. Thane was just lying there trying to comprehend what had just happened. He now had a murderous look about him, and death lingered around him.

"Relax, he'll send her back and she will be fine." Klaus said.

"How do you know? You killed her to get Thane back! You put his life above your granddaughter's! My baby!" She pushed him away from her.

"Keep your hands off me, Bianca!" he snarled. "That will be the last time, and only time you are ever allowed to touch me. I will allow it this time because of the situation." He demanded and shoved her back.

"Stop it!" Tobias got between them. "Father, you will not threaten my wife, or talk to her that way!" Tobias shouted, glaring at Klaus while looking him straight in the eyes without blinking. Which was a sign of disrespect and challenging when yelling at each other.

"The Dark Guardian will return her. He has no reason to keep her while she is an infant. She will be of no use to him," said Klaus.

"You better hope so," Bianca screeched. Tears were rolling down her face in despair. She pulled little me close to her body and ran out of the room. Tobias followed her closely without saying a word or looking back. Klaus was just standing there looking at Thane, studying him, waiting for him to make a move.

I was dead; my grandfather killed me for his own selfishness, to get his son back because he couldn't deal with the loss. I was just collateral damage. The fire burned within me. I was angry at him, wishing I could take him out at this moment. How would he know I would be returned? I must have been returned since I am alive now. I see I had powers before this, and then they were taken away. What must have happened? I had to find out. Just as I turned and was about to follow them out of the room, Thane sat up and got off the bed. He stumbled a bit getting to his feet.

"Take it easy, son; it's like learning to walk again." He said. Thane looked over and saw Stella lifeless, dead on the floor with her neck slit. His heart ached and stopped beating at the same moment. He took a deep breath in, as it rippled through him like a tornado.

"No! Stella!"he yelled and tumbled over toward her. He fell next to her on his knees and pulled her ice-cold body close to his chest. He was sobbing so loudly, I am sure the whole inside of the caves could hear him. He sat there rocking back and forth, holding her. He was inconsolable.

"It's time to go, son. We must clean up this mess, and you need to control yourself. I didn't teach you to be a crier. It shows weakness. They can't see you being weak." Klaus said, flicking his hand at him to get up.

"Fuck you! You never cared about anyone but yourself! Only what you have to gain to get more power. Not everyone is like you. Did Scarlett do this to her?" he questioned.

"Of some sort. She has been taken care of; you don't have to worry about her anymore." He explained.

"Where were Slade and Brock? Why didn't they help defend her? What could have been more important than being with their leading officer?" he asked.

"They showed up too late. It was her undoing for always wanting to be close by for you. Now, I said this is done, everything is taken care of, no more questions, no more digging, leave it alone, Thane. That is not a request, that is an order! Do you understand?" he demanded, with a snarl, and he stomped his foot on the ground.

"Loud and clear, Father!" Thane shouted back at him.

"Now, collect the things you want to keep and exit the room. You know what has to be done to get Scarlett's scent out of this room," he demanded. He turned away from Thane and left the room.

Thane got up off the floor, wiping his tears away. He leaned down and picked up Stella's body and placed her on his bed. He covered her up with an extra black sheet he had pulled out from under the bed. He gathered a few of his belongings, then went to his armoire and looked around to make sure no one was watching. He grabbed a red and gold chalice. It had old markings on and looked to be ancient. He slid it into the pocket on his robe. He grabbed some clothes and placed them on top of the weapons closet and then dragged it out of the room as quickly as he could. He didn't look back. All that was left in there was pain and betrayal. He vowed to never be vulnerable again with anyone.

He went forward, and going forward, he would bring revenge and destruction to whoever got close to him again. They would all surely regret the events that led to this unforeseen turn of events in his life. He closed the door behind him.

Cecilia stood there for a moment collecting her thoughts. She wasn't alone for long when the door opened again. It was a familiar face. She looked her straight in the eyes when she came in. It was Raven. Did she know I was here? Two guards followed behind her to collect Stella's body. They lifted her up, exited the room and took her to the burial pit.

Raven glanced around the room and smiled right at Cecilia. There was no mistaking it now; she knew she could see her.

"You might want to leave this room unless you want to be burned to a crisp." Raven demanded.

"Why can you see me, but no one else can?" asked Cecilia.

"Why do you think, girl? I am tied to all life and I can feel when life forms are near whether they are dead, alive, in spirit or have traveled." She explained. Cecilia nodded her head and started walking toward to door. Raven grabbed her by her wrist.

"You're lucky that my lady lord has asked me to leave you be and allowed you to observe, or I would have killed you where you stand." She quietly whispered in her ear. "It is my last command and tribute to her life."

Cecilia pulled away from her. "You should listen and let go of me then!" She snarled. Raven shoved her toward the door. But Cecilia didn't leave all the way; she stood peeking her head in the door. Raven was spraying an elixir all over the room, and then she snapped her fingers. A ball of blue fire appeared in her hand. She tossed it and the room went up in raging flames. It was contained to just the room.

Through the flames she could see the images of memories in the room that contained Scarlett. From the first time she walked into the room as a teenager to hang out with Thane, to their first kiss, to Raven brushing her hair after she lost her mother. Even to all the horrible and good things that happened in this room. It even showed the first time she had given herself to Thane.

The last thing it showed was Thane telling her they would all pay for what they had done to him. She always pleaded and tried to see the good side in him that no one else saw. But in the end, she lost herself and lost control trying to save someone that couldn't be saved; she had enough and ended it all.

The flame died down slowly, condensing into a small ball of flame. Raven snapped her fingers again, and the ball of flames floated to her hand and snuffed itself out. Raven had a single tear running down her cheek. She put her hands up and sealed shut the window, then the fireplace. The room became pitch-black, empty, and cold. Cecilia saw Raven walking toward the door, so she moved away toward the hall, still watching her every move. Raven shut the door behind her; placing her hand upon the door and sealing the room shut. It looked like a normal rock wall, like there had been nothing there at all. It was as if the room never existed, along with all the memories of the room within it.

Cecilia watched as Raven walked away and then glanced over her shoulder. She knew Cecilia was watching; she whispered. "Don't ever trust anyone. Even your shadow will leave you in the darkness."Then Raven continued her walk down the slightly lit hallway.

"Cecilia," she heard whispers of her name echoing in the hallway. She followed the noise without hesitation, without question. She walked down the same hallway Raven had just gone toward. She came to a room with the door wide open. It was little Cecilia's room. She walked in and noticed it was smaller than the other rooms. It had plain stonewalls, with nothing adorning them. There was no fireplace, had one armoire to the left, a wooden rocking chair, a few toys scattered on the floor, and a wooden crib placed in the center of the room with a big brown area rug underneath it. To the right of the room there was a curved entryway into another room. She could only suspect that was her parent's room. Walking into the other room, she saw her parents on either side of her lifeless body, while she lay on their bed. Raven was sitting next to little Cecilia with her hand placed on her forehead, the colors of her eyes red.

"He's giving her back, but with conditions," said Raven.

"What? Why with conditions? We did nothing wrong," said Bianca.

"He's going to strip her of her Empusa powers for now, until she is ready to use them. He is tired of people taking advantage of her to use her abilities for their own gain or using them against her. She should be the only one to use them since he gifted them to her." Raven explained.

"It's not our fault or hers; he used her. We told him not to. How will she protect herself and us?" Bianca whined.

"Find another way. His mind has been made up," Raven said. She whimpered, trying to hold the connection with him; you could see the sweat dripping off her forehead.

This time when she opened her mouth to talk it wasn't Raven's voice, but that of The Dark Guardian's.

"One more request, a demand, a soul for a soul."

Shivers went down their spines, all the way down to their feet. They knew he meant it. Raven's eyes flipped back to normal. Her hand started to sizzle and burn, so she pulled it away from little Cece's head. Raven stood up next to my father, who had his arm wrapped around my mother, both looking terrified.

Little Cecilia was turning white and she was starting to glow. The whole room was so bright from the light protruding from her body. There was a sudden flash of white light throughout the room, and then a reddish burning almost like fire within her. Then there was complete darkness engulfing the room, then a popping noise. All of a sudden, there was the sound of a baby giggling.

Bianca looked down and Cece's eyes were open, but they were black, the black then seeped out of her eyes and turned into a cloud of smoke. It formed and floated out, leaving the room. It went down the hallway.

Her eyes were now solid white, then she blinked, and then they were normal. She was kicking her legs and swaying her arms in the air to be picked up. My mother picked her up and just hugged her, keeping her close to her chest.

Something didn't seem quite right. They could all feel the monster had left the room. There was an eerie silence surrounding them and throughout the caves. Then a bloodcurdling scream echoed throughout the halls. Not just any type of scream, one that made the hair on your arms stand up, the kind that made your skin crawl with goose bumps.

All you could hear was my grandmother screaming his name.

"Klaus!" They all scattered toward the bedroom door, knocking into each other. They took off running down that hall like something was chasing them. Cecilia followed close behind. They couldn't get there fast enough. They already knew what had happened; he chose him. I had only ever heard the stories of my grandfather's death. Now I got to witness it.

We had reached his bedroom door, and all we could hear was sobbing. She just kept repeating, "Come back, come back!" Tobias put his hand up and told the others to wait.

Tobias opened the door slowly, so slowly it was creaking as he opened it. He poked his head in the door.

"Mother?" Tobias said in a shaky voice. He was trembling from head to toe, afraid of whom or what he might see.

"He's gone," she whimpered. She was on the ground lying over his body; he was completely white, pale like a ghost, like all the blood had been drained from him, and was cold to the touch.

"We need Cece," she begged, tears streaming down her face.

"No, mother," he said with regret on his face.

"What do you mean no? This is your father! He can't be dead. Do it now, go get her. I demand it!"She screamed at him, pointing her finger at him. She was shaking from head to toe in shock.

Raven stepped into the doorway, looking at her, trying to have as much compassion as possible.

"I am sorry, Iris, we can't anymore. He has to stay dead."

"But why? I don't understand!" She screeched. Iris was confused because they had just brought Thane back. Why couldn't they bring Klaus back too?

"It mustn't be done. We barely got Cecilia returned to us. Haven't we had enough loss today, mother?" Tobias said.

"You just don't want to do it because you want to be king! Is that it? You boys have never really loved your father." Iris proclaimed. She was irate and being irrational, saying hurtful things.

"Enough!" he shouted, raising his hand next to her, about to strike her. She cowered down next to him in fear. He put his hand down and felt bad for what he was about to do, but what she had said was out of line and was not true. His boys loved him, but they didn't respect him for how cruel and callous he was. Iris stood up and straightened out her white silk robe, tucked her hair behind her ears, and wiped her tears away with her sleeve.

"I want to know why. Once I know, I'll drop it." She demanded.

"We could only have Cecilia returned to us if he was able to take a life of his choosing. We didn't know it was going to be Klaus, we swear it." Raven said.

"Cecilia died? He didn't tell me that," she stuttered and caught her breath, grabbing her chest.

Bianca now showed herself in the doorway holding Cecilia. "Of course he didn't, why would he? I am glad it was him; I would do it again if I had to. Better him than my daughter!" she shouted.

Iris lunged for the door to go after Bianca, but Tobias caught her on the shoulders with his hands, pushing her back.

"No, mother! You will not go after her. She is to be queen now, and I am your king. Your authority and you must respect that!" he shouted.

Iris smacked him across the face. "How dare you! Your father isn't even burned yet, and here you are taking his place for the Clans. If you were to make her your queen, she is human and will live a short life and die. What will you do then?" She snarled at him.

"We'll figure it out together, with you," he said.

"No! I want nothing to do with any of it. I blame your brother for all of this. If he hadn't treated Scarlett in the manner he did, she wouldn't have lost her marbles. She wouldn't have gone crazy killing him. Then we wouldn't be in this mess. It's his fault she lashed out. You need to exile him from our land; there are only worse things to come, I know and feel it." She said.

"No, we are all in this together, and in time we'll need each other for support. Not turn our backs on one another," he said.

"You'll see that I am right. You're going to have to make hard choices that you don't want to make. Don't come crying to me when it all blows up in your face." she snarled.

"Let's get the celebrations of life ready. We'll pass the crown then." Tobias demanded.

Raven looked over at me and whispered, "That's all for now," and snapped her fingers.

I opened my eyes, and I was lying in straw. Just like that, I woke up from whatever hell I was in. My head was throbbing, I had a massive migraine. I had Zeke, Vilhauer, Siren, and Anton standing over me, staring at me, all looking concerned. I had tears running down my face. I opened my mouth.

"It's not Efron!" I screamed in terror.

Chapter Sixteen
Efron: aka Maverick

I was flying, wings wide open, and free in the sky over the open waters. This body is like nothing I have ever experienced before. I can fly, I am strong, I have stamina, and I just fucked a beautiful woman and still could run for miles. What more could I ask for? I also keep getting a whiff of this amazing smell. I am not sure what it is, but I am chasing it because I need to find out what it is. It is leaving a burning sensation in my throat. I want it, I need it, and I must have it. I'll continue to follow it, to sniff it out, to hunt it. The smell is orgasmic, I can't fight it. I can feel the need in my bones, in my flesh, the craving. It's calling me.

I feel like I have been flying for days. I am cold and wet. I have seen only a few islands on the way, but that is not where the smell is coming from, so I kept going. It's not where Thane is calling me to. I made him a bargain; I promised him that if he released me from the Versatory, I would help him. I owe him for freeing me from that prison. Until I pay that debt, the force won't release me from the grasp he has holding over me.

I finally came to another island; it was already dark. There in the bay was a huge wooden ship docked. As I got closer, I could smell it. A sweet, un-resistible scent that caused my gums to hurt. I reached to touch them, to rub them, and soothe them, when fangs burst out. Aaaah, now it makes sense: the blood lust, the thirst, the pain in my throat, the calling to feed.

I landed on the island, next to the docks, and walked on the sandy land toward the big wooden gate. It was left cracked open, but I pushed it open some more, because it wasn't open wide enough for me to get through. It squeaked when I pushed on it, I guess I could have flown over it, but I was already on the ground. Everything was so quiet and still, and it had a very eerie feeling about it. There it was again. I had found where the smell was coming from. I sniffed the air again, only to have my eyes burn. I reached up to grab them and felt veins on the sides of them. I had never been in a vampire's body before. Everything was heightened: my sense of smell, my visibility, my hearing. I could hear a heartbeat, and the closer I got to it, the louder it got. I approached a house and could hear a bunch of heartbeats. I heard a snap and quickly turned around, and there he was.

"Nice to see you, old friend," Thane said with a smirk on his face. He was standing tall with his arms crossed. He had landed on a twig and snapped it in half.

"Scarlett sends her regards," I replied, taking a step forward toward him, looking him straight in the eye.

"Drop the look," he said. "Unless you wish to challenge me? I don't think you want to do that after just arriving, not knowing for sure how that body works." Thane demanded.

"You sound like your father."I snickered. "I'm just messing with you."I looked away and stopped staring him in the eyes.

"Don't mention that asshole; he's not my real father, anyway." He snapped.

"So what's the plan, boss?" I asked, turning my head and taking a look toward the house and taking in another deep whiff of blood. It was so tantalizing, it almost knocked me off my feet.

"I am assuming that's for me?" I smiled and took in a deep gulp and swallowed.

"Yes, I rounded them all up for you; they are all in one house hut. You'll need to feed; once you do, you will have a lot of blood in you, and that will keep duplicating the source." Thane replied.

"The source? From what, may I ask?" looking confused.

"You have Dragon transitioning blood in you. You were brought back into this body with my granddaughter's blood, and her blood creates new dragons. Once you feed, you will have more blood, and it will duplicate, then multiply. I needed her at first, but now I don't because her mother was naïve enough to give me her blood in you," he explained.

Thane looked proud of himself because he could finally carry out his plan that he had been waiting to do for years.

"That's devious. How will it work?" Maverick looked concerned that he was now going to be a blood supply to create new beings.

"How about you stop asking so many questions and just do as you're told. Go feed, then we will discuss what the process is and what I have planned." Thane demanded. "The door is that way," he pointed.

"Whatever you say, boss, you're in charge." Maverick said sarcastically. Honestly, he didn't care; he wanted to taste the blood. He trotted toward the house hut and opened the door.

There was a mirror directly on the wall next to the door; he closed the door behind him. He looked at himself in the mirror, which was directly behind the door. He found his eyes were jet black with black veins protruding out of the sides. He had huge yellow wings behind his back that were tucked in and horns on top of his head. There were yellow scales on his face and throughout his body. There were also a few tribal tattoos on his arms.

He never knew anyone that was both a dragon and a vampire. He would be able to be out during the night and walk in the sunlight during the day. As he was standing there admiring himself, the scent of blood came across his nose.

He took a deep breath in and then exhaled. Oh, that smells so very good, he thought. The hearts he heard pounding were light and gentle. He turned the corner from the entry way and there sitting, waiting for him, were about 20 of them, no screaming, no terror on their faces. They just wanted it over; they were tired of being bred for food.

Maverick walked over toward the first human and grabbed him by his shirt collar, pulling him off the floor. He pulled him in close and could hear his pulse pounding, and see the veins throbbing in his neck.

He bit down into his neck. The man squealed in pain. It was warm; he dug his teeth in and sucked. A warm tingling sensation filled his body; he was tingling from head to toe. The blood flowed quickly into his mouth as he continued to suck the life from this man. He could feel the energy draining from the body; the soul was beginning to disappear. He felt stronger, more powerful as sucked again and again, until nothing came out. He had drained him dry; there was nothing left to eat. He removed his teeth and had bright red blood dripping down his mouth and off his chin. He let go of him, dropping the body to the floor. Thud was the noise the body made as it hit the ground. Then they started to scream in terror.

"Who's next?" he said with a smile on his face.

They were all cowering down in a corner of the room. Well, as close as they could get to each other and the corner. Maverick was standing there staring at them, ready to walk toward them and pick his next entrée, when one of them kicked another out from the crowd. He was flung across the room onto the floor and landed in front of Maverick.

"I see we have a volunteer as tribute," he said, laughing. He bent down to grab him by his hair. "Are you scared of me?" He addressed them all. Some shook their heads up and down in agreement, while some spoke out loud screaming, "Yes!"Others had covered their faces in horror.

Maverick had a look of pleasure on his face, with the side of his lips at an angle not quite smirking, but not quite smiling either. He had the look of satisfaction.

"You should be," he replied. He put the second victim's neck to his mouth, still holding him by the hair. The man was screeching and clawing at him trying to get free, but it was useless; he was too strong. The man finally gave in and gave up. He couldn't fight any more, and his body was just hanging there like a puppet slumped over. When Maverick was done, he released his hair, dropping him to the floor on top of the other guy.

The heartbeats in the room had grown so loud it was like an annoying thumping in his ears.

"Calm down!" He said. He then huffed a breath, "I am famished; this is happening, you can't change it, so accept it and step forward." He demanded, snapping his fingers.

The room got quiet, and they all went calm. There was now a slower, more peaceful heartbeat throughout the room. He kept killing them one after another until only one was left. She was standing tall and proud in the corner, wearing a navy blue dress. She had mocha-brown hair that covered half her face, with blue eyes and long lashes.

She was the most beautiful woman he had ever seen. Her heart was slow and thumped, not because she was scared, but because she was mesmerized by him. He smelled something in the air. It wasn't his appetite calling to her directly, but something else entirely. She smelled different. She moved her hair out of her face, and opened her plump red lips and said, "Change me."

He just stood there looking at her, drawn to her. He had never felt that way before, for anyone. He didn't know what it was.

"I knew you were coming. I felt you," she said.

"What are you?" he said. She looked at him with tears in her eyes from being overwhelmed with emotions inside and not sure how to express them.

"I am yours," she whispered. He dashed across the room and picked her up by her thighs, pushing her up against the wall. He kissed her, blood still on his face and soaked throughout his shirt. He had to have her now. He then carried her over all the bodies and opened the only other door that was in the hut.

There was a bed in the corner of the room. It was covered in light and dark brown sheets, a round window with bars on the wall behind it. He closed the door behind him with his foot and carried her to the bed, not taking his mouth off hers for a moment.

He plopped her down on the bed and bent her knees up. Her legs were quivering not in fear, but in excitement.

"Alright, I don't want to hurt you. I can't," he murmured. He lifted her dress and found her naked underneath. She had been waiting for him. He put his face between her legs and feasted on her. He started by licking her up and down in her most sensitive spot. She was ready and moist. Her leg started twitching, and she grabbed his hair and pulled hard.

He groaned and released his wings. They now took up over half the room. He used his teeth and scraped her just a bit for fun to see if she would like it. She moaned with pleasure, arching her back, and bit her lower lip. Shortly, she had reached her climax; her whole body trembled and shook. He could feel her pulsating on and around his tongue. When she stopped, he gave one last lick that made her jolt, and then he lifted his head.

"I don't know what this is between us," he said, "but I want to find out," he said. He remembered what Thane said about his blood. He put her dress back down. Grabbed her hand and pulled her next to him.

"We'll finish that later," he purred. He tucked his wings back in, put his arm to his mouth and bit. Blood was dripping from the wound; he immediately put it to her mouth. "Drink it," he said. And without hesitation she opened her mouth, wrapping her lips around his wrist and drank. You could hear her slurping and taking in big gulps. "Enough!" he said with a gruff tone. She obeyed and took her mouth off.

His arm started to heal immediately; he looked at her and smiled. She looked a bit nervous and was trembling; he then put his hands on each side of her head.

"You will be fine," he said. He then proceeded to snap her neck, and she was dead. He gently laid her on the bed, then stood over her, opening her mouth and began releasing his venom from his fangs into her mouth. It all landed in the back of her throat. It burned and sizzled as it was expelled from his teeth. It hurt, but for her he would endure it.

She started to change quickly; twitching a bit in place while the venom was taking over her veins. She reclaimed her body quickly as the dragon blood rushed throughout her body and took control of it. It made its way through her swiftly. At first, she had sharp brown claws that grew in place of her nails, then dark orange and yellow scales started appearing on her arms and covered her whole body. Finally, two brown horns grew out from the top of her head.

She opened her eyes almost immediately afterward; they began glowing orange, then she blinked and went normal. She looked stunned. She opened her mouth and her fierce teeth showed; two dominant fangs in the front to feed on flesh. She took in a deep breath and blew out, but no fire appeared, just smoke. She coughed, and then snorted.

"You're beautiful," he said. He felt even more of a connection to her, a bond that couldn't be explained. She started to open her mouth to speak. She had tears in her eyes, and she couldn't believe what she was feeling.

"I had only ever heard stories about souls connecting; I thought it was just a myth. But it's true. I will be yours until the end of time. I am your Mate, and now Sired to you," she said.

"You're… my Mate," he replied. He was in shock. Oh no, he thought, this can't be happening now. What will Thane do with this information? His face was flushed, and he felt like he would be sick and turned away from her. She sat up and grabbed his face.

"What is wrong? Isn't this all anyone wants to find in this unpredictable, unfair life we have?" She asked.

"I didn't even get your name. What is your name?" He asked.

"It's Rolandra," she replied. While they were both talking and gazing into one another's eyes, the door was kicked in, and it flew across the room, startling them. They both went into defense mode. Maverick pushed Rolandra back against the wall, and he stood strong and tall with his body in front of hers and hissed. It was no one other than Thane.

"I was wondering what was taking you so long, so I thought I would come in and check on you. I see you decided to take it upon yourself and use my blood!" he yelled. He was obviously pissed. He glared at Maverick with a look that could kill.

"It's not like that. I couldn't control it." Maverick said. He was feeling nervous, not knowing how Thane would react; he was trembling all the way down to his bones.

"I am his mate," she whined. Thane took a good look at them and then shook his head back and forth in disbelief.

"Well, this is about to get real fun," Thane said sarcastically. "At least we know the transition works. Don't get in the way of my plans, and I'll leave you alone." He grunted, looking straight at her. "But good luck with Cecilia, hence that isn't your body Maverick, so you can deal with that all on your own. I got you out of Versatory, so I owe you nothing, but you still need to keep up your end of the bargain. We have only just begun. Now, let's go! I have things to do," he demanded.

Thane walked out of the room, with Maverick and Rolandra follow him. They walked out the front of the hut, leaving the massacre behind. Thane turned and faced the front of the hut, letting out a big huff; he then blew fire out of his mouth, catching the hut on fire. It went up in flames almost instantly. He turned away from the hut and started walking down the sandy path toward the boat dock.

"Follow me," Thane demanded. They followed closely behind, hand in hand. Maverick looked back, and the fire had spread to other huts. He then noticed in the far distance beyond the huts a woman running from the fire. She must have gotten missed when Thane gathered them all up together. He didn't say a word and just let her go.

They boarded the boat, where human servants were patrolling the deck. Thane walked down below deck, and they continued to follow. The door was shut behind them as Thane led them down a shallow hallway, his shoes clicking with every step. He stopped in front of two steel French doors.

"I don't understand why we don't just fly?" Maverick said. Thane grabbed the door handles and then swung them open. "Because they can't," Thane said in a booming voice.

"Fuck!" Maverick yelled. There were vampires everywhere, and he knew what that meant. Thane walked into the room and they all were staring at him.

"Now who's hungry?" Thane said, with a villainous look on his face.

Chapter Seventeen
Maverick

I could feel acid backing up in my throat. I felt like I was going to pass out. This can't be happening; I stood there in shock and disbelief. There were about forty vampires in here, and Thane was going to have them feed on me. I couldn't focus or breathe; I wanted to run but couldn't leave Rolandra, because I knew he would kill her.

They were all just standing there staring at me with black eyes, and fangs exposed. One yelled and said, "Where are the humans we are to eat?" Thane shook his head and rolled his eyes in annoyance.

"Do you not remember the promise I made? For you all to walk in the light once again, and you wouldn't have to be human to do it? I just need you to stand by my side and help me take back what is rightfully mine." Thane pleaded.

They all shook their heads in agreement. One of them said, "Anything to walk in the day again, and look at the sun." Thane grabbed me by the wrist and flung me to the floor in front of them. He then grabbed Rolandra, flinging her next to me.

"What? Wait, wait, wait! Why her? I'm the one with the blood," I said. I grabbed her and pulled her close to me. She was shivering in fear.

"Well, you changed her, which in turn gave her the blood as well. So, now the transitioning will not take as long, since now there are two of you to feed off of," Thane replied.

"But she wasn't part of the bargain. You said you would leave her alone." Maverick begged and pleaded with fear in his eyes.

"Well, I changed my mind, and maybe next time you won't disobey me and follow the rules." He demanded.

"You didn't give me any rules to follow!" He snapped.

"I didn't think I needed to imply about not turning anyone without my consent." He snorted and glared at Maverick. "Just relax; it will hurt only a little. It's not like you're going to die again. You're in an immortal body. You'll heal; you might not even feel it." Raising his eyebrows. "You can't back out of it now; you're bound to deliver on my request." He snarled.

"What if I can get a new bargain with the Dark Guardian?" Maverick said.

"You can't. One bargain has to be fulfilled before a new one can take its place. If he hadn't accepted my bargain with you, he wouldn't have allowed you to return in Efron's body." Thane remarked matter-of-factly.

"Let's get it over with then." He said, looking scared and holding onto Rolandra. She had tears rolling down her face, and she was shaking with fear. The vampires started to creep closer to them.

"So, since you are all vampires and don't need venom, all you will need is to feed on the blood and you should turn. You shouldn't need a lot, just a few swallows." Thane explained. One of them said, "You want us to feed on Efron? He's a vampire dragon, there's nothing special about him."

They were all whispering to one another and were getting frustrated and started to all go sit back down at the tables they had gotten up from.

"Smell him, he carries the daylight blood, it's different. All you have to do is feed and you will become what he is, and be able to walk in the light." Thane said.

As I lay there, they all approached us. We were lying on the ground, terrified. I felt like I could throw up at any moment. They got on their knees and surrounded us and started sniffing at us like a pack of wild animals. One of them even sniffed my ass.

"They do smell different," one of them murmured. The first bite came fast and swiftly. Then I felt another, that was two and another three and they just kept coming, I lost count how many there were. I could hear Rolandra start to scream. It was high-pitched at first, and then died out. I was holding her hand, but she let go. There was nothing but air in my grasp. I am sure she was feeling the same pain, if not more. I could feel her misery down to my bones, to my core, and there was nothing I could do to stop it. I had to let it happen.

I started to shake, hyperventilate, and have a seizure. I just wanted to die; I didn't want to hurt anymore. I didn't want her to hurt anymore. Finally, as fast as it started, it was done, and the last vampire removed her teeth, lifting her head off my abdomen.

I had bite marks over every inch of my body. I was bleeding profusely, but I was starting to heal instantly. I could feel the binding from under my skin fuse together. I looked over at Rolandra. I could see her chest rising and falling. She was still breathing. I could still feel her presence.

I sat up and pulled her close to me again, wiping the blood out of her face and moved her hair out of her eyes.

"It's over," I whispered in her ear. She opened her eyes and just stared at me. I felt like she was looking into my soul. She sat up; she had her mouth full of blood. She then proceeded to spit it out toward Thane's feet. "Fuck you!" she said.

Thane squatted down toward her and grabbed her by her cheeks with his hand and squished them together.

"Good girl, a part of us has to die in order to evolve into whom we have to become to live."He snarled. "But do that again, and I will kill you where you stand."

He let go of her cheeks and stood up. "Keep her in line or I'll take care of her," he demanded and looked at Maverick wiping his hands off on his shirt.

"Now look, you're both healed already, no harm, no foul," he said with a grin.

Within minutes the vampires started changing. There were slight popping sounds in every corner of the room. Their fingernails turned into sharp claws. Their bodies were taking shape one by one. Several different colors and shades of vampire dragons were revealed. There were different shades of green, blue, and yellow, orange, purple, and even one black one.

They all glanced at each other in astonishment at what they were seeing. They couldn't believe their eyes. Thane called the black dragon forward to the front of the room. He walked up slowly standing in front of Thane. He stared at him in amazement because there were so many resemblances between them. Thane was the only other black dragon.

Thane put his hand on the man's shoulder. "You look amazing, but there's a problem." The man looked confused; he didn't understand what he was talking about. Thane released his claws and sliced them through the man's neck, severing his head clean off his shoulders. His head tumbled to the ground with his eyes still open. His body fell to the ground.

"There can only be one black dragon, and that's me!" he said. He wiped his claws off on his shirt and retracted them back in. Everyone in the room jumped in shock. They were stiff as a board and not sure what he would do next. A blue dragon ran to the front of the room and yelled, "No! You bastard! How could you?"

Fire burned in her eyes. "He was my arranged mate!" She hissed at him and went to strike him. He blocked her and shoved her backwards.

"Stop! Unless you want to be terminated next, and joining him," he said, snarling at her.

"Let me make this clear…There needs to be no more arranged mates. You can find your fated mate, go after lust if you wish, but it's only after you have helped me with the revolution and completed the bargain that you have made with me. Then you will be free, with no rules to follow ever again." He said. They all stared at one another and started whispering amongst themselves.

"What do we eat?" one said.

"You can eat regular food like a human, or drink blood since you are now a hybrid, but when you deprive yourself of blood, you won't be as strong as you would be if you were to feed." He replied.

"Will any type of blood be satisfying and replenish what we need? Say, for example: dragon blood?" one asked.

"That's what I am counting on," he said with a wicked smile on his face.

"So, we no longer need the servants on the ship?" Said another.

"No, you don't. Do with them as you wish. Although I wouldn't touch the captain at this time because he is steering us to Ashores Land," he replied.

"What is the Ashores Land?" They murmured.

"Where a new beginning will start," Thane replied, and then left the room out the double doors.

Most of them started to walk out of the confined room that we were in. Some of them stepped over Rolandra and me. They started searching every room on the boat for who knows what. You could hear screams echoing from the hallways within. I can only imagine that they were killing the human servants.

I started to wonder to myself if all this was worth bargaining with Thane to escape the Versatory? This place didn't seem any better. Soon it would be covered in blood and death of all the innocent people and creatures. But was I innocent?

The people don't even know what's coming; they have no idea of their demise soon to hit. All of this taking place just to free my soul from The Dark Guardian's grasp. I stood up to my feet and I grabbed Rolandra's hand and started to escort her out of the room. Right before I reached the door, I heard a voice.

"Hey! I know you're not Efron," he said. A man started to approach me from behind. It stopped me in my tracks; I turned around quickly to face him and pushed Rolandra behind me, blocking her. "I mean, it's obvious, isn't it? You have some woman we have all never seen before and you're protecting her like your mate. We all know you are bound to Cecilia," the man said.

"Well, we are allowed to do what we want now. Who says I have not taken on two mates?" he replied.

"That's preposterous and unbelievable at most, even for Efron." The man said, while glaring at me.

"And what if I am not him? What do you plan to do about it?" He snarled back at him.

"The man started laughing. "Well good, I never liked Efron anyway, and he was always such a smug, kiss-ass. My name is Gunner; it's nice to meet you." He put out his hand. "What's your name?" he said.

"I'm Maverick, and this is Rolandra," I replied, shaking his hand in a friendly introduction.

"We are going to need alliances on the land when we get to battle, so I figured I would introduce myself." He said. Two more dragons stepped up behind Gunner; one green male and the other an orange female.

"This is Klark and Daria. They are part of my new forged clan. I mean they have always been by my side it just seems more formal now since the transformation," he said.

Maverick shook his head in a nod to say, "Hello."

As they were standing there discussing their new lives and what it would be like to walk in the daylight and fly, all of a sudden they heard a big boom and the room they were standing in started to tilt. They grabbed onto one another and the entire furniture in the room slid to one side, crashing into the walls, and everyone was sliding out of control down on the floor and the boat slammed down on its side, the boat had gotten flipped.

"What the bloody hell!" Maverick yelled. They needed to get out or they would be underwater fast. Within seconds, water was pouring in. "Get out now!" You could hear Thane yelling from down the hallway. "We are under attack!"

My first instinct was to grab Rolandra and head for the hallway. The water was already up to our torsos at that point. It was completely dark in the hallway. I didn't know where I was going; there were three people in front of me, and Rolandra was directly behind me. There was also a small group of people behind her.

We were all holding hands to keep track of each other and get out together. The water was ice cold. I felt like I was turning blue and stiffening up. I could barely move. We were heading out toward the exit, which was the way we had come in. When we reached the corridor to the exit, the door was already open. It was still dark outside.

"You're not getting away!" Echoed a shrilly voice in the hallway. Rolandra's arm was tugged, and she was starting to be pulled backward, going under the water more than she already was. She had been submerged in it since she was holding onto the other dragons that were behind her.

"Let go, Rolandra!" screamed Maverick

"Let them die?" she said.

"Yes! And who says they would die; they are immortal." He said.

"Efron died. And here you are," she replied.

"Well, if it's someone attacking us, I am pretty sure they know what kills us. Now let's go!" he demanded.

She released them as he turned around and pulled her behind him. He then felt a fire in his stomach and throughout his body. Smoke started to come out of his nose, and he opened his mouth. The fire came raging and fast. You could see the blue serpent dragon with her mouth open, biting off one of the smaller dragon's head. She had just dropped it as the fire hit her in the face.

You could see the confusion and disbelief in her eyes, as if she couldn't believe what was happening. She started to talk, but all that got out her mouth was, "Ef —." The blue dragon had killed all the vampire dragons that had been behind them. Maverick just burned her to a crisp. The water they were in turned red from all the blood. Rolandra started drinking it, thinking it would make her stronger. They all followed suit and started to do it as well, except for Maverick. "Let's go!" Maverick said, and he went out the exit.

The screams were loud as they got out into the open air of the sea. The breeze was cold, and hit your skin like ice every time there was a gust of wind. There were stars above in the night sky and just water below. The boat had completely flipped over at this point. They were now standing on the hull fighting; it was slick with green algae and smelled of mold. The boat seemed to stay floating from where it was, even though it was swaying back and forth.

We didn't even know who these dragons were that were attacking us. We didn't know what they wanted or who sent them. We didn't do anything to them, but apparently they wanted us dead, so we had to kill them. I noticed Thane was up in the air, hovering. He wasn't anywhere near the water. He just kept spitting fire toward the dragons. They returned shards of ice. They were both missing each other. This seemed like it would go on forever. Only a handful of us had wings from the transformation. So I am assuming the only way out was to fly out of here.

On the other end of the boat, there was a struggle.

"Do you know who I am? Let go of me, they will have you killed. I am the captain of this ship. I am in charge of the vampires!" The short, stocky man struggled to get away. He eventually stopped squirming and got tired and just stood there.

Maverick looked at Rolandra. "When I make a move, I want you to fly. Do you understand me? No questions, just do it! Those who can should follow you, and if they don't, they will die. We can't save them all. We have to save ourselves." She shook her head in agreement. She let go of his hand. He took off running toward the end of the boat, toward the one named Adonis. He had to act fast before he was seen.

"So, you're the reason these vampires are now dragons? You brought them here? Dragons are secret creatures." The dragon with the crown on top of her head hissed in his ear.

"I am Callie, and I am the Lady of the Anchors Clan, and you will die by my hand. You never make a species. They can't be controlled. They are either born or they don't exist."

She squeezed him tight with her arms, her tail wrapping around him so he couldn't move. She opened her mouth; cold air breathed on the back of his neck, and soon was followed by icicles. They shot straight out of her mouth like missiles and went through the back of his skull, killing him instantly.

She let go of his body. It dropped to the ground, rolled off the boat and sloshed into the cold sea. She went to turn and all she could see in the corner of her eye was fire in her face. Her whole body was engulfed in it within seconds. It was as hot as an inferno and burned her straight down to her bones in seconds. She was incinerated and gone within seconds. All that was left in the place she stood was a burn mark on the boat and her crown that fell to the floor, making a tinkling sound when it hit the boat's surface.

Maverick jumped into the air as fast as he could and opened his wings, taking flight. Shards of ice shot toward him as he went into the sky. One tore through his wing and left a small hole. Rolandra and others were already waiting in the sky for him. There were maybe fifty of us left after that battle. Any of the ones that were left on the boat's hull and in the water were immediately terminated by the Anchors clan.

As we were flying away from the scene of battle, you could hear the agony of the Anchors dragons screaming and crying in pain for the loss of their Lady.

Chapter Eighteen
Cecilia

I got up from the straw bed feeling nauseated and unable to move, how could I not know? I have known him since we were children. My family was hiding a lot more secrets than they wanted me to know. I now knew I was chosen to have these powers, maybe even born with them, and I shouldn't give them up to anyone. There was a reason for all of this, and only one person could tell me the answers I was seeking, and that was The Dark Guardian.

"I have to go; I can't feel her through the bond anymore!" Anton shouted. He took off in a sprint and then started running toward the exit of the cell chambers, tears streaming down his face.

"What was that? What does he mean through the bond?" Cecilia said.

"It's when you have a sire bond and you fully accept it, you can talk to each other in your minds, you can feel each other's pain, the joy, the love, there's nothing like it," said Zeke. While glancing at Siren.

"I am such an idiot, that's what it was with Efron and me. We had a sire bond. We could talk to each other. When he came back, it was as if he were silent. I didn't know that was a thing," she said.

"Really, wasn't it obvious?" said Siren, shaking her head at Cecilia.

"Look, I don't need any lip from you; it didn't help with you trying to kill me," Cecilia snapped.

"Oh, you got your gabs in too, lady." She fired back lippy.

"So then, Anton's mate is gone?" Cecilia asked.

"It would appear so, but something is coming and we need to prepare now." Zeke said.

"Don't lock us in here! We can help. We have proven that, haven't we? If it weren't for us, Cecilia wouldn't be here right now. I promise to protect her at any cost," said Vilhauer. Siren nodded in agreement. Zeke looked at them both worried, but what other choice did he have? The more people to fight, the better advantage they would have.

"Don't make me regret this," he said. They all started rushing toward the exit together.

"Is there any dragon's bane on the island?" Cecilia asked.

"What? No, we have never needed it," said Zeke.

"Obviously you are kept in the dark," she said.

"What is that supposed to mean?" he asked.

"Exactly what I said. It means you don't know anything that is actually important or going on. You don't know what happened to our uncle to make him the way he is. The fact that he is not blood-related, and that Efron is his son. Crazy, I know. I wonder what else they are hiding." She said.

"If you don't trust him, or us, then why are you even here?" Zeke said.

"I really don't know who to trust at this point. I don't know what to do. All I know, is I don't want to hurt you or have you get in the way of my plan." She said.

"And what is your plan, Cece?" he asked.

"I am not sure; I am just kind of winging it at this point." She explained.

They reached the end of the caves and exited to find Tobias was waiting for them. He informed them that Thane was on his way here by flight with hybrid vampires that they had made into dragons. They were coming in fast, and they didn't have much time to prepare for battle.

He explained to them what happened and how the boat got flipped, how the Ashores killed some of them but not all. Some of them had taken flight, and that Callie was lost and couldn't be brought back.

"I can bring her back," I said

"You will do no, such thing!" said Tobias.

"You will not tell me what to do; I will make sure she is okay! I will help her, just like I will help Efron when I get him returned," said Cecilia.

"I said no, there is nobody to return her to. She wouldn't want to be brought back. It isn't natural. The soul you returned to Efron's body killed her because he is sired to Thane until he fulfills his bargain! There is no getting Efron back." Tobias declared.

"Liar! I can get him back! I need the knife." Cecilia said.

"What knife?" he said.

"Don't play dumb with me; I need it to send your brother back and to get Efron back. I am the only one that can do it and you know it." She snarled at Tobias.

"I said, No! And how do you know about the knife?"He said quietly, his face growing cold and looking a bit pale.

"Raven showed me something's, that I am assuming were relevant to help this situation we are in." She said.

He stood still and motionless, like he had just seen a ghost, once he heard Raven's name.

"Just tell me where Klaus is buried. I'll get it myself. Last time I saw the knife, he had used it on Thane. He put it in his pocket, unless it wasn't buried with him. But, knowing you, that's what I am assuming you did with it. Unless, you have it hidden somewhere else, which I wouldn't believe, because if it was me, and I didn't want it used again, that's where I would put it." She argued.

He just stood there staring at her; he couldn't reach for the words to tell her. He couldn't talk, like someone stole his voice to keep a secret.

"Tell her if you know dad," Zeke demanded.

"What's the matter? Does the cat have your tongue?" She said. "Let me help you," she put her hand up and raised it toward him and went into his mind. Her eyes went white, and she stood in a daze.

She could see back to the day when they were doing the celebrations of life party for Klaus, and Stella. But there was something different; there were two more bodies. I noticed that Slade and Brock were lying next to them in the burn-offs. Everyone stood around them in a big circle. They were in dragon form. They blew fire out of their mouths; first they lit up Stella, Slade and Brock, and then tried to burn Klaus' body in the send-off, but he wouldn't burn. He instead had a red glowing aura around him that was blocking the fire. It was shielding him somehow. She couldn't understand why. She could see the edge of the knife in his pocket.

She looked around at all the people and noticed someone was missing from the party. She noticed movement from the corner of her eye and jumped back. It was Raven. She was looking her straight in the eyes.

"We have to stop meeting like this," Raven said.

"Well, I have to get my information from somewhere, and if no one tells me anything. So, I have to forcefully take it and if you're here I guess the pleasure is all mine. How did Slade and Brock end up like this?" Cecilia asked.

"I think you already know, do you really need to ask who did it?" she replied.

"It wasn't their fault. Who made the call?" Cecilia said.

"No one made the order. Thane killed them in cold blood, and he blamed them for Stella's death. He said they should never have left her alone. He made them watch each other while he tortured them to death.

Their Sire mates heard them down their bonds and felt every ounce of pain they had, and then once he knew they couldn't heal or be saved he dropped them in the fields when he was done with them. We looked everywhere for them in for days. Their mates almost lost their lives as well from the mental pain; they are still recovering in their quarters. Cecilia was starting to feel nausea thinking of the things he would have done to them. "Where is Thane now?" She asked, her voice quivering.

"No one knows. He's been exiled and is not allowed to return." Raven answered.

"Why do you choose to help him?" I said.

"Because if I don't, he will have no one, and maybe just one person will make a difference." She said.

"Look, I didn't really come to chit-chat and try to save him. It's too late for him. I am looking for something and it's kind of time sensitive," Cecilia said.

"I know, and I am not sure I can let you have it because if you use it. You will bring something back that's more dangerous than what you are dealing with now." Raven pleaded and grabbed her arm.

"What?" Cecilia said, looking confused and pulling away from her, not realizing she could make contact with her here.

"You won't understand until it's too late for your own selfishness." Raven lifted her arm and moved her hand toward Klaus' body. She snapped her fingers, and then he was gone. Everyone looked over at Raven in confusion, but didn't question her.

"What are you doing? I needed the knife in his pocket. You know that's why I am here, to see what happened to it." She shouted at her.

"Like I said, it's for your own good." She whispered.

"What's wrong Raven? You don't want them to know that you see me from the future, that you can't stop what's coming? You didn't even try to stop it, but I am sure you know that. So why does it matter to you?" She replied angrily.

"Because ever since you were chosen, I have seen what the future holds, and I am trying to save your soul, to save all of you. Shouldn't that be enough?"

"Why? What's so important to you that you have to save me from my destiny?" She mocked her and rolled her eyes.

"It's not the monster in front of you that you should be afraid of, it's the monster you haven't found yet. It hasn't crawled out of the darkness yet or made itself known. You have many unknown things to face. You will lose everyone you love if you don't control it and balance everything correctly."

"What is that supposed to mean?" She asked.

"I guess, you will have to figure it out. Hopefully you will do what is right. No one can guide you on what path to take, but you. Until you decide, I will be waiting for one of our meetings or waiting for you to end me. I guess it's whichever comes first." Raven replied.

Cecilia looked confused and then closed her eyes. They turned back to normal, and she stood looking at Tobias. Her face was flushed. Tobias started coughing and dry heaving from his dry mouth. She just shook her head.

"Apparently Klaus wasn't burned at the Celebrations of Life and no one is going to be able to tell me what happened to him. Raven has him hidden and doesn't want him found." She said.

"But why wasn't he burned? That's a tradition and a disgrace otherwise. Why would he be hidden?" Said Zeke in confusion, looking at his father.

"Why don't you tell him, Father? Oh wait, you can't," Cecilia said sarcastically.

Cecilia was looking at Tobias in disgust and felt defeated. Then she noticed he had a familiar green emerald amulet wrapped in gold around his neck. It looked similar to the one she saw Klaus wearing before. Tobias saw her staring at it and went to cover it with his shirt, taking a step back from her.

"Was that your fathers?" She asked.

"It gets passed down to each king. It's a family heirloom." He replied.

"Let me have it!" She demanded. She reached for his neck and tried to grab it. He swatted at her hand.

"You all seem so scared of Thane, and this Dark Guardian, maybe it should be me that you should be scared of. Don't make me ask again." She said. Tobias grabbed the amulet from under his shirt and pulled it over his head, handing it to Cecilia.

"What are you going to do with it?" asked Zeke.

"I am going to do a locator spell and find Klaus' body." She said.

She laid her hand open with the amulet in it and placed her other hand on top of it. She tapped her fingers around on the top of it, and a red light started to glow.

"Find your original owner." The jewel inside the necklace started to glow green, then lifted from her palm. It started to float in the air and took off slowly toward the underground caves. It floated through to the underground chamber cells.

They all followed closely behind. The amulet floated all the way to the end of the walkway to the biggest cell, specifically the one that once held Scarlett. When it got there it banged on the floor three times, then dropped and stopped glowing. Cecilia picked it up and handed it back to Tobias.

"Stand back," she said

"Wait, do we really want to do this? What if this isn't the way?" said Zeke.

"I am all ears, if anyone has any better ideas? I need the knife that is in Klaus pocket to terminate Thane permanently." She said.

"Be truthful, that's not all you want it for!" said Tobias.

"Yeah, you're right I need it to get Efron back. He's not himself right now, it's someone else, and so I need to fix that too." She explained.

"What if you can't?" Asked Vilhauer.

"There is no can't, he would do it for me." She said with tears in her eyes, they were starting to run down her face.

"This isn't supposed to happen. Bad things are to follow," Tobias said. He looked pale and scared.

"Why don't you try standing up and not being a coward for once dad? Try fighting back, instead of always running and hiding. Grow a pair of balls." Cecilia snapped at him.

"Don't talk to him like that; you don't know the battles he's faced, that we have faced." Zeke said.

"Well then enlighten me, because all I have seen are lies." She scolded him.

"I am going to say this one more time. Stand back everyone, or I will consider you in my way. I will forcefully move you, and you don't want to make an enemy of me." I said.

They all stood behind me, off to the sides, so they could see in front of me. I started waving my hands in the air. I started bending the bars of the cell in front of me. You could hear the creaking and squealing of the bars and the smell of rust. Even though they were very old, they were making a lot of noise.

I bent them into a ball and flung them aside. Next I used my hands in a digging motion and the dirt started to dig up from the ground. It didn't take long, maybe about three feet deep down into the hole. I came to a layer of bricks. I removed those and tossed them aside. There was a wooden coffin under that. I plucked the old, rusty nails out of the wood and removed the lid.

There was a blanket over the top of him. There was also quite a bit of dust on top of it. I blew into the air and it cleared the dust off him, and we all started coughing. I walked over and leaned into the shallow grave; pulling the blanket off him. There he was with his long blond hair, still intact and not decayed one bit; it was the infamous Klaus, my Grandfather, the original Dragon King.

Chapter Nineteen
Cecilia

I couldn't waste any more time. I climbed on him and reached into his pocket, finding the knife I had been looking for. It was the same knife I saw Scarlett kill Thane with. The same knife Klaus stabbed Thane with, over and over again. This knife was cursed. It had death all over it. But I needed it to terminate Thane and get Efron back. I placed the knife in my pocket and climbed out of the hole. Tobias just stood there, staring at his father for a moment.

"You look like him. I am sorry, I never got to know him," said Zeke.

"I am not. You were better off without him." said Tobias.

"We have to go; they will be here soon if they have not already made it to the beach shore." Said Cecilia.

They all walked together and left the darkness of the dungeon cells. When they reached the caves, they could hear the chaos already taking place outside. The noises were echoing off the walls from outside, taking place in the field and beyond. We all took off in a sprint and started to separate at the cave exit.

"Don't separate completely, always stay in pairs of two, and if you see anyone alone make it a trio!" Zeke demanded. Tobias nodded at Cecilia, agreeing with the order.

Cecilia grabbed her hair and pulled it back tight."It's going to end here," she said.

Zeke looked at her and said, "You got this, Cece, I am behind you on your left."

"It's good to know I can count on someone," she said. Cecilia and Zeke blasted into the crowd, claws out and Cecilia with her fangs exposed. Her eyes were red. They hit them so unexpectedly that it threw some of them into the air.

"Vilhauer, you and Siren are with me. We are stronger together. If my daughter can trust you, then I can to." said Tobias.

"We won't be able to help once the sun comes up, but you've got us until then." Siren warned.

All three of them ran into the crowd. Tobias' claws transformed, sharp and ready to kill like daggers. Steam and smoke appeared from his mouth, getting ready to blow fire. There were a small handful of them; there was no way they were going to lose this fight.

Tobias' crew was out here fighting; Brogan and Una were surrounded. Una had a green vampire dragon latched onto her neck with its claws dug deep into her back. It appears they didn't really know how to fight; they just bit you and drained your blood as vampires do.

Brogan was trying to get them off Una, but they were starting to overtake him as well. He opened his mouth as wide as he could and bit the vampire dragon's head off. The dragon was still stuck on her back, twitching and convulsing with no head on its body.

They immediately started latching onto his limbs and then his torso. He fell to the ground in pain, groaning, screaming, and they just kept coming. They kept feeding and wouldn't get off him. No one could help him. He tried to get enough energy to produce fire, but only blew out a puff of smoke. It was too late, he was gone. They sucked him dry, and then they started to use their dragon teeth to eat the meat off his bones, they continued onto Una's body and didn't let up until there was just nothing but bones left. You could hear Brogan's mate with her blood curdling screaming from inside the caves.

Rolandra came face to face with Cecilia toward the shoreline next to the water. "I can smell my mate on you. Where is he?" Cecilia said.

"You, mean my mate! He is no longer yours, yours is terminated!" She shouted.

"Oh, he's coming back, but right now you're about to join him." She warned. Her eyes glowing bright red, and puffing steam out of her mouth toward her. She took the knife out of her pocket and twirled it in hand. Rolandra bared her vampire fangs at Cecilia in intimidation.

"That's cute. Is that supposed to scare me? I have some too, but mine are much larger." She hissed at her and bared her teeth, and flicked her tongue.

Rolandra charged at Cecilia. She flung her hand up at her, pushing her back, and ended up in the water.

"You see, I have more than just weapons up my sleeve. I could squash you like the little parasite that you are," she threatened. One of the water dragons appeared and wrapped itself around Rolandra and squeezed tight. Rolandra started gasping for air. Cecilia just stood there and watched.

"That's enough, Mae, she's mine." Cecilia said. Mae flung her back onto the land. Rolandra tripped and landed on her face.

"Now, don't make me ask you again." She demanded. Rolandra looked up at her as she pointed up the hill to the left, beyond the caves. There was smoke coming from up there. You could see there was a light, which meant a fire was burning. Cecilia grabbed Rolandra by her hair and started to walk up the hill, dragging her.

"Try anything and I will end you, do you understand?" Cecilia demanded.

"Ouch! Where are you taking me?"Rolandra cried out.

"We are going on a little field trip. Let's get moving and don't drag your feet." She demanded. They started to make their way across the field, up the hill, and through the crowd, walking over some dead bodies along the way. It looked like we were winning this fight. There was blood and body parts flying everywhere you looked.

They finally reached the top of the hill as it turned flat on the top. Looking out over the island, you could see everything around, and below you. There was some kind of stone structure in a circle at the top of the hill with a blazing fire placed in the middle of it.

I looked straight ahead and there he was… Thane! He stood there, tall and dark with his wings spread. He was almost black as night and blended into the darkness with Efron at his side. There were some unknown faces I had never seen before; they also had Vilhauer, Siren, Zeke, Tobias, and Iris captured.

"You know, it is said whoever creates you, you have to abide by their every rule until your bargain is paid." Thane said.

"So I have been told," Cecilia replied, moving closer to the fire, pulling Rolandra by her hair and pushing the knife against her throat.

"Maverick," she whined.

Thane grabbed Siren; she squirmed for a moment, but then gave in. He was much stronger than she was. Thane grabbed Maverick and cut his arm with his sharp claws, then put it to Siren's mouth. She moved her head away and begun to spit. He forced her head back and she hissed, which made her teeth exposed and he pushed her, making her latch onto his arm.

He then begun to hold the back of her head onto him and plugged her nose so she had no choice but to breathe through her mouth and suck. The blood came rushing in though her mouth. Thane let go of her nose. The hunger took over she had been so hungry and couldn't remember the last time she had eaten. She started to suck harder and it hurt Maverick.

"Enough!" Maverick said, and smacked her off his arm. She hit the ground and landed on her hands and knees.

"Sorry, I don't know what came over me," she said as she wiped the blood off her mouth with her dirty hands from falling to the ground. She then immediately curled into a ball on the ground groaning in pain, the transformation was starting.

"You know, all this is happening because you made Efron's body my personal supply," said Thane, with a wicked smile on his face.

"Do anything else and I'll kill her. Cecilia pushed the knife deeper to Rolandra's neck, blood now dripping down her throat. Maverick was getting edgy watching Cecilia handle her, he looked like he was going to pounce toward her any second.

"Do you think he cares about her, Efron?" Cecilia said

"My name isn't Efron, and I am not your mate so quit acting like you know me." he replied.

"Once he's done using you, you're gone. He's incapable of attachments and love." She said.

Cecilia started to move around the fire circle toward Maverick. He started to move at a faster pace, but before he could gain momentum, Vilhauer jumped in front of him. He was holding a sword that was embedded with dragon's bane in his hand, which Tobias had given him before the fight.

"It would seem I have the higher ground." Vilhauer spat at him with his fangs out and hissed.

"You really think that will kill me?" Maverick laughed.

"Get out of my waaayyy!"Just as he got those words out of his mouth, Thane had gotten behind Vilhauer. He had grabbed him and stuck one of his claws straight through his neck, almost cutting his head clear off his shoulders. His other claws went through his chest. He pulled back, releasing him, and dropped kicked his lifeless body into the fire.

I gasped in horror. I couldn't believe what I was seeing. Vilhauer's body burned within seconds and sounded like glass shattering. I'll never forget that sound.

"You'll pay for that!" I screamed. Siren was still lying on the ground in agonizing pain, screaming for help, which was taking way longer than the rest of the vampires that had changed earlier that day. I picked up Rolandra by the back of the neck and projected her over the fire. I just hung her there over the fire, burning, being tormented. She just hung there screaming for help. Soon her clothes burned off and her hair burned till she was bald; her skin started boiling then became charcoal. Maverick started to run toward Cecilia, but she put her hand up and stopped him in his tracks, he tried to push through the barrier but couldn't.

"That won't kill her," Thane said.

"Oh, I know," she replied. "But this will," she threw the knife she had in her hand at her, and it went straight through her chest where her heart was. She snapped her fingers and the knife retracted and went back in her chest, from her back then returned to her hand. Rolandra then burned to ash; her body floated away in ashes and was gone. Maverick was screaming.

"How could you?" He said, tears streaming down his face.

"You are not supposed to be here, and I am going to fix that." She said. Looking him straight in the eyes with the dagger in her hand.

"You need to leave it be, things need to be balanced, hasn't there been enough termination?" Tobias said.

"No, I need Efron back, and this has to end here today, right now! She said.

Everyone went quiet for a second, and it felt like the island rumbled for a moment. Siren stood up off the ground and puked. She had changed into a dragon, and no one had noticed. She was not just any ordinary dragon. She was a fully black dragon with one line of yellow, orange, green, blue, red, and purple scales, and she was bigger than Thane. Thane was distracted by her beauty and started heading toward her. Thane looked at his mother and asked,

"What does this mean?"

She looked white as a ghost and was looking off into the distance.

"It is said, when The Mother of Dragons is born, the King of Dragons will rise."

"She's the most beautiful dragon I have ever seen," said Zeke.

"There's no way the prophecy is true. That's absurd," said Tobias.

Sure enough, they looked off into the distance and saw his shadow. Through the fire his blonde hair swayed in the wind. He looked the same as he did the day he died all those years ago. He walked straight up to Iris and untied her and Tobias. He looked at Thane with a disappointed look.

"What do you think you're doing, boy?" were Klaus' first words.

Thane didn't seem so masculine now that his father was talking down to him. You could feel the tension in the air. Like somehow talking to him turned him into a child again.

"What, you just come back from the dead and we are all supposed to fall in line? I don't think so," Thane replied.

"Life for a life, remember? I am supposed to be here. You are not. Things need to be corrected." He said.

"You don't get to make that choice. You are not the Dark Guardian." Thane said.

"No, I am not! But who do you think sent me back? Who allowed all this to happen? I see by the facial features of that one, that he's your son. He needs to be sent back too, because I know that is not his soul in that body," Klaus said.

Thane was distracted and had his back turned to Cecilia. Now was her chance. She gripped the dagger tight in her hand; it was so tight she could feel her hand pulsating. She used her other hand to keep the other dragons in their places where they were standing. As quick as she could she sliced Thanes wings off his back, he was screaming in agonizing pain. Falling to the ground on his knees, the blood squirting from the wounds on his back in all different directions. He was kneeled on the ground in front of Siren. She looked at him with a grin and smiled. Siren opened her mouth wide with her new, sharp teeth. She then proceeded to bite Thane's head clear off his shoulders. She then spit his head out into the fire. She started to gag a little bit afterwards and threw up again. Cecilia moved his body with her free hand and picked it up, tossing it into the fire. It went up in flames and the flames turned black. Thane was so consumed with his family and revenge it became his undoing.

Cecelia looked around and said to the remaining vampire dragons.

"You are free now from his madness. This fight is over. If you don't believe that or still want to continue the fight we will end this right now and you will be terminated."

The sun was starting to rise and there were a few vampire dragons that started to get hot and burn and go up in flames. After they diminished we found out from Siren, if they were turned by Rolandra's blood the transition wouldn't work because it had to be Efron's blood to work because it came from the source directly. Siren wasn't just the Mother of Dragons apparently, she knew their origins and where they came from, but she wasn't able to tell us.

"It is time for me to go," Klaus said.

"But you just got back, and Thane is gone," said Iris.

"I shouldn't be here. I died a long time ago, so I must restore balance and take those with me to be returned to Versatory. Goodbye my love and take care, you will do fine without me," he said. He kissed her on the forehead and walked away.

Klaus walked over and grabbed Efron's body from behind in a bear hug. He wrapped his arms around him. Maverick tried to break free but couldn't. He then put a force field around them and they were glowing red, they started floating and went over the fire.

"What are you doing? I need his body to return him to." Cecilia yelled. She knew by the color of the power it was the Dark Guardian that wished this.

"No, you have done enough, the Dark Guardian doesn't permit it, and Efron has died and is not returning." Klaus replied.

"No, stop it! Put him down!" she was screaming. Tears were streaming down her face uncontrollably.

Maverick was screeching in pain. Their flesh was starting to melt off their bodies; their skin was boiling with bubbles, you could see the bone underneath, and smell the cooking flesh was rising in the air. It was nauseating.

"Stop! Please!" She yelled, "I'll fix him!" she cried...She tried everything in her power to get through the force field, wielding her hands, throwing balls of fire at it, putting explosions toward it. Throwing objects at it, pulling it apart, she even tried to put the fire out, it didn't work.

"Nnnnooooooo! You can't take him from me, I need him!" She begged on her knees, sobbing. "Ppppllleeaassee!" she yelled one last time. She just sat there in the dirt until nothing else came out, until her voice was hoarse and her mouth was dry. They were gone, the fire had burnt out. She picked up the dagger off the ground that was next to her and placed it tightly in her hand. She looked at her family and then she looked at Siren straight in the eyes.

"Tell him, I am coming for him," she yelled with one last breath.

"What?" said Siren.

Cecilia stabbed herself in the chest with the dagger and fell to the ground, she killed herself.

When she opened her eyes, it was dark, and she was in an oval cage. She had chains on her wrists and she was in a red dress that was torn and on her knees. She had horns atop her head, and her hair was red, she could feel her eyes burning with fire within. She felt different but couldn't put her finger on it. She lifted her head and saw him; he was tall, had broad shoulders, long red hair, with two big long horns atop his head with pointy ears, with orange fire blazing in his eyes. He had the top of his chest sticking out of his red armor suit. She could only suspect that it was The Dark Guardian standing in front of her. He looked her right in the eyes and smiled.

"I have been expecting you…Wife."

To be continued…

www.ingramcontent.com/pod-product-compliance
Lightning Source LLC
Chambersburg PA
CBHW071406100726
47908CB00004B/1080